The
Pearl Wars

SKYSHIP ACADEMY

NICK JAMES

SCHOLASTIC INC.
New York Toronto London Auckland
Sydney Mexico City New Delhi Hong Kong

MIDDLE SCHOOL

ISBN 978-0-545-44869-7

Skyship Academy: The Pearl Wars copyright © 2011 by Nick James. All rights reserved. Published by Scholastic Inc., 557 Broadway, New York, NY 10012, by arrangement with Flux, an imprint of Llewellyn Worldwide Ltd. SCHOLASTIC and associated logos are trademarks and/or registered trademarks of Scholastic Inc.

12 11 10 9 8 7 6 5 4 3 2 1   12 13 14 15 16 17/0

Printed in the U.S.A.   40

First Scholastic printing, January 2012

Book design by Steffani Sawyer
Cover design by Kevin R. Brown
Cover illustration by Derek Lea

1

My fingers grip the ledge, searching for cracks. The rest of me dangles into empty sky like some demented human windsock.

I hear him approach from the other side of the rooftop, footstep by footstep closer to crunching my fingers until I let go in agony and plummet twelve stories to the cracked pavement below. Splat goes me.

Cassius Stevenson, his government badge reads. When he showed up I thought maybe he was here to help us. Maybe the Academy sent him down in case we messed up. He can't be any older than fifteen, same as me. I didn't even know the government trained people that young. But apparently they do. And apparently he's not here to help us.

"Can't say I expected *this*." His voice is every bit the spoiled Surface kid, complete with a lilt that he must think sounds sophisticated. In reality it's just mass irritating. "I'd about given up finding anything interesting out here in this wasteland. And then I bump into you and your little friend. I gotta tell you, you guys saved my day."

He's talking about Skandar, my teammate, who should be up here helping me. Too bad Cassius already immobilized him downstairs. Eva's gone too, off with our Fringe contacts. I'm the only one left. I don't know why I let Skandar talk me into exploring this rotting hotel in the first place. This Cassius person is instant karma for straying from our mission objective.

Cassius flashes me a smile as his face comes into view. "I'm in awe, buddy. I've never seen someone actually trip off the side of a building before."

He stares down at me over the ledge, his dark bangs touching the top of his hazel eyes. He wears a spotless navy sport coat over his lean, muscular body. A silver badge sparkles with the reflection of the unrelenting sun. There's no mistaking that familiar lightning bolt emblem surrounding his name. He works for the Department of Energy Acquisition—a Pearlhound. That means he also works for the Unified Party. And that makes him my enemy.

"What's your name?" He coughs and shields his eyes from a cloud of dust kicked up from the rooftop. "There's gotta be some kind of record book for the stupidest ways to get yourself killed."

"Jesse Fisher," I answer, and instantly regret it. What kind of secret agent gives up their name first chance they get? A mass failure kind, for sure.

Cassius gives me a thumbs-up before grinding down on my fingers with the heel of his shoe. I muffle the string of curse words fighting to fly from my mouth. The arid wind beats at the side of my face. Syracuse's atmosphere isn't regulated by a Bio-Net like New York's Chosen Cities. This would sure be less of a struggle in a decent temperature. A hundred and fifteen degrees isn't exactly workin' in my favor right now.

I dig my fingers into the hot brick, straining to lift myself while trying to find footing on the side of the building. Beads of sweat drip down my arms. I'm like a human sprinkler. It's the dang heat. I don't know how Fringers live like this. I'm waiting for the moment when my muscles snap. I suck at pull-ups. This is like one endless endurance test.

Cassius's smile widens as he watches my pained expression. "So the question is, who do you work for? I saw your shuttle back behind those buildings. You're Skyship, aren't you? I bet you guys are down here looking for a Pearl. Illegally, of course."

He pauses, waiting for me to answer. My vocal chords have shut down and gone home, but I know I've gotta say something. Keep him talking.

"We already found it." I struggle to form each word. All I really want to do is cry out for help, but there's nobody around to hear it. The town's deserted. Most Fringe Towns are. And even if there were people here, they'd be as far away from the sun as they could get. "You've got the wrong person. I don't have it."

Cassius squats, his eyes never leaving mine, his foot pressing harder and harder on my fingers until it feels like they could break off. "Well, obviously," he chuckles, "but the fact that you're even down here without clearance makes you an enemy of the state. Come to think of it, I'll probably get a gold star for getting rid of you."

"Please." One minute in and the begging's already started. A more experienced agent would pull out some complex, psychological argument to convince this guy to reach down and save me. And here I am with my pathetic "please."

"Who's got it, then? Not your ridiculous friend downstairs?"

"No." I inch my free hand across the surface of the ledge. If I can just grab onto his ankle before he notices, maybe I can take him by surprise and pull myself up.

"Don't tell me there are more of you Shippers running around." He grabs onto the sleeve of my windbreaker, yanking my arm up off the ledge.

"Don't drop me!" I shout, about as far away from an intimidating hero command as you could get.

A gust of wind batters my left side, throwing hair into my face. The world is a sea of blond for a moment before I manage to whip it from my eyes.

"Then don't try anything funny." He hoists me up a few inches by the thin material on the arm of my jacket. "I'm going to give you another chance, even though you don't deserve it. Where's the Pearl?"

"My friend's got it," I stammer. "She's on the ground, in an alleyway behind the hotel."

Cassius grins. "There. Was that so hard?"

I look up at him, hoping for a hint of mercy in his eyes. Instead there's something else: a playful coldness, like a kid sneaking into his parents' room to open birthday presents two weeks early. He's actually gonna do it. He's gonna kill me. For fun.

And before I have a chance to do anything, he lets go of my jacket.

"Oops." He grins.

I struggle to grab onto the top of the ledge as my arm falls to my waist, but I miss it by a good inch. My body lurches to the side as the muscles in my right arm tense with the added weight. I'm left scraping at the bricks with my fingernails, desperate to regain my grip. Nothing at the Academy's prepared me for this.

I twist around in the air, hanging on by five fingers, soon to be four. Three. Then ... I can't even think about it.

"Oh god." Cassius covers his mouth. "Why don't I have a camera right now? Your face is priceless. You really should see yourself. You'd be laughing."

I glare at him as I pull myself back to a more stable position, using every ounce of remaining strength in my rubber-band arms. I've gotta project confidence. No begging. No crying.

I press the tips of my boots against the side of the building. The shirt under my windbreaker clings to my body, heavy with sweat. I consider reaching for the taser on my belt, but it's too risky to try.

Cassius sighs and crosses his arms. "You just won't quit, will you?" He crouches. "Maybe I underestimated you Shippers. I mean, you'd be used to heights, living up there your whole life." He points to the thin layer of clouds above us before focusing back on me. "You know, I've always wondered. Is it a superiority thing? Do you enjoy looking down on us, this 'failed country' you couldn't stand to be a part of anymore?"

I wanna shout at him, spit in his face. But if I did it'd only come raining back down on me.

"It's okay," he continues. "You don't have to answer. You're all a bunch of cowards, running away. All that does is get you in trouble, just like you're in now."

"I told you I don't have the Pearl," I sputter, trying to think of something mass heroic that'll get him to leave. "The longer you stay up here, the less chance you'll have of finding it."

Yeah. Good one.

He shrugs. "I guess we'll have to get this over with, then." He grabs my ring finger and twists it back until my nerve endings scream out in pain. He laughs, but I'm too busy wriggling around to notice. Every last instinct wants to reach over and stop him, but if I do that, I'll fall.

Then suddenly the pain disappears, replaced by a numbness that shoots back from the tips of my fingers, up my arm, and into my chest. At first I'm convinced that Cassius has destroyed some vital part of my nervous system and left me paralyzed, but then his eyes widen and I know he feels it too.

He tries to pull away, but his hand sticks to mine as an invisible whirlwind sucks our fingers together. Sparks kick off from our fingertips, tiny green things shooting out from within our hands. They should be hot, but I don't even feel them. Everything above my wrist is numb.

"What are you doing?" Cassius strains his arm as he continues to pull. It's no use. We're completely stuck.

I don't feel pain anymore, not even in my strained muscles. It's like I'm floating.

A soft humming joins the suction where our hands meet as the sparks amp up. They shoot across the rooftop and disappear. The humming vanishes with them.

Silence.

The pain returns. It starts in my toes, moves up to my feet, legs—all the way to my arm. I feel it rise through my hand and into my fingertips. When it can go no farther, an explosion of force pries our hands free.

Cassius and I separate violently, thrown back with the strength of a hurricane. We fly apart, which isn't so bad for him because he's got the rotting Fringe hotel rooftop to land on.

Not so good for me, as I'm looking down at twelve stories of freefall. I don't have time to grab onto the side of the building. I don't have time to grab onto *anything*.

The dust-clogged air tugs on my windbreaker, ruffling

the material as I fall backward. I panic, combing through training modules for something I can do to stop myself before hitting the ground.

Rows of shattered windows pass by above me in a blur, faster and faster until I'm mere feet from smashing into the ground.

This is it. All I can do is close my eyes and pray.

2

I land hard beside a metal dumpster with a sickening thud. Whatever's inside reeks. The fact that I can smell it at all is more than a little surprising.

For a moment I'm sure that I'm dead. I can't feel anything. Not my arms, not my legs, not even the intense heat swirling around me.

I look up at the rooftop. From down here it seems a mile away. No way could I survive a fall like that.

And death isn't really all it's cracked up to be. I may not be able to feel, but nothing's changed around me. Same old dustbowl Fringe Town. Beyond depressing.

I try to push my body up off the ground, but everything's gone limp. My mind tells me my arms are moving in the dirt, but there's nothing pressing against my skin. I can't feel the wind pushing on my face either, or the sun frying my jacket. But I can smell the dumpster. And I can see.

Then, out of the corner of my eye, I watch three lanky teenagers dart out from a nearby alleyway and run over to me. Their hair is cut short—nearly shaved to the skin. They wear mass filthy, hole-ridden tank tops over rail-thin bodies. Their dark arms are blistered. The "Surface Tan," we call it.

Suddenly I know I'm not dead. There aren't any Fringers in the afterlife.

One look at their faces and I can tell they're not like the peaceful Pearl Traders we met outside the abandoned hotel fifteen minutes ago. These guys are lawless. They're out for blood.

Another moment and they're on me. I watch helplessly as one grabs my neck, lifts me up, and throws me against the wall, knocking the feeling back into my body.

The fall catches up to me, or maybe it's the wall slamming into my back. I fight to stay conscious as the pain tingles down to my feet. The second Fringer grabs my arm while the first releases my neck and pins my left side tighter against the brick.

"Search him!"

The third rummages through my pockets, stopping at the belt under my jacket.

I kick at his shins. My nerves cry out with a sharp pain each time I move my leg. I'm so dizzy and uncoordinated that I nearly topple back to the ground before I can do any damage. I'm mass threatening.

The Fringer manages to unbuckle my belt and rip it out of the loops, whipping it into the street. I watch as my com-pad flings out and rolls into the dirt, along with my surface goggles. They've got the taser now, too. Even on my best days I'm no match for three angry Fringers. Without a weapon I might as well just crawl into my casket now.

"Pockets are empty," the Fringer mutters. His breath smells as bad as the dumpster.

The guy on my right leans his torso against my arm and grabs my cheek with his free hand, pushing the side of my face into the hot brick. My skin roasts on the wall. I bottle up a scream.

"Not used to the heat, are you sky boy?"

The second guy moves down to my hand, forcing it onto the wall. "We don't need no vultures coming down here and picking from our scraps."

His friend pushes harder on my cheek, spreading the skin up to my eye. "Maybe we'll fry you up and pick at *your* scraps."

I wince at the thought of it. I wanna defend myself, but I can't even talk. My mouth's pulled at such an awkward angle.

Just as the guy's about to crack my skull open, an explosion rattles the street.

All three Fringers release me and spin around. I crumple to the ground, face on fire.

Framed by their tense, ready-to-pounce bodies, I see the silhouette of Eva Rodriguez. A trail of sandy smoke winds up into the air beside her like a serpent. It came from a detonator, the spherical shell of which lies on the cracked pavement in front of her right foot.

She looks older than her fifteen years, and far more intimidating than me with her cropped hair and well-practiced battle scowl. A bulky burlap pouch hangs over her shoulder, barely containing a radiant green glow. Resting inside is the Pearl we were sent down to retrieve.

Before the Fringers can move, she pulls a pistol from her belt. It's only a stunner, but there's no reason for them to know that. Her brown skin glistens in the sun. Her arm is five times as buff as mine.

"I've got more where that came from." Her dark eyes lock onto each of them as she moves the barrel of the pistol from one to the other. "Leave. Now."

The Fringers exchange glances before realizing that it's not worth it. Snatching up my belt from the dirt, they take off. Eva watches them disappear around the corner of the nearest building before walking over to me. "I was looking for you." She reaches out her hand. "I should have known to follow the screaming."

I grab her wrist and lift myself to my feet. "Remind me why we trade with them?" My voice comes out muffled and scratchy, like I've swallowed a ball of dust.

She holds up the pouch. "Pearls. Besides, you know they're not all violent. The ones in the alley were nice enough. You should have stayed and talked for a while instead of wandering off." She squints and grabs my chin, pushing it to examine the side of my face. "That's gonna hurt tomorrow."

"It hurts now."

She frowns. "Where the hell were you, Fisher?"

"I just—"

"And where's Skandar? This is why we stay together. You know it's dangerous out here."

"Mr. Wilson said this city was deserted."

"Well, he was obviously wrong." She straps the pistol onto her belt. "They got your stuff too, didn't they? Thank god you're not authorized for stunners yet. You'd have shot yourself in the foot."

I rub my cheek, wishing I had some cold water. "Hey, as far as I'm concerned, we shouldn't even be here. I mean, leave the combat missions to the adults."

She sighs. "If you and Skandar would have stayed in the alley like you were supposed to, then this wouldn't have turned *into* a combat mission. I know this was your first time in the Fringes. I know Skandar's a bad influence, but you need to think of the consequences, Fisher. This isn't a game!" She lays her hand on the pouch, further muting the green glow from inside. "This is what it's all about, Jesse. Not your nursery-school curiosity."

I ball my fists, eager to punch something. "Yeah? Well ... " I struggle to find a comeback, something to get her off my case. "I just fell off a building!"

Her face falls flat. "That is the dumbest thing I've ever—"

"No," I start. "It's true." I point to the rooftop. "See that building? I just fell from the very top all the way to the ground and I don't have a scratch on me. What do you have to say about that?"

She glances up, then back to me, and shakes her head. Then she punches my left shoulder. Hard.

"Ow! What did you do that for?"

"You're not invincible, Fisher. Grow up."

I rub my shoulder, glaring at her.

"Now let's find Skandar and get out of here before you bring the whole Unified Party down on us."

A gun cocks in the distance. Eva spins around immediately, stepping back until her shoulder touches mine.

Halfway down the block stands the Pearlhound, Cassius, pistol in hand pointed in our direction. Just my luck.

Neither of us heard him approach. He's in one piece, though his shirt's untucked and his tie juts down at a screwed-up angle. He takes two steps forward and stares at me, ignoring Eva.

"What did you do up there?" he sneers, eyes narrowed.

I shake my head. It's all the explanation I've got.

Luckily, Eva's all words. "Who are you supposed to be?"

His eyes meet Eva's for the first time. "You must be the third Musketeer, huh? I'm sorry your teammates let you down, gorgeous."

"You call me gorgeous again and I'll rip your face off."

That's Eva. Mass charming.

She squints, crossing her arms. "That a government badge?"

"Madame's finest."

She chuckles. "I'm so sure."

"So you're the one with the Pearl." He steps forward. "Hand it over, then."

Her chuckle devolves into a full-blown snort. "You've gotta be kidding."

His response comes in the form of a gunshot aimed an arm's length from my head. I wince as the bullet slams into a building behind us. Cassius smiles. "You may be shooting to stun, but this is the real thing. Hand it over and I'll let you crawl back to wherever you came from."

I wait for Eva to react, to dupe him into thinking that she's packing more than stun darts. Instead, she looks over her shoulder with an expression that would make a baby cry. "Your fault, Fisher," she whispers, "your fault."

She slips the pack off her shoulder and tosses it to Cassius. With it, we lose all hope of passing our super-secure mission. Not like dying's a better option, but returning to the Academy empty handed isn't exactly high on my list either. Mr. Wilson's counting on this Pearl, and now because of my supreme lameness he's gonna have a handful of nothing instead. Maybe death by road-splatter isn't such a bad fate after all.

Cassius catches the pouch by the end of the strap and slings it over his back, keeping his aim steady. For a second I'm convinced he's gonna shoot, but I guess he's got some screwy sense of honor because he backs away instead and darts into the nearest alleyway, out of sight.

I wait until he's gone to whisper to Eva. "Are we going after him?"

She turns to me, frowning. "With what? You've lost your entire arsenal, remember?"

"But the training mission—"

She sighs. "You didn't seem too concerned about it twenty minutes ago when you left me alone in the alleyway with the Pearl Traders. Besides," she takes off at a brisk pace through the empty street, "I'm not going to have you killed. Even for a Pearl."

"Where are you going?" I follow.

"Skandar. We find him and we get out of here."

·"Oh."·I point to a rotting wooden door a few yards away. "He's in there."

Eva stops, resting her hands on her hips and looking at the entrance to the building. Like all structures in the Fringes, it's a sorry reflection of what it used to be. Long planks board up the windows. The paint is mass faded and cracking. Two columns that had once supported a portico now stretch into the air, weathered down to round stubs at the top.

A fat, dark rectangle stains the space above the doorway where a sign used to hang. In its place is a black "x" about two feet in each direction, paired with a confirmation code designating Syracuse as a Fringe Town—part of the forgotten lands after the government set up the Chosen Cities. Several lines of spray paint cover the code numbers.

"Charming," Eva says. "I can see why you two had to scurry off and explore this treasure trove."

"It was Skandar's idea," I mutter as she pulls open the shaky door.

My eyes take a moment to adjust to the darkness as

we step into the entryway. Little more than strings of sunlight poke through cracks between the ancient, dust-caked blinds. Whittled-down skeletons of chairs lie in one corner of the room. On the opposite side squirms Skandar Harris, his hands and feet bound together by plastic bands.

He pauses as he notices Eva and me. Dirt from the ground covers his brown hair. A pair of cracked goggles hang around his neck. The floor's been long since stripped of carpet. Only the wooden boards remain.

Eva shakes her head as she walks to the center of the entryway. "I'm surrounded by idiots."

He frowns, renewing the struggle with the bands around his wrists. "I nearly had him. Showed up outta nowhere." Only a sliver of his British accent remains after living at the Academy for so long. Now it's just a weird Skandar accent.

Eva kneels down next to him. "Maybe we should drag you home like this, roast you over a spit."

He rolls over to smile at her, his faint freckles covered in a layer of dust and sand. "Have mercy, Eva."

Her eyes narrow. "We lost the Pearl."

His face hardens and he tilts his head to look over at me. "It was *his* fault. What'd you run up to the rooftop for, Fisher? It's a dead end."

"No duh," I shoot back. But he's right. I should have known better.

Eva sighs as she pulls a knife from her pocket and flips it open. "You were trying to lose him, right Fisher?"

"Yeah." I stare at my feet. "That's what I was trying to do."

"Sure," Skandar rolls over so Eva can cut the bands behind his back. "Take *his* side."

"Trust me," she lowers the knife and begins sawing through the plastic. "I'm not on anybody's side. I'm embarrassed to be seen with the both of you."

Skandar pulls his hands free as Eva moves on to his ankles. When she's finished freeing him, he wobbles to his feet and shakes the feeling back into his hands. Red marks encircle his wrists. He only made them worse by struggling. I'd call Skandar Harris many things, but a quitter isn't one of them.

"Hey Jesse," he rubs the dust from his face. "How did you get out of the building? I never saw you come back down the stairs."

Eva puts her knife away, glaring at me the whole time.

"I fell."

He stands still for a moment before busting out laughing. "Off the rooftop? Good one."

"No, it's true. It didn't even leave a—"

"Time to go, gentlemen," Eva interrupts me. "And I use that word in the loosest of ways."

She marches out the door without another sound. Skandar and I follow, resigned to our fate. Sure, I'm feeling mass lucky to be escaping with my life after all that just happened, but the trip back to the Academy isn't gonna be filled with ice cream and sing-alongs. This was a test. I failed miserably.

"You really fell off the roof?" Skandar whispers as we shield our eyes from the baking sunlight.

"Yeah."

"Like, from the top of the building?"

"That's the one."

He pushes my shoulder, nearly sending me flying onto the pavement. "You're such a weirdo."

I want to press the issue, but then I realize how ridiculous it sounds. Jesse Fisher, least promising agent-in-training at Skyship Academy, falls off a twelve-story building without a scratch on him. I'm not so sure I didn't imagine the whole thing myself.

"Next time." Skandar shakes his head. "We'll have our revenge next time, right Fisher?"

Eva checks the nearest alleyway for trouble before entering. "With our track record, there won't be a next time. Now keep on alert. Apparently this city isn't as deserted as Wilson said it was."

Skandar stops in his tracks. "Fringers?"

"Fringers," she replies, "unfriendly ones. Fisher already got a taste."

He crosses his arms. "You got to have all the fun, didn't you mate?"

"Yeah," I mutter. "Fun."

I plug my nose as we make our way through the alleyway. Trash litters the ground. The heat enhances the already rotten smell, cooking and congealing mystery liquids that run into the dirt in thin streams. We step around the worst of it and funnel into the next street. Patches of brown, crinkly grass sprout from cracks in the pavement before us.

As we cross an empty intersection, I keep my eyes peeled for Fringers, hoping that my attackers were an anomaly—an angry street gang from a neighboring town. The Pearl Traders were friendly enough, content to exchange their discovery for the rations and purification tablets inside our shuttle. Now that we've lost the Pearl, all those crates of Skyship food will be marked as lost inventory. Lucky Fringers. Not-so-lucky us.

The top of our transport shuttle comes into view. I half expect it to be decimated. After all, if those guys were so keen on grabbing my belt, they'd lose their marbles over our ship.

The shuttle's saucer-shaped with three retractable, rusty legs resting on the pavement. It's the only dash of color on the street—a deep red.

Despite my aching body, I run through the street, eager for the cool, climate-controlled air inside the shuttle. When I reach the front end, I slide open the plastic guard and punch my authorization code into the keypad. The door lifts and three steps tumble out from the bottom. I barely use them. The recycled air hits me immediately. Sanctuary.

Eva and Skandar follow, shutting the door and taking their seats. I fasten my belt as Eva grabs the wheel, flipping the ignition and retracting the landing gear. Then we're off.

I recline and watch as Syracuse pulls away from us. My eyes linger on the hotel rooftop for a few moments. It juts from the flat brownness, taunting me. Something happened back there. Something unexplainable. That Cassius guy felt it too. He'd looked as unsure as me before he escaped. It wasn't part of his plan, and it sure as heck wasn't part of mine.

I close my eyes, letting the adrenaline wash off my body. First trip down to the Fringes and it nearly killed me. I managed to disappoint my teammates and utterly fail our mission objective. Maybe Mr. Wilson will be more forgiving than Eva. Wishful thinking, sure. But wishful thinking is what I live on.

3

Cassius Stevenson strode through the halls of the Lodge with a noticeable swagger. Slung over his shoulder rested the brown pouch containing the Pearl. He hadn't let it out of his sight since leaving the Fringes. He hadn't stopped to shower or change clothing. A trail of dust followed him through the hallway. The custodial crew would clean it up.

Even through the burlap, he could feel the warmth of the Pearl on his back. It didn't burn like the undiluted sun outside. It was a different kind of heat. A mother's touch, maybe, or a loved one's embrace. He didn't have a lot to compare it to, raised the way he was.

He'd been lucky to stumble across a Pearl so easily. Madame would be exceedingly proud, enough to forgive him for breaking the rules and sneaking outside of the Net to get it. On the way to Syracuse, he'd considered turning his ship around several times, but days of tedious simulation training had taken their toll. He needed to get out. Plus, it was fun to see if he could bypass security and do it.

Cassius couldn't remember life without Pearls. They'd been falling from space since he was a small child, drawn to the parched Earth. Charity from the stars. Some people, like the evangelists of Heaven's Rain, considered them God's gift. But Cassius didn't put much stock in Pearl-worshippers. To him the space rocks were a natural resource, as simple as oil. Back when oil existed, of course.

Pearl energy powered the Bio-Nets that protected and cooled the Chosen Cities, which separated the order and comfort of his home from the blazing chaos of the Fringes. Just one Pearl could power a city for months. He grinned and clutched the bag tighter.

Window after enormous window framed the Lodge's lush manicured lawns as he continued down the corridor. The sprinkler system had shut off for the evening. The sun lingered at the edge of the horizon.

He knew he was privileged to live where he did, on the outskirts of the city. Those who didn't work in energy acquisition made do with government-approved living quarters—300 square feet per family. The Bio-Nets were only so big, and cramming everyone into the fifty Chosen Cities required more than a little sacrifice for most folks.

But the extravagance of the Lodge wasn't without a price. Inside, candidates were prepped to enter the Pearl

Retrieval Squad, and harvesting Pearls could be dangerous, especially when Skyshippers found them first.

Cassius scowled. Shippers.

There had always been separatists, even before the bombings. Rebellious factions began to make themselves known mid-century, upset with the government's increasing secrecy. They were small in number and unorganized, just as the Fringers were now. All they needed was a rallying cry—an event significant enough to bring them together.

The Scarlet Bombings changed everything.

Named for the enormous red clouds that engulfed the six largest American metropolitan centers on that afternoon twenty-two years ago, the chemicals not only killed millions, but continued to plague the country decades later, vaulting the temperature in the Fringes to dangerous levels. Folks back then assumed the clouds were red because of all the blood in the air, the way the chemicals dissolved people. As far as Cassius was concerned, that was a bunch of fear-mongering. Blood wouldn't float in a cloud.

Regardless, when everything finally settled, the country was left without its leaders. Worse yet, there was no telling when it would happen again, or why America had been attacked in the first place.

The Unified Party sprung from the ashes, an anonymous, efficient protector of an increasingly fragmented country. Retaliation was swift. The President ordered a full-scale assault on all terrorist-harboring countries, blasting entire chunks of Asia and Eastern Europe into rubble.

Cassius knew it was the right call, protecting the country from another attack, but others disagreed. The Separatist movement demanded evidence that retaliation was necessary. When the Unified Party refused to comply, the Seps hijacked the government's Skyship Program weeks before it was christened and founded a nation above the clouds—the Skyship Community. There was fighting. Some called it a civil war. Then came the Hernandez Treaty. Things hadn't been the same since.

The conditions of the treaty kept Surface folk and Skyshippers apart—a pair of sovereign states separated by the International Skyline. Travel across the border was unlawful without proper clearance, but for as long as Cassius could remember, he'd been part of a rat race between the Surface and the skies. All for Pearls—the ultimate energy source.

The treaty, of course, was nothing more than a piece of paper. Shippers ignored it, sneaking down to harvest Pearls that legally landed in Surface territory, or trading with Fringers. The President of the Unified Party buried his head in the sand, as nameless and anonymous as when he'd first been appointed. If Cassius knew who the guy was—if *anybody* knew—he'd know who to blame for ignoring Skyship's growing threat. But no one could talk to the President. He spent his days giving orders from secret bunkers stationed around the country. It was up to people like Madame to put words into action.

Cassius rounded the corner, suddenly wishing he'd

been less compassionate with the Shippers back in Syracuse. Next time.

Ahead of him lay another lengthy hallway, identical to the one he'd come from. A newcomer might assume the Lodge stretched on forever in this way, but Cassius knew better. After all, he'd spent his whole life here.

It was irregular, him growing up in the Lodge. New trainees didn't arrive until after their thirteenth birthday, when they were transferred from their schools after scoring high on skill proficiency exams. For many years, Cassius had been the only child under the age of thirteen in the building. Those were the best years, when he garnered Madame's full attention. Now she was always so busy.

He'd never met his real family. His mother disappeared quickly after childbirth, hooked on black market Serenity. Any other infant would have grown up in the workhouses or been tossed into the Fringes, but Madame had found him first. Though she'd never declared it outright, Cassius had always considered her his adopted mother, even when she didn't act much like one. Most Surface kids grew up in blissful ignorance, spending weekends with their friends, hooked up in one of Rochester's twenty-five online pavilions. Cassius had been raised amidst stealth and weaponry—frantic calls to the President in the middle of the night.

A few more steps and the dark mahogany doors of Madame's office came into view. He hesitated a moment before knocking.

Silence.

He stared at the ornately carved designs on the panels of the door. Within the familiar lightning bolt emblems were cut hundreds of names—high-ranking officials that died when the terrorists blasted the White House into a pile of dust.

"Cassius, come in." Madame's soft, hypnotic voice startled him. He looked up to see a round speaker above the door. "You're always welcome."

Clutching the burlap pouch closer, he dusted off his sport coat, pulled on the silver door handle, and entered. Madame always knew who stood outside of her study. She'd had the entire Lodge covered in cameras and microphones ages ago—a necessary precaution for the head of the Chronic Energy Crisis Commission.

She sat at her large rosewood desk at the end of the room. Her dark hair was pulled back behind her in a fastidious bun. A pair of spectacles rested on the end of her tiny nose as she set down her personal reading device. The Lodge's students had a standing bet on her age. Late forties seemed to be the consensus, though her latest Face Freeze kept her ageless.

The curtains behind her were drawn shut in anticipation of the impending darkness. Bookshelves bordered three walls of the small room. Traditional books were outlawed in favor of electronic files, but Cassius knew that Madame had a penchant for antiques.

Madame leaned forward, eyes slit, and stared intently at his face. "And to what do I owe this pleasure, Cassius?" Her calm expression soured as she noticed the state of his clothing. "You're filthy."

He allowed himself a smile. "Yeah. Sorry."

"Just ... don't drag it all over the rug. It's Persian, or so they tell me."

He stopped in his tracks, momentarily flummoxed. "I'll go around."

He tiptoed to the side of the oval rug, careful not to press too hard on the ground with his dusty feet. His Fringe stink choked the lavender scent hanging in the air.

Madame's gaze followed him the entire time. When he was within reach of the desk, her eyes darted down to the pouch. "Bearing gifts, are we?"

Without an explanation, he gently set the bag on the ground, unbuttoned the flap, and lifted the Pearl out from within. It weighed very little, but instantly illuminated the darkened room with a shimmering green glow, casting hypnotic waves of soft light along the walls.

Consuming no more space than a fortune teller's crystal ball, it rested comfortably in the palm of his hand. Beneath its surface pulsed a raging, chaotic hurricane of energy— strands of light constantly in motion. He could stare at it for hours if she let him, but he placed it into her eager hands instead.

Her expression remained still as she laid both hands on the Pearl, examining it. But Cassius recognized the familiar glow in her eyes. She hungered for it, just as he did.

After a moment of silent admiration, Madame's gaze

wandered back in his direction. "This is quite a surprise, Cassius. We haven't authorized you for Pearl exploration. You went outside of the city to get this, didn't you?"

He clasped his hands together behind his back. There wasn't any sense in lying. "I got bored. I took a tracer with me and it picked up an energy trail outside of Syracuse."

"A Fringe Town." She cradled the Pearl in her arms. "I see." She sighed. "Now, I know the teachers go on and on about your progress but that doesn't mean I like the idea of you going out there on your own. It's dangerous, especially wearing a government uniform. You know how they feel about us on the outside."

"I was ready."

"You keep this up and you're going to make my department look bad. How could we have missed a Pearl falling right under our noses?"

"I . . . uh . . . I don't think it *fell* in Syracuse," he responded. "It was transported."

"Ah." She leaned back in her chair. "Skyship agents?"

"Not exactly. They were kids."

"Kids?"

"Teenagers. It was an exchange, I think. With Fringers."

"Kids." She shook her head. "Skyship's audacity never ceases to amaze me. It's bad enough that we've got adults crossing the Skyline without clearance, but children? Can you imagine being asked to do such a thing, Cassius?"

He bristled at her words, being called a child. He wasn't. Not compared to the morons he trained with.

Madame drummed her fingers on the edge of the desk, then stopped suddenly. "How many?"

"Three." He met her eyes. "Pathetic, though. I mean, it was embarrassing."

"I'd expect as much. They undoubtedly haven't benefited from the intensive field experience that we have. You know, when we first passed the Skyship legislation to ease the population, we never dreamed it would be used against us like this. This is how it starts, Cassius."

"How what starts?"

"War," she said. "It's a trickle, at first. Small, seemingly unconnected moments. You hardly even notice them. Then there's a warning sign, like the terrorist attacks on New York City at the turn of the century. Ignore that and ... well, look where we are now." She frowned. "I was never a fan of the Hernandez Treaty. We gave them too much power."

A moment of uncomfortable silence hung in the air. Cassius tried to think of a clever response, a way to engage in intelligent political discourse.

Madame didn't give him the chance. "I spoke to the President earlier today. Seems Representative Fifty-Four had to jet across the Atlantic for an emergency meeting with the remnants of the Commonwealth. So, the timetable's made its rounds and it looks like it's my turn to speak with the Tribunal. I think I'd like you to accompany me."

"Go up to Skyship?"

"To Skyship Atlas, yes. It's simply procedural—collect their activity reports, sign some papers. Dull, monotonous details. I'm required to bring two others with me. My body-guard will be joining us, of course, but I'd like to offer you the second spot."

Cassius tried to contain his smile. He'd never been invited to participate in important government meetings before, especially ones off-Surface. "Why me?"

She clasped her hands in front of her. "I'd like to give them something to think about."

Cassius shifted uneasily, unsure of what she meant.

"But we'll save that discussion for tomorrow." She cleared her throat. "The meeting's not until Thursday. Now, back to the matter at hand. It won't happen again, will it? Going outside of the Net without clearance, I mean."

He shook his head, though he knew he couldn't promise it. Being cooped up inside the Lodge all day was so boring.

"Good." Madame's attention returned to the Pearl. "Though I can't argue with your results." Her fingers danced along the top, mirroring the weaving energy inside. "Marvelous little baubles, aren't they? To think that we ever lived without them. I still remember that first winter after the bombings. Seventy-six degrees in the middle of December. In Boston, no less." She chuckled. "People thought it was great. Impromptu vacations. Christmas at the beach. That was before the insects started multiplying and crops began to die. I wish you could have seen it, Cassius, the way it was. Real snow, not that nonsense the Weathermen program into the Bio-Nets. Just pure white, stretching out as far as the eye could see."

Cassius strained to imagine it. The only large-scale weather event he'd ever experienced was the arid, dusty wind of the Fringes.

Madame smiled. "You know, I've never been a very religious person, but every time I hold one of these in my hands I feel like we're not alone in this universe."

Cassius chuckled nervously. Despite growing up with her, he still found himself tongue-tied around Madame. Mostly he just let her do the talking.

"I'll have someone put it into stasis right away," she continued. "I look forward to our trip up to Atlas. It'll give us some time to catch up. It feels like I've hardly seen you these past few weeks."

"You've been busy."

She nodded. "True, but that's a lazy excuse, isn't it? This is an important time in your life. I'd regret missing too much of it."

Cassius was about to respond when a powerful wave of heat rushed through his chest, like someone had lit a fuse and buried it deep inside his body. The room fractured and spun, a kaleidoscope of carpet patterns, bookshelves, and Pearl energy. He staggered sideways, nearly toppling over onto the floor before catching himself and straightening his posture.

Madame stood immediately, revealing a slim figure covered with a fitted blouse tucked into dark trousers. "Cassius, are you all right?"

He rubbed his head. "Yeah, I just got a little dizzy there for a second."

"You've been outside the Net for too long," she spoke with a tremor of concern. "You should go lie down."

"Maybe." His heart pounded at double time as his chest continued to burn. He cleared his throat, making sure to conceal his discomfort in front of Madame.

Her eyes narrowed. "Are you sure nothing happened to you back in Syracuse?"

His mind raced back to the rooftop—separating from the Skyship boy, thrown across the ground. "Yeah," he lied, careful not to stumble on his words. "I'm fine."

She frowned, unconvinced. "All right. We'll talk tomorrow. Get some rest and a glass of water. And please call the infirmary if you feel ill."

He nodded and turned to leave the room, desperate to get out before he did something stupid and embarrassed himself in front of her.

"And Cassius?"

He looked over his shoulder. "Yeah?"

"I'm very proud of you."

Her words comforted him as he staggered out the door, gripping his burning chest. He continued down the hallway, each step echoed by a thudding pain inside of him. Heat. Everywhere. So hot.

The hallway weaved into diagonals. He stumbled into the wall twice before making it to the dormitories. Panic consumed his thoughts. Cassius wasn't use to panic, and that was the worst of all. Something was wrong inside of him. He knew it immediately, at a gut level. This wasn't a simple stomach pain. It wasn't the Fringe heat, or the chemicals.

He yanked open the door to his room, slamming it behind him and slumping face down on his perfectly made bed. He'd always been healthy. Rarely sick, he healed from injuries faster than most of his peers. But he hadn't even been injured. Scuffed up a little maybe in Syracuse, but nothing serious.

A sharp pain stabbed below his heart and prickled to his feet. Each moment that followed was an exclamation point on an already panicked state of shock. He'd heard of people having heart attacks, dropping dead minutes after they felt pain, but a fifteen-year-old? There's no way.

Desperate for water, he carefully lifted himself off the bed and stumbled toward the bathroom.

A jolt up his spine stopped him in his tracks, sending him crashing to his knees. His organs sizzled, as if his insides had started leaking poisonous acid into his body. He bit his lip to keep the scream stuck inside.

Then, just as unexpectedly as it had arrived, the pain disappeared.

Cassius ran his hand over his forehead, breathing hard. Sweat dripped from his chin to the floor. He tore off his jacket and threw it toward the bed, untucking his shirt and loosening the top buttons.

Pulling himself off the ground, he struggled to a standing position and sat on the edge of his bed. His legs wobbled. He'd just been through war.

But it wasn't over yet.

The pain returned, nearly knocking him from the bed. This time he felt fire—flames consuming him from inside out.

This time, he screamed.

The fire burst through his skin. Like a human bomb, he exploded. Torrents of flame shot around the bedroom, engulfing every corner. His clothing seared into ashes and fluttered from his body.

It took seconds.

Seconds, and the once spotless room was a charred shell. The flames began to eat through the walls, threatening neighboring quarters. His skin remained pale, his body intact. The fire spread. The warmth inside him diluted. The pain disappeared.

Cassius slumped off the edge of the skeletal bed frame and onto the floor. Face down. Unconscious. Flames danced all around him.

4

As our shuttle bursts into Earth's stratosphere, I dream about Pearls. I dream there's this giant robed guy lounging around on an asteroid somewhere chucking them down at me, one after another. I stand on the Surface, watching them burn through my body as they hit, leaving swiss-cheese holes until I'm hung together by nothing more than gooey threads.

"We've hit 30,000 feet." Eva's call knocks me out of my frustratingly short nap. I pry my eyes open and look out the side window. The vast outline of Skyship Polaris blots out most of the evening sky, just out of reach—a floating, metallic castle. A string of drool hangs from the side of my mouth. Charming.

We passed the Skyline hours ago, back on the East Coast. Ever since then I've been able to relax a little and get some shuteye. I've heard stories about Shippers getting shot for landing on the Surface without credentials. We were lucky not to run into border patrol, though I guess it's kind of hard to police every square inch of the Skyline.

Skyship Academy, a dinky, self-contained ship compared to some of the bigger models, hovers above the California-Oregon border, give or take a few miles. Puttering back all the way from New York, we've been cooped up in this shuttle for going on two hours. Stir crazy. I told Mr. Wilson that it was a mass stupid idea sending us all the way out to the East Coast, but he kept saying that the "opportunity was too good to pass up" (a.k.a., "we're gonna give you losers the safest possible city with the safest possible Pearl Traders so you don't get yourselves killed").

Yeah. That went well.

Eva flips a switch on the ceiling. "I'm stabilizing and setting the auto-pilot."

"Go for it," Skandar answers half-heartedly. Eva's always been one for protocol, though she knows she doesn't need our advice. She's the best pilot in Year Nine. I don't even have my learner wings yet.

Skandar unfastens his belt and moves across the shuttle, sitting backward on the seat nearest to me, face pressed against the window. "Polaris." He grins. "I heard they've got this hotel . . . and there are these women, right? You walk in and they'll do—"

"Please." Eva groans. "Please stop."

He makes a face out the window, though it's meant for her.

My eyes follow the enormous ship as we pass by. The neon towers stretching up from the top level create an unnatural glow in the atmosphere. The hull is dark and wide—

wedge-shaped, with space for thousands of tiny little rooms and corridors. The more money you've got, the higher you get to live. Nobody wants to try and sleep next to the thrusters on the bottom level. That's why it's reserved for docking bays. But Polaris isn't much of a "settling down" ship, anyway. Not if you want peace and quiet. "We flew over there a couple years ago, right? For the opera?"

Skandar rolls his eyes. "Ugh. The most boring night of my life. I'm telling you, mate. Someday we need to highjack a shuttle and sneak onto Polaris. Head up to the casinos. That's where the real action is."

Somehow I can't imagine that happening. After today's little adventure, I wouldn't be surprised if Mr. Wilson kept us locked up in the Academy until we all turned eighteen.

Skandar's com-pad flashes at his side. He detaches it from his belt, reading the line of text on the shiny black surface. Rolling his eyes, he tosses it to me. "Romeo's been buzzed."

I fumble with the device, glancing down at the words on the screen.

Jesse, why are you ignoring me? Are you all right?
- Avery

Eva shifts in her seat, peering at the rearview mirror. "Is it Avery again?"

Skandar nods. "You mean Fisher's girlfriend?"

I flip down the keypad, typing. "She's not my girlfriend."

"Not if you keep denying it," Skandar replies.

"I don't care who she is," Eva huffs. "Academy CPs are not meant for socializing. How she's managed to hack her way into our channel I'll never know."

"She's good at that kind of stuff," I mutter, pressing the send button.

Not ignoring you. Lost my CP, but I'm ok. - Jesse

Seconds later, another message appears on the screen.

Just wanted to congratulate you on your first mission. Dinner tonight? - Avery

My heart swells as I reread the words. With all the negativity floating around this afternoon, the prospect of dinner with Avery Wicksen is more than enough reward for me. Ever since she was transferred from the Academy on Skyship Mira three years ago, she's been the calm oasis after increasingly embarrassing mishaps—the only one I can really talk to. I quickly type a nonchalant "yeah" into the com-pad and send it.

Eva frowns. "Give me one good reason I shouldn't tell Mr. Wilson about you two abusing the CPs."

I toss it back to Skandar. "Um . . . your kind and generous nature?"

She snorts with laughter.

"Come on, Eva." Skandar attaches the com-pad to his belt. "Have a heart. Fisher's gotta work on his game." He slaps my shoulder. "So what'd you tell her?" He purses his lips, adopting a ridiculous deep voice. "*Hey, baby, come to my room so we can get it on.*"

Eva rolls her eyes. "Real subtle, Harris."

I shrug. "I pretty much just said 'yeah.'"

He rolls his eyes, leaning back. "Well, that's lame."

Our shuttle continues to zip along the thin layer of cirrus clouds beneath us. Soon Polaris is nothing more than a dot in the distance. Creeping up next on the radar is the Horizon College of Liberal Arts. We call it Skyship Academy.

And we don't study liberal arts. The school's a front to keep the Unified Party off our backs. Under the Hernandez Treaty, Surface representatives can inspect any part of the Skyship Community with a warrant and "documented suspicion of duplicitous activity," which can basically be turned around to mean just about anything. Places like hospitals, churches, and schools are exempt. Safe havens. So in all its infinite wisdom, the Tribunal runs all its secret Pearl-snatching operations through a handful of "schools." Lucky us.

We file activity reports, but nobody in the Skyship Community knows what we're really getting up to: secret reconnaissance missions, Fringe-trading, anything that helps us grab Pearls before the Unified Party finds them. Read the e-feed and you'd think the Skyships are stable, with enough Pearl Power to last as long as we need. The truth is, we're one dry year away from having to sacrifice a good chunk of our ships. But the Tribunal would never admit it to the community.

Eva unfastens her belt and joins us in the passenger cabin. "Visitation Day on Friday."

Skandar drags his hand across his face. "I hate wearing suits."

"It's only for a few hours. We have to look like any other school and that includes giving tours. Right, Jesse?"

"I'm with Skandar on this one."

Every semester on Visitation Day, hopeful students follow our teachers around all wide-eyed and grinning, mass eager to learn about philosophy and literature and heaps of other stuff that we don't actually teach. None of them ever make it through our "selective" admissions department. Skyship Academy's only new recruits are agents' kids or transfers from other training facilities. Count me among the former, though I can't really remember my parents. They died when I was two, part of a government sting operation. In other words, they died heroes. Kinda sets expectations for their only kid.

"Well," Eva continues, "I don't think it hurts for us to remind ourselves that we're going to be agents soon. It's not bad to look professional every once in a while."

Skandar grimaces. "What, are you like forty years old?"

"I'm just saying . . . a little bit of maturity goes a long way."

I frown. "Tell that to Mr. Wilson when he flunks me out of the program."

She leans forward and lays her hand on my knee. It's

mildly creepy. "That's not going to happen, Jesse. You've got three and a half more years. The only way to go is up."

Skandar chuckles. Eva shoots him a look that silences him instantly. "*You* on the other hand ... everything's a joke to you, isn't it?"

He shrugs. Eva's face bristles. I can tell she's about to slap him so I half-heartedly point out the window. "Looks like we're home."

After one last glare in Skandar's direction, she stomps back to the cockpit and flips off the autopilot.

The Academy hangs in the sky before us, a dark gray ornament against a backdrop of fuchsia sunset. It's shaped like the world's biggest spinning top, widest at its peak and curving down all the way to the jagged spire at the bottom that sweeps through the wispy clouds below like a needle through dry ice. Unlike a top, we don't spin. Skyships rarely change coordinates at all, unless there's a security breach.

We live on one of the smaller models, less an airborne city than a massive, flying house. Extending from the top center is the central tower. Inside, Captain Alkine—our number-one-cross-him-you-die commander—makes all the important calls. A transparent fiberglass dome cuts through the tower halfway, arching down to surround Lookout Park, a green oasis in the middle of the sky. Not only does it grow most of our food, but it's the place to be after lessons. There's no such thing as a cloudy day at Lookout. They're all rushing by below our feet.

Six levels of living quarters, training classrooms, and

research labs fill the rest of the ship, narrowing as they near the bottom where the docking bays lie open in anticipation of our shuttle.

We pull closer to the Academy. Dark, weathered siding fills the air outside my window. A pink sunset streams in behind us, hitting Eva right in the face. In an hour it'll be completely dark. The canteen's probably closed except for a few leftovers. There goes dinner.

I run my fingers through my dusty hair, sitting up and stretching as the shuttle veers into docking bay number three. The floor vibrates as the landing gear retracts. The cabin lights flicker off, replaced by the soft glow from inside the bay.

Eva shuts off the power as soon as we touch down. With a quick hiss of air, the door rises open and the steps collapse. Skandar and Eva head out first. I stand up. My head spins.

I grab the back of my seat to avoid falling over, but the dizziness gets mass worse. My pulse quickens until each thump feels like it's gonna send my heart flying out of my chest. I let go of the chair and stretch my arms, closing my eyes and breathing deep. I just need a drink of water, that's all. I mean, after what happened today, it's a wonder I'm still alive.

Carefully, I step out onto the metallic floor panels of the docking bay. Aside from a couple of mechanics working on a decommissioned shuttle in the far corner, the place is deserted. The last sun rays, now a vivid orange, flow up into the mouth of the bay behind us and cast our shadows on the far wall. We look huge in shadow form. In reality I don't think we're so impressive.

I take a deep breath and follow my teammates past the chemical scanners to the ground level of the Academy. The wide windows of the circular hallway heat the incoming sun until it feels like we're back on the Surface. We intersect the corridor and head for the central elevator shaft—the Academy's spinal cord.

Skandar thumps his fist against the white walls as we march down an unremarkable hallway. With nearly a thousand of us onboard, the upper levels are packed this time of night. It's dead silent down here.

My heart beats twice for every step. I stop and close my eyes, hoping that when I open them the hallway will stop spinning. It doesn't.

We turn the corner into a second corridor. My strides shorten, feet dragging.

Skandar pauses and leans against the wall. "You okay, mate?"

I hold up a hand. The other one's clutching my chest, trying to get my heart to slow down. "I'm fine. Just a little dizzy."

Eva turns, hands on hips. "Probably the heat. You rehydrated on the shuttle ride, didn't you?"

I nod, taking a deep breath and straightening my back. "I'll be okay."

She sighs, but doesn't press the issue.

A few more moments and we're at the elevators. Skandar presses the button and stares at me while we wait for the doors to open. I don't look back at him. By the time we're crammed inside, my heart slows to a normal pace again.

I watch the screen beside the doors as we ascend to Level Five.

Meeting rooms. Mr. Wilson.

As head teacher of Year Nine, it's Wilson's responsibility to put us on track for graduation and to train us in the grand arts of Surface survival and Pearl Retrieval. He doesn't like me. He's never liked me. Any crumb of affection left between us oughta be wiped out tonight.

The elevator doors spread open. My back-to-normal heart lumps in my throat. We slump toward the meeting room with all the excitement of a funeral procession. When we finally take our seats at the crescent-shaped table inside, I'm about to pass out from all the stress. An old wooden desk in front lies empty for now, waiting for Mr. Wilson.

There's no decoration, no windows, nothing but a ripped projector screen hanging from the ceiling and a barren table pushed into the corner. A weeping plant clings to life against the opposite wall. It probably hasn't been watered in weeks. Fluorescent light blares down from a tube directly above us. Hell's waiting room.

I take a sip of water from a glass in front of me. We sit in silence. Bad kids in detention. Nobody knows what to expect. Mr. Wilson's not a yeller, but there's a first time for everything.

The door knob twists and Mr. Wilson strolls in, wearing a

drab, unbuttoned sport coat and jeans. Focus real hard and the hint of a bald spot creeps up from under his combed-over hair. I like to see how fast I can find it. Today it takes me longer than usual. Go Mr. Wilson.

He's got a bundle of books tucked under his arm that he sets on the desk before treating us to a mass dorky, come-on-impress-me smile.

"Well," he begins. "It's reassuring to see you all back unscathed. I hope your shuttle trip was comfortable. There's supposed to be a storm passing through below us tonight."

Nobody responds. We can barely meet his eyes.

He picks up on this immediately, crossing his arms and leaning against the desk. His lips shut and settle into a frown. The buzzing of the overhead lights is deafening.

He claps his hands together. I nearly jump out of my seat. "I guess we'll get right to it, then. Where's the Pearl?"

Crickets.

"The Pearl," he repeats, like we didn't understand the first time. "Come on, kids."

I raise my head and meet his eyes. "We ... um ... we kind of don't have it."

His expression falls blank. "You *kind of* don't have it, or you *don't* have it?"

"We don't have it," I mumble. Might as well rip off the bandage all at once.

He drags his hand across his face, rubbing away the last remnants of anticipation. "I need to sit down." He crawls behind the desk, grunting and sighing with dissatisfaction.

"I told Alkine this was a bad idea," he mutters. "What happened?"

"We were ambushed," Eva replies. "Just after unloading the last of the rations."

I wince. Technically, *Skandar and I* were ambushed, and we weren't anywhere near the rations.

Mr. Wilson's face drains of color. "Ambushed? Syracuse is deserted. We made sure there weren't any hostiles before sending you down."

Eva frowns. "He was one of Madame's. No older than us, sir."

Wilson leans forward. "By himself?"

I glance over at Eva. It would be so easy to concoct a dramatic story with government blockades and cruisers and tanks. It'd be less embarrassing, too. Less consequence. Less lectures. But by the time I open my mouth, it's already too late.

"Yes, sir," she says. "By himself."

Mr. Wilson shakes his head. "So let me get this straight. Some fifteen-year-old punk from Madame's crew shows up in the middle of the Fringes and manages to single-handedly take on three of my trainees *and* steal our Pearl?"

"It was Fisher's fault!" Skandar points at me.

"Hey!" I glare back. "It's not like you weren't tied up on the ground!"

"I had it in my hands," Eva interrupts, "but Jesse got himself in trouble with some of the locals and I had to help him. The guy snuck up on us. I did everything I could, sir.

It wouldn't have happened at all if Fisher and Harris hadn't been screwing around. I would recommend—"

Wilson holds up his hand to stop her. "All right." He sighs. "Enough. I got it. You've had a very long day. As much as I'd like to, this isn't the time to run through all of the mistakes that could have been prevented. Eva, Skandar, head over to the canteen and get something to eat. We'll talk about this in detail tomorrow."

I glance around the room. "What about me?"

"*You* stay here." His eyes pin me to my seat. "Alkine wants to talk to you."

Skandar flashes me a sympathetic look, but wastes no time slipping out the door. Eva follows right behind.

"I think a round of Bunker Ball is in order tomorrow, so get some sleep!" Wilson calls after them as the door shuts. I sink down into my seat, barely able to make eye contact.

A silence falls over the meeting room. My heart does somersaults. Sweat drips down the sides of my torso. Usually when I'm forced into a meeting with Captain Alkine I layer on a gallon of deodorant beforehand. I may smell like a flowery garden, but at least he doesn't see what a nervous wreck I am.

"Fisher, Fisher, Fisher." Mr. Wilson shakes his head. "What are we going to do with you?"

The scary thing is, I don't know. I don't know what the hell they're planning to do with me. Alkine's a busy guy. He doesn't have time for unscheduled meetings.

I contemplate bolting for the door and locking myself

in my bedroom, but before I know it, Captain Alkine enters the room. His heavy combat boots clomp on the floor as he walks to the desk. He's gotta be a full foot taller than me at least. Impossibly tall. His skin is weathered from years of living on the Surface. A scar runs down his left cheek—a battle wound from his days as a soldier. His dark hair is all but gray now, turned by years of overseeing a Skyship full of children.

Mr. Wilson stands, whispers something in Alkine's ear, and leaves. Alkine moves behind the desk and stares off into the corner of the room for a moment. Then his eyes fall squarely on me.

"Jesse Fisher."

I bristle at the sound of his deep voice. I try to look anywhere but at his face. It's not that he's a bad guy. It's just that, well, he scares me. And not knowing why he's here? That's even scarier.

His words sit in the air, detached. I can't tell if they were supposed to be a statement or a question, so I keep my mouth shut.

He sighs. "For god's sake, straighten up in your chair. You look like you're about to drip onto the floor."

Amazing. He's managed to put into words exactly how I feel inside.

"So you lost the Pearl." He clasps his hands in front of him. "Big deal. It's happened before, it'll happen again. It's only training."

My shoulders relax. Maybe I'll get away with this after all.

He clears his throat. "Do you want to be an agent, Jesse?"

Crap. I give my best fake nod, wondering if he can see through it.

"Then you've got to focus. And work hard." He pauses. "What's on your face?"

I touch my cheek, still tender and warm from the brick wall. "It's ... uh ... a burn."

"Clumsy," he replies, shaking his head. "I regret that I haven't been able to play a more active role in your life, Fisher." He scoots closer to the desk. A shiver runs down my neck at the thought of Captain Alkine wanting any part of my life, or even thinking about me at all with the hoards of trainees running around up here.

He sighs. "Your parents would have wished for you to realize your full potential, you know. I'm concerned that without a steady guide things are becoming ... stagnant."

I look down at the table at the mention of my parents. I can count on one hand the kids at the Academy without family. No need for Alkine to remind me.

"I never thought I'd be taking care of children up here," he continues, "but let's face it, children are our greatest hope."

I nod, unwilling to make eye contact.

"The Tribunal's been on my back about getting all of our medical reports in order. There are some additional tests I've arranged for you at the beginning of next week, things you've missed."

I groan inwardly. It's been the same since I was a kid. The Academy loves its checkups. Something about the Tribunal wanting to make sure trainees are in tip-top shape, they say. All I know is that I hate needles, especially when they're poking into me.

He pauses, waiting for me to say something. I keep my eyes on the table.

"Aside from losing the Pearl, how did it go today? Did it feel different being on the Surface?"

My mind flashes back to the rooftop. Falling off. Living.

"Hotter," I reply.

He smiles. "Yes, yes of course. That certainly can't be helped with the Unified Party in charge." He laughs, though it's more like a grunt. "*Unified*. What a joke. Unified in vengeance, maybe. It's ironic, you know? In fighting their so-called terrorists they've only become more like them. Secretive, scared—a silent dictatorship. They're like a bug turned over on its back, wiggling its little legs, lashing out at everything else in hopes of flipping back around." He chuckles. "If the Tribunal gave me the go-ahead I'd be down there right now, with a big boot to squash them before they turn themselves over. Sometimes I feel ridiculous up here, running this school. I'm not a teacher. I'm a soldier."

I want to point out to him that an illegal training base isn't technically a "school," but I keep it to myself.

"Did I ever tell you I served in Operation Blackout?"

"Several times, sir." In fact, during school lectures he

never shuts up about it. *The defining moment that turned the tides of the Chinese-American War*, he says.

Alkine nods, crossing his arms. "Best days of my life. I guess some of us are just born for battle."

I glance at the door. Some of us were born to get out of this room.

"We came so close to a nuclear war," he continues. "Thirteen years later...we thought it was all over and *bam*!" He pounds his fist on the desk. I jump in my seat. "Guess that's what you get for turning a blind eye. Never look away, Fisher. Never."

Taking the cue, I meet his eyes for a moment and keep my attention glued to his face. Well, more like his shoulder. The face is too threatening.

He laughs. "I remember this one night on the Chinese border, decades before we nuked them. There was this kid, couple of years younger than me at the time. Come to think of it, you remind me of him. Not a soldier in the strictest sense, but the potential was there.

"Anyway," he continues, "the two of us were on a rendez-vous assignment...guy from inside the country was meeting us with schematics, stuff we'd need to get in and out of their facility alive. It was a simple mission, just waiting around to grab a bundle of papers. But as you discovered today, simple missions are never as easy as they sound. Turns out someone tipped off the border patrol. We were outnumbered. But worst of all, we were unprepared."

My eyes stray back to the table. "What happened to your friend?"

He frowns. "Died. Round of bullets right through his chest. Wasn't quick enough."

I fidget in my seat. And this guy reminds Alkine of me? "Sir, do you ... uh ... want something?"

He blinks twice. "Am I boring you, Fisher?"

"No, sir," I mutter.

"Well, you're getting to that age where decisions must be made. I don't want you to end up with a round of bullets through *your* chest. Your peers and teachers are all well and good, but I want you to feel free to come to me if anything's wrong."

"What would be wrong?"

"Nothing, nothing," he says. "I just ... well, I know how it can be, growing up with the pressure you kids experience. It's a rotten card you've been dealt some days, being born into the program. I also know that Mr. Wilson isn't particularly impressed by the limited progress you're making. Frankly, neither am I. It's important that you have a strong male influence in your life. I'm trying ... that is, I *would like* to be that person."

I look up. A lopsided, uncomfortable smile sits on his face. It's worse than his frown.

This is majorly screwed up. Alkine doesn't interact with students. He leaves that for the teachers. He said it himself. He's a soldier. "Does that mean that we'd have to, like, spend time together?"

He sighs. "Jesse, what I'm trying to say is: if you have a problem, you come to me. Should I make that an order?"

"No, sir."

"Okay." He slaps the top of the desk. "Then go join your friends. Get something to eat."

Without waiting for him to change his mind, I jump out of my seat and head for the door. He doesn't call after me, thank god. Forcing me to listen to old war stories is punishment enough.

I head out into the hallway, traveling double speed. Trying-to-be-nice Captain Alkine is ten times scarier than normal Captain Alkine and the fact that I'm on his radar at all is yet another thing to add to my list of reasons why I'm getting out of here as soon as I turn eighteen.

5

Cassius's eyes parted to see Madame's flawless face staring down at him.

She perched over his bed, her lips forming a grim frown that took a few seconds to fade into something less disconcerting.

"Cassius." She smiled. "You're awake. Thank goodness."

He blinked several times to make sure it wasn't a dream. His skin felt tingly and raw, like he'd been submerged in a bath of ice for the past week.

He sat up in the bed and analyzed the spare white room. A counter ran along the wall beside him. A chair stood vacant in the opposite corner with a freshly pressed uniform hanging over the armrest.

An infirmary recovery room.

"We were very worried," Madame continued. "A couple hours longer and you may have required serious medical attention. It's lucky you're such a strong boy."

"What happened?" He hardly recognized his groggy

voice. He looked down to see a hospital gown tied tightly around him. "What time is it?"

"You were unresponsive all evening after the accident."

"Accident?" The ceiling lights above the bed forced him to squint.

Madame smiled. "You mean you don't remember? Your room's gone, Cassius. We're lucky you didn't take out the entire second floor while you were at it."

"I don't..." He trailed off, trying to remember the events of the afternoon. Sneaking out into the Fringes, finding the Pearl, heading back to the Lodge.

"Fire." The word spilled from his mouth almost automatically. "There was a fire."

"Yes." She nodded. "There certainly was."

"A blown circuit?"

"No."

He stared up in confusion, waiting for her to continue.

"It was you, Cassius."

"I'm sorry," he stammered, realizing how mad she must be. Yet she didn't seem mad.

"I don't think you're understanding me." She laid her hand on his leg. "*You* started the fire. It came from inside of you."

He stifled a laugh. He'd heard urban legends about people spontaneously combusting, but that's all they were. Legends.

She frowned. "It's really not a laughing matter."

He searched her face for any hint of a joke. Then he remembered. Madame never joked.

"The damage is extensive," she said.

He looked down at his still-tingling hands. His s. was abnormally smooth. Gone were the scrapes and sores from the day before. He was paler than usual, too. "That's impossible. *I* caused the fire?"

Madame nodded, squeezing his knee.

"I ... I don't understand. I remember feeling sick when I left your office but everything after that's a blur."

She eased her grip. "I'm sure your body was struggling to keep control. Perception ... things of that nature fall by the wayside during traumas such as these. After all, it was the first time."

"Wait," he started, "did you know this was going to happen?"

She sighed and moved to the counter to pour a glass of water. "There are things we don't talk about, Cassius. I'm sure you've noticed. And the truth is, I'm still not confident that I'm ready to address them." She paused a moment in thought. "But you've forced my hand."

"I didn't do anything."

Her eyes narrowed as she handed him the glass. "You went outside the Net, Cassius."

"Plenty of people live outside the Bio-Nets."

"You met a boy."

"What? Who?"

She sat down at the edge of the bed "His name is Jesse Fisher, and he complicates things."

"Jesse Fisher," he whispered, searching his memory. "The Shipper on the rooftop ... "

Her eyebrows raised. "Rooftop?"

He took a sip of water and looked to the side, uneager to talk about his failure in front of her. "I had him hanging on—barely. He was about to drop off the ledge when he ... I don't know what he did. We separated and he fell twelve stories to the ground. I thought he was dead."

She nodded. "But he wasn't, was he?"

"It's impossible. He was just a scrawny little coward."

She laughed. "Impossible? Impossible like burning down a dormitory without so much as a matchbook?"

He met her reassuring eyes, shaking his head in disbelief.

"He's dangerous, Cassius. He ignited this inside of you. This ... sickness. And it's through him that we'll cure it."

Cassius set down the glass. He held his hand in front of him, spreading apart the fingers, trying to imagine flames shooting from the tips. It was crazy. It couldn't be real.

"In the meantime," she removed a small envelope from her pocket and set it on the bed in front of him, "we can do our best to control the situation."

He picked up the package, opening the top and peering inside to find three tiny white pills. "What's this?"

"Insurance," she replied. "Very expensive, too. The medication will slow your heart rate and calm your system to a level where you'll be able to control any further outbursts."

He winced, struggling to give voice to his next thought.

The words came out slow and muttered. "I'm not sure I believe you."

Madame pursed her lips. "Cassius. I could be … very angry with you right now. Your lack of judgment in traveling to the Fringes has caused me a great deal of unnecessary stress."

"Kids don't burst into flames."

"And planets aren't meant to grow unlivable," she countered. "We live in uncharted territory, and you're going to have to accept that. Things happen. You're a very special young man. You have a lot to accomplish yet. I didn't want this to happen. Not until we were ready."

"Ready for what?"

"It's a numbers game. Always has been, ever since the Seps took to the sky. I've been lobbying the heads of the party to do away with the birthing limits for years now. We need bodies." She crossed her arms, drumming her fingers on her cashmere jacket. "They're right above us, Cassius. Have you ever actually considered what that means? We thought we had it bad with the terrorists, but they were half a world away. Shippers could drop down on us any minute. And to be honest, I don't think we're ready."

"For war," he whispered. "Like you were talking about last night. And this Jesse Fisher … him triggering this … thing in me has got something to do with it?"

She nodded. "It has everything to do with it. In fact, if we don't take care of this situation quickly, he may just be the lynchpin that triggers the opening shot. I do not wish that to happen. Not yet. Not while there's a chance we could lose."

He rubbed his hands together, trying to work some warmth into them. "Why's he so special?"

"That is on a strictly need-to-know basis."

He scoffed, then caught himself as Madame shot him an icy look. "Well," he muttered, "considering the circumstances, I think I *need* to know."

"You need to trust me," she replied. "Fisher has his uses. He's very important."

"He's just a kid."

"Pearls," Madame responded. "Without Pearls our empire would crumble. We would be left in the dust like the Fringers. They would tear us up and burn us all, Cassius. The Skyships would lower to the ground and reclaim the country. We need Pearls."

Cassius winced. "So what's Fisher got to do with all that?"

"Pearls," she repeated. "That's all you need know."

He looked down at the bed sheet, avoiding her fiery gaze. "How are you going to capture him, then?"

"Not me," she paused. Her expression softened. "*You.* I need you to help me with this. You're going to make a detour after our meeting on Skyship Atlas."

"You know where he is?"

She nodded. "I have operatives stationed all over the Skyship Community. How do you think I know he exists at all?"

"But the Hernandez Treaty—"

"Oh, Cassius. Nothing was ever gained by playing strictly by the rules. Do you think they don't have people spying on *us*? They're not that naïve." She clasped her hands, staring at the empty counter. "Jesse Fisher's training at an academy. They use schools because they think we're stupid enough not to check up on them. Maybe the President's that gullible, but not me."

"Does the President know that they're doing this? Using schools?"

She smiled—a cold, disenchanted smile. "There's a reason the President's in hiding, Cassius. He'd like everybody to think we're as unified as our moniker suggests, but things are never that simple. Remember what I talked about last night? Small, unconnected moments. Sometimes it takes a person of fierce awareness to connect the dots. The President is not that man. He's better suited to pacifying rebellious Fringers than worrying about Skyships and Pearls."

"Well, if this kid is so important, why are you sending *me* to get him?"

"I trust you, Cassius. I wouldn't be telling you any of this if I didn't. I cannot trust anybody else in the Unified Party. As I said before, there are … things that we don't talk about, that *I* don't talk about. Things I've seen, things I know. Things I must keep a secret, even from you."

He shook his head. "About Jesse Fisher."

She nodded, glancing in his direction. "About a lot of things." She cleared her throat. "Besides, an adult agent would never make it inside Skyship Academy undetected.

They're having a visitation day at the end of the week and you're going to board their ship as a prospective student. I've already arranged a passport for you. We'll wire a skin graft over the identification code on your wrist. Luckily your little stunt in the dormitories seared most of the residual Surface chemicals from your skin. Their scanners shouldn't be a problem."

"You really think it's safe? You think I won't be caught?"

She shook her head. "It's as safe as we can make it. I've gone to a lot of trouble these past hours, Cassius. You shouldn't have gone to Syracuse, for your own sake."

He opened his mouth to apologize, but realized it wouldn't do any good. As always, he couldn't discern what she was really feeling. Her face remained stony and impenetrable.

After an uncomfortable gap of silence, Madame broke from her trance. "As Head of Energy, I have access to whatever military force I deem necessary. If anything goes horribly wrong, you will be well-supported. But I would prefer to keep this off the radar. For now." She sighed. "Before I go, I've got something to share with you. If nothing else, it should inspire you to take on this mission." She reached below the bed to retrieve a small black cube—about half a foot wide and equally as tall. "This is from your mother."

"But—"

"Your *real* mother." She ran her fingers across the smooth, shiny exterior. "When you came to me, so did this."

Cassius analyzed it, trying to figure out what the cube

had been carved from. It looked almost like marble, though it couldn't have weighed much judging by the ease with which Madame had hefted it. The only mark was a small keyhole at the top center. No dings or scratches, though it was obviously very old.

"What's inside?"

"A cure, I hope. For the fire within you." She set the cube in front of him. "Other than that, I have no idea."

Cassius touched the side of the cube. It felt colder than the rest of the room, like touching a tombstone. He glanced up at Madame's face. His birth mother was certainly one of the subjects they never talked about. There wasn't much to say. Why care about a pathetic junkie? But then again, he'd never known a junkie to carry around such a strange object. His mind raced with ideas of what could be inside. Inheritance, birth certificates, photographs. The last thought made his heart skip a beat. He'd never seen a photograph of his parents.

"Where's the key?"

Madame frowned, pointing up to the ceiling. Cassius knew exactly what that meant.

Skyship.

He nodded. "Fisher."

"Find Jesse Fisher, and in addition to a cure, we'll get you that key." She stood up. "Now if there's nothing else, I'm going to see about getting you some food. We'll start briefing tomorrow afternoon. I'll need you strong from the get-go. I laid an extra uniform on the chair over in the corner. I'm sure you're eager to get out of that hospital gown."

She grabbed the cube from his lap and took a few steps toward the door before pausing and turning around. "And Cassius, remember this is just between you and me. Please keep it that way."

He nodded.

"Fantastic." She exited the room without a goodbye, leaving a mountain of unanswered questions in her wake.

6

I swirl a spoon through a bowl of the canteen's leftover mystery chili, mentally replaying the events of the day. A janitor mops the floor by the kitchen. It's just me and him tonight.

I sit at a circular table in the corner of the room. The chili's cold. It tastes even worse than it smells. I can't say our cooks know how to do Mexican. They should stick with what they do best—opening cans and dumping them into serving bowls.

The walls around me are the same color as the seven pitiful pieces of melted cheese that congeal into a rubbery disc in the center of the bowl. I would have been better off sneaking a couple pieces of fruit down to my room and calling it a night.

"Well," a figure enters the canteen, "I can't wait to join this fun little pity party."

I look up and smile, even though she's twenty minutes late.

Avery Wicksen: fellow orphan, snoop extraordinaire, and totally unattainable eighteen-year-old post-grad.

She skips over to the corner of the room, plopping down on the seat next to me. Her straw-colored hair's tied up away from her face. She wears a pale-blue tank top and loose-fitting jeans, and couldn't be more beautiful if she tried. She stares down into the bowl, shaking her head. "That is a crime against nature. They should be ashamed of themselves."

I push the bowl away. "I was wondering if you were gonna show up."

She grins, the faint cluster of freckles on each side of her smile dancing up and down. "Ran into some trouble with Dolores. *Trouble* in the sense that I couldn't escape her. I swear that woman is in love with me."

I lean against the wall, facing her. Dolores Anderson is the fossil-old librarian that Avery works with during the day. Given her less-than-stellar training record and knack for ditching classes, the teachers stuck Avery with mass boring library work rather than graduating her to full-blown agent status. Hanging out with her is like taking a look at my own future. If only our similarities were enough to hypnotize her into falling in love with me. "You two have tea again?"

She nods. "Ever since her husband died she's been so clingy. Part of me wishes they'd just send her off to one of the retirement ships. Rigel, maybe."

"Yeah, right. Once you're up here, you're here to stay. Unless you wanna let the Tribunal do a full mind wipe."

Avery shrugs. "*Nature's* doing a mind wipe on Dolores. Sometimes I think she mistakes me for her daughter." She pauses. "But enough about her." She grabs my wrist. "How are you?"

"Been better," I reply.

"Do you wanna talk about it?"

"Not really."

She leans in closer, squinting and placing her fingers on my cheek. An orchestral symphony swells inside my body. For a second I'm convinced that she's gonna kiss me. My mind frantically searches for the right thing to do. Lean forward, grab her shoulder, pucker up. Then she opens her mouth.

"Are you aware that you have an imprint of a brick on the side of your head?"

My inner symphony hits a bum note and the orchestra lights flicker off. "Yeah, I'm aware. It hurts like hell."

She chuckles. "Did someone brand you?"

I lean back, knowing that the red mark is the least of my worries. "I told you I don't want to talk about it."

"Okay." She pulls away. "Just saying. Us poor little orphans have to stick together up here."

I sigh, resting my chin on my knees. "We lost the Pearl today. I lost my belt. Everything. If Eva hadn't stepped in when she did, I might be dead."

Her green eyes fill with concern. "Dead? On a training mission?"

"Yep," I reply, pressing on the table with my thumb. "And if that doesn't define my life up here, I don't know what would."

"So you think it was your fault."

"I *know* it was my fault, Avery. There was this Pearlhound, not even an adult. I should have been able to take him, but I panicked."

"This guy have a name?"

"Cassius Stevenson." I sigh.

Her brows raise.

I meet her eyes. "What? Does that mean something to you? Is he like some super macho legend I should know about?"

"No," she responds. "Just curious."

"Oh, and by the way, Eva's pissed about you hacking into our CPs. How do you do that, anyway?"

"A lot of time and a lot of reading." She shrugs. "But look, I've seen Skandar in action and he ain't so hot. And Eva may think she's some warrior princess, but I heard she still sleeps with her old teddy bear blanket."

I smirk. "Really?"

"No," she replies. "I made that up to get a smile out of you. Truth is, Jesse, it doesn't really matter. The teachers make it seem like Pearls are the be all and end all, but there *are* other things in life. Don't obsess over the parts you can't control. Jeez, if I spent time wallowing about my failures I'd have jumped off the ship ages ago."

"I wasn't wallowing."

She laughs. "Oh, you're wallowing. That is the most wallowing bowl of chili I've seen in my life."

I glance over to the lonely bowl, considering her sage advice. It's times like these that I'm convinced the two of us should just hijack a shuttle and take off for Polaris or Vega or some other fun ship—a ship where they don't train children for illegal, dangerous work and then mock them when they're not up to it.

"Speaking of," she reaches over and grabs the bowl, "you got any enemies, Fisher? We can pick the lock on their door and dump this on them while they're sleeping."

I chuckle, despite myself. "That sounds like the worst idea you've ever had."

"Oh, come on. I've had worse."

"Well, there is August Bergmann..." I wince as I say his name, imagining how he'll spin my little Surface adventure once he hears about it. The guy's had it in for me ever since Year Six.

Her face lights up. "Yeah! Now there's a perfect candidate for a late-night chili dump."

I shake my head. "But I'm already in trouble. Alkine's *concerned*." I frame the word with air quotes. "They're all concerned."

She rolls her eyes. "They're *always* concerned. If they weren't, they'd be concerned about *that* too." She pushes the bowl away. It flies across the table, nearly toppling off the edge.

"There were Fringers," I continue. "Not friendly either. Hence the lovely mark on my cheek."

She rests her chin in her hand, staring at me. "It's actually kinda cute. Think of it as a temporary tattoo. Real badass."

"Yeah." I smile. "Temporary tattoos are the definition of badass, right? They might as well have just scrawled 'loser' across my face. Bergmann's gonna have a field day with this one."

She shrugs. "There's always the chili. Just sayin'."

I nod, relishing the idea of August Bergmann with cold chili dumped all over his body.

"Seriously, though," she leans closer, "you'll get over it. After my parents died ... when General Campbell had me transferred over here, it was the absolute loneliest time in my life. Sometimes this place is like a tomb. You just wanna get outside and breathe in fresh air for once, but people keep pulling you back. I mean, who cares about Pearls and stuff when your whole world falls apart, right?"

I nod.

"But then I started hanging out with you and things weren't so bad. The teachers may be concerned about you, Jesse, but they're boring, stuffy people. They don't matter."

"I don't think they'd agree."

"Trust me," she says, "you'll be wasting your effort trying to please them. Wilson was *born* disappointed. Alkine, well ... if you ask me he's not exactly the sympathetic war hero he'd like everybody to believe. You make me laugh, Jesse. And there are maybe three people onboard who can do that. Should count for something, right?"

I smile. "Thanks, Avery."

"For what?"

I pause, holding back what I really want to say. "For coming up here. For talking."

"Hey, no problem."

I stare at her face for a second before glancing away, realizing that I look like a stalker. "I should get to bed early tonight. Wilson's making us do Bunker Ball tomorrow morning and my legs are killing me."

"I'll walk down with you."

We stand up from the table and take off through the empty canteen, leaving the chili in the corner to harden.

When we reach my room on the second level, I input my code and crack the door, turning around. An awkward pause comes between us.

There's always an awkward pause. If we were really boyfriend and girlfriend I'd lean over and kiss her goodnight, or at least give her a hug. Instead, I offer a meek "goodnight" and she smiles, heading down the hallway. I watch her go for a moment before slipping into my room, kicking myself for wasting yet another perfect opportunity.

Before plopping onto my half-made bed, I walk to my desk and run my fingers over a pair of medallions hanging on the wall. They belong to my parents, which means technically they belong to *me*. The Tribunal had them shipped over in honor of bravery and sacrifice and mass heroic stuff like that. They've been a permanent fixture in my room for as long as I can remember. The Tribunal destroyed all photographs for security purposes. My parents weren't the keepsake type, either. These medals are all I have—a constant, glistening reminder of how fearless they were. Not like me. I can't even handle a Pearlhound trainee.

I drop the medallions and let them clank against the wall, reaching for the entertainment console at the end of the desk. Then I slump face-first onto the bed and purge the day from memory with the most mind-numbing program I can find on Skyship TV.

7

Cassius hadn't slept well. Four times he'd woken up, covered in sweat. Each time he was convinced it was going to happen again. Fire. Everywhere. Another room destroyed.

Part of him still couldn't believe that it was true. He'd seen what was left of his room. He'd heard what Madame said, but he held onto the hope that there was another explanation.

Now he was on his way to her office for mission briefing. They would be traveling up to Skyship Atlas tomorrow afternoon. If Madame stuck to her word, it would be his last full day at the Lodge for a while. He wasn't sure if finding Fisher was an opportunity or a punishment.

He paused outside the Office of Research and Development—the Lodge's nerve center. Madame was expecting him in half an hour, which meant he'd have time to browse through the Lodge's database in search of more human combustion episodes. Not that he didn't trust Madame, but he wanted to see if this had ever happened before, to anyone else. After all, there was nothing special about him. He couldn't be the only one.

"Stevenson?" A man's deep voice issued from a speaker above the door. "Is that you out there?"

The voice belonged to Lieutenant Henrich, one of the head instructors at the Lodge's training division and one of Madame's most trusted allies.

"Yes, sir," Cassius replied, annoyed to have been spotted so soon.

"Come inside and give me a hand," Henrich said. "You've been given the access code, haven't you?"

"Yes." Cassius plugged in his code beside the door and entered. Madame had just granted him access to the office two weeks ago. He was the only student privileged enough to receive it. Another perk of being her favorite.

Once inside, he passed through rows of computers and bookshelves. It was a tight space, longer than it was wide. At the far end, below a curved glass window, sat the central computer system, responsible for tracking Pearls as they hurtled through the stars and estimating Surface coordinates once they landed.

"Over here." Henrich's voice came from the Stasis Laboratory, a small room connected to the main office. A green glow spilled out from the open doorway. Cassius passed through an aisle of bookshelves, hoping that whatever Henrich wanted wouldn't take long. He needed to find out what was happening to him. Madame's cryptic answers weren't enough.

Green light washed over his body as he entered the laboratory. Lieutenant Henrich stood before a wide counter, wearing a white undershirt and dark trousers. His black hair was slicked back as usual. A Pearl sat in a shallow basin before him. A wall of television screens beamed just beyond the counter, each displaying security footage from one of the ten entrances to the Bio-Net around Rochester. Many of the Lodge's rooms shared this feature. A precaution.

"Stevenson." Henrich greeted him with a lopsided smile. "Come over here and help me attach this stasis equipment. Fraggin' thing's already getting buggy on us."

Cassius moved next to the Lieutenant in silence. He didn't much like one-on-ones with instructors. It felt awkward. The adults at the Lodge didn't interact with the trainees outside of instruction time.

"Hand me that harness over there." Henrich pointed to a claw-like device on the far end of the counter.

Cassius picked up the heavy instrument. A wide tube attached to the top stretched into the wall. The claw portion would leech the energy from inside the Pearl and funnel it through the tube where it could be stored in the city's energy terminals. It was advanced machinery. If Skyship hadn't gotten their hands on the schematics a decade ago, the race for Pearls would have been over before it had started.

Henrich grabbed the harness and twisted the knobs on the side to open the claw to a suitable width. He laid his hand on top of the Pearl. "I hear we've got you to thank for this beauty."

"Yeah," Cassius mumbled, "but I stole a shuttle to get it so Madame's not too happy."

Henrich positioned the harness around the Pearl and tightened the clamps to secure it. "You're lucky she's taken a shine to you." He checked the tube for holes. "You don't want to get on Madame's bad side. Honestly, I'm surprised she gave you clearance to this office. You should feel pretty good about that."

Cassius looked up at the monitors. All ten entrances to the Net were still and empty, except for the guards, slumped over and yawning.

"Some fire last night," Henrich continued. "You're a lucky kid, I'll tell you that. We're doing a sweep of the electrical systems later this afternoon. I don't know what could have happened."

Cassius glanced over to him, expecting to see a hint of a knowing smile. Lieutenant Henrich was one of Madame's right-hand men. But then Cassius remembered what Madame had said: *I cannot trust anybody else in the Unified Party.*

Satisfied with the strength of the tube, Henrich powered on the harness. Cassius watched as the device whirred to life, absorbing the energy from inside the Pearl and sucking it out. In a few hours there'd be nothing left but a hollow, translucent shell—an empty fishbowl.

"It's amazing," Henrich started. "All these years and we're still not able to break through the outer layer. That's some strong material there. It'd have to be to withstand impact,

I guess. I'd hate to be standing in the way of one of these when it fell."

Cassius agreed. There'd be no surviving it. A falling Pearl burned through anything it touched before hitting land. They were only safe after they stabilized.

"So you're heading to Skyship tomorrow." Henrich leaned on the counter. "Be prepared for protestors up there. Flip the Tribunal the middle finger for me, okay?"

Cassius kept his eyes on the emptying Pearl. "Do you know why Madame picked me?"

"You're her kid, Stevenson. She's giving you an opportunity the other kids don't get. It's an honor."

He thought back to the infirmary room, to his raw, tingling skin. An honor. Right.

Henrich frowned. "Listen, I've known Madame longer than you've been alive. Let me tell you what I've learned." He scratched his nose. "It's all about Pearls. It's all she thinks about. How to find them, what to do with them. Bring her Pearls and you're golden. Stand in her way and ... " He chuckled. "Well, you don't stand in Madame's way." He ran his fingers over the emptying Pearl. "If she's bringing you up to Skyship, chances are it's got something to do with these little babies."

Cassius was about to respond when he noticed movement on the top-right security monitor. "Hey," he pointed to the screen, "what's that?"

Lieutenant Henrich craned his neck over the counter to see the screen. Cassius watched as a crowd of people—

twenty or so—converged on the seventh Bio-Net entrance. He recognized them as Fringers immediately. Their clothing was filthy, little more than torn rags covering their gaunt bodies. Their skin was dark with the Surface Tan.

"Second group this week." Henrich shook his head.

Cassius moved closer to the display, trying to make out details. The Fringers carried something in their arms. Sunlight glinted off of metal. Weapons.

A monitor in the opposite corner whirred to life showing footage from a nearby ground camera. He could see the rectangular entrance clearly, as well as the closest Bio-Net connectors—large, solid Xs climbing into the sky, growing fainter the higher they were placed.

The group sped up as they neared the entrance. Ever since the Unified Party had erected the Chosens and shut out anyone unable to pay the environmental tax, the cities had become targets for bands of Fringers, incensed with the government's lack of support to those on the outside.

Cassius turned to Henrich. "Why are they allowing them to get so close?"

"Just wait," Henrich replied, fixated on the monitor.

The group of Fringers stopped mere feet from the entrance and drew their weapons. The video feed didn't pick up sound. Cassius wondered if they had fired any shots.

Henrich smiled. "Can you believe this? They think all it takes is a couple of guns to break into a Chosen City."

"This happens often?"

He nodded. "We're coming up on the anniversary of

the Chosens. Perfect time to stage a coup, right? Expect the crowds to get bigger before they die down. Doesn't matter, though. Watch."

Cassius turned his attention back to the screen. The Fringers stood still, probably making demands of the guards.

A blinding beam of light filled the screen. The ground exploded. Dust shot up from below, engulfing the crowd in a swirling brown cloud. Limbs fell in a tangle to the ground. Weapons flew into the air.

"Automated defense systems." Henrich chuckled. "Stupid Fringers forgot to look up. Bam!" He laughed.

Cassius turned to him. "Dead?"

Henrich nodded. "Dead and gone."

A chill ran down Cassius's spine. He'd seen people killed before. Even tortured. But something about the video stuck with him. The efficiency of it. The silent feed.

"And still they try." Henrich shook his head. "I guess if you've lived outside the Net so long you've gotta have more than a few screws loose, huh?"

Cassius kept his attention on the display, watching as the dust faded to reveal a pile of bodies. He didn't respond.

"*That's* why you don't mess with Madame," Henrich said proudly. "Or the Unified Party, right Stevenson?"

Cassius nodded, turning back to the draining Pearl. Maybe he shouldn't go snooping through the research files after all.

———

Cassius walked the hallway in silence. Before he could take the last few steps to Madame's office, her door swung open. A brown-haired boy stepped out, a determined frown on his face. Their eyes met for a moment, but the boy pushed past Cassius without a word and took off down the hall. Cassius turned to watch him round a corner and disappear.

He was young. Too young to be in her office.

Cassius caught the door before it shut entirely and slipped into the office. Madame sat behind her desk, speaking on a headset.

"I understand, Prime Minister." Her voice was calm, though she spoke through gritted teeth. "Yes," she answered. "I know it is a larger fee than you'd prefer, but you need to understand what we're dealing with. Shippers are crossing the Skyline more and more frequently. It's as if the treaty means nothing to them."

She flipped the headset outward so Cassius could hear the Prime Minister's voice. It was muffled, but he could still hear the man's thick cockney accent. "If they're breaking the law, why not arrest them?"

Madame sighed, bringing the headset back to her ear. "If it were up to me we'd do more than arrest them, but the President is fearful of a war. We need Pearls, Mr. Hughes. We're not crammed together on an island like the Commonwealth. We're spread out, surrounded by miles and miles of Fringe Towns. Granted, it gives us more landing space ... greater access. But Fringers are teaming with Shippers, and the Unified Party must have Pearls to stay strong.

My terms remain fixed." She paused, motioning for Cassius to take a seat beside her desk. "Fine," she muttered, and flipped off the headset, giving a great sigh.

"Cassius." She removed the earpiece and glanced over to him. "You're early."

"Who was that?" He motioned to the doorway.

She frowned. "I don't know what you're talking about."

"That boy," he replied, "that just left your office."

She removed her glasses and rubbed her eyes. "Oh, don't you worry about that."

Cassius turned back to the door. He *was* worried. Madame never let students into her office. Cassius was the exception. The *only* exception.

And that's the way it needed to stay.

Madame opened a drawer beside her and pulled out a small black bag. "Prime Minister Hughes wishes for more leniency from the Unified Party." She set the bag on the table. "It seems the European Commonwealth has fallen on hard times. They're attempting to mimic Canada's Polar Cities in Scandinavia. He reckons the project would move faster with Pearl Power."

Cassius knew that the Polar Region, with its Arctic Ocean, was the most stable and desirable area on the planet. It would be in the Unified Party's interest to keep the Commonwealth from building there.

Madame leaned forward in her chair. "It's not my fault their piddly little country is low on landing space. I upped the fee to eight million euros per Pearl. He is not a happy Englishman."

Cassius smiled. Pearls targeted land, and North America was one of the biggest chunks of civilized land left. A large percentage of Pearls fell in Unified Party territory. And with the recent purchase of Africa's landing space, Madame could ask whatever she wanted for them. Europe would have to pay.

"We should have never sold them the schematics to our stasis equipment." She unhooked the bag's top buckle. "But it was not my decision to make. McGregor was in charge then. I'm more worried about the Fringers now. Reports came in this morning that a town in south Texas got their hands on a disk of stasis schematics from Skyship agents. I've sent down a troop to level the entire community if necessary. If Fringers find a way to harvest Pearl energy it's all over. It's bad enough that they're trading with the Seps."

She sighed, reaching into the bag and removing three items. Cassius watched as she set a pistol, a Skyship passport, and a folded suit on the desk in front of him. "This is all you'll have to rely on in your search for Fisher," she started. "The pistol is constructed entirely from plastic and filled with a trace of diluted Pearl energy. It is twenty times more effective than any bullet and, more importantly, won't register on any Skyship scanners.

"The second item," she continued, "is your passport. It will get you onto Skyship Polaris once we've left the Tribunal meeting. From there you'll board a ship to the Academy.

For security purposes, your name will be Michael Stevens. I've uploaded details onto your com-pad. Study them. You will be questioned."

Cassius ran his eyes over the three items, a lump in his throat. "And the suit?"

"As I told you in the infirmary, you'll be arriving at the Academy on Visitation Day. You'll need to be presentable, without a government seal in sight."

Cassius frowned as he looked over at the pistol, picturing situations that would force him to use it. "You're sure this is a good idea? You're sure I won't get caught?"

"My methods don't fail," she replied. "If you get caught, it will be through fault of your own. But we've trained you well, Cassius. I'm not worried."

"But what if—"

"Fire?" She interrupted, seemingly reading his mind. "That's what the medication is for. Listen. Don't concern yourself with what ifs. It's a hole you won't be able to dig yourself out from. We'll discuss your journey from Atlas to the Academy in detail, as many times as it takes for you to feel comfortable. And if you are still nervous, let it be a lesson. You disobeyed me, Cassius. Stole a shuttle and went outside the Net. Actions have consequences." She grabbed the pistol and stuffed it inside of the bag.

Cassius struggled to think of a response. An apology would feel pointless and insincere. Madame seemed more resolute and hardened than usual, as if she was on a race to defuse a time bomb before it exploded. No time to hold hands or take baby steps.

One thing he could be certain of: this mission was starting to feel more and more like punishment.

8

A detonation ball whizzes past my shoulder, missing me by a fraction of an inch. I hurl my body behind a crumbling brick wall and slow my frantic breathing. An eerie quiet falls over the battlefield. Then several detonations puncture the stillness. Someone swears. It's nobody on my team, but that doesn't mean I'm safe.

Nine a.m.

I'm not sleeping. I'm not eating breakfast, either. No, I'm up to my ankles in sweat and frustration. It's Bunker Ball time. Mr. Wilson said he wanted to see how some of us Year Nines worked as a team. I'm convinced he just wants to punish me.

The joys of Bunker Ball should be reserved for convicted felons. Instead, the teachers gleefully strap up two teams of teenagers with detonator pellets and set us against each other. It's a full-blown war zone without the casualties, unless loss of dignity counts as a casualty. It's all good for Mr. Wilson, though. He gives us the whole war experience without the danger.

"Fisher!" Wilson's voice reverberates through the speakers in the ceiling. "Move your butt!"

I groan. He's perched up on the balcony, watching our every move. Worse yet, he's pitted us against Year Sevens. Thirteen-year-olds. And it's a testament to our supreme suckability that we're still losing.

One of the Year Sevens slumps over to the bench at the border of the training field. We're finally even.

Manjeet and Paulina, two kids in my year, sit beside him. I'm happy not to be the first one out today, but those two are pretty much super-geniuses, so it's not like they've gotta be good at this combat stuff. Besides, I'm only alive because I'm a good hider. The whole "battlefield" of sand dunes, brick walls, and bushy trees they've constructed is supposed to make things more challenging. I just use it to hide. I'm not completely without my merits.

I pass behind a massive boulder, drawing my arms inward to become less of a target. The training landscape changes each time we're in here. Sometimes it's a dense forest, other days a demolished cityscape. Today it's something in between. I think they were going for a desert theme, but there's also random walls and trees and stuff. Kind of impractical. I'm not exactly sure what this is supposed to be teaching us.

Skandar rushes past me, grabbing my arm and half-yanking me to the ground before I regain my balance and run alongside him.

"Wilson told you to move, mate," he says through labored breaths. "Gotta get your head in the game."

Before I can respond, he climbs up onto a sand dune, gives a mass ridiculous battle cry, and chucks a detonator at Asha Mutombo. She dives out of the way. The detonator sails past her shoulder, landing somewhere in the sand.

"Frag it." Skandar frowns before retreating behind the dune.

I unhook one of the seven remaining detonators from my belt and cradle it in my hand, wondering if I should go after someone or just let myself get hit. Only the fear of pain stops me from surrendering altogether. The plastic feels cold in my hand. I roll the thing along my fingers, a wicked, silver baseball of death.

"Hey, Fisher." Skandar breaks from his mad pursuit. "Mind if I borrow one of your detonators? I've only got two left."

"Knock yourself out." I toss him mine and pull another from my belt.

"I saw that, boys!" Wilson's voice rains down on us.

Skandar cups his hand around his mouth and shouts up to the balcony. "It's teamwork, sir!"

Wilson doesn't respond. We're each supposed to register a certain amount of "kills" today. Skandar's good at this sort of thing. I'm the one who needs the practice.

"Follow me," Skandar whispers as we sneak around the dune.

"Where's Eva?" I whisper back.

"On the other side of the field. Asha and Chan are somewhere in the middle. If we all sneak up and surround them, it'll be three against two."

"What about Alexis?

"To hell with Alexis." He leads us farther around the dune, out toward the open. "She's no threat to us."

I'm about to argue when a detonation nearly deafens me. For a second, I'm convinced that I've been hit. But there's no pain. I glance over at Skandar. The expression on his face says it all.

"What the hell?" He spins around. "Who hit me?"

I turn to see Alexis White standing behind us, a Cheshire Cat grin on her face. The smallest girl in their year and she managed to knock Skandar Harris out of the game.

"Jesse, don't just stand there! Hit her!" Skandar shouts.

I hurry up and throw the detonator. It strikes Alexis's right leg just above the knee. Her face winces with pain as the shell explodes, but it's not enough to completely wipe away her smile.

"It was worth it," she says.

"You cheated," Skandar mutters.

Alexis shakes her head. "It's not my fault you two were having a little tea party back here. Watch your backs next time."

Skandar holds up his last detonator to hit her again, but remembers the rules and stops himself before doing anything stupid.

And with that, it's Eva and me. And I don't even know where she is. Some teamwork.

"Rush them from the sides," Skandar whispers in my ear before pacing off the field in disgust.

I wipe the sweat from my forehead and hold down the button on my earpiece. "Eva? Where are you?"

Her voice comes in all fuzzy. "South end of the field, Fisher. What's up?"

"Skandar just got hit."

"Skandar? You mean you're the last boy standing?"

"Trust me," I say, "I'm as shocked as you are. We got Alexis, though."

"That leaves Asha and Chan."

"Skandar said we should rush them from the sides."

"Where are you?"

"Um..." I look up at the ceiling, hoping to judge my position from the light fixtures and the familiar water stain at the northwest corner. I spot it almost instantly. "Northeast, I think."

"Fine," she says. "Move inward slowly. Keep your head up and if you see anything move don't hesitate to attack. You can't hesitate, Jesse."

"I know." I roll my eyes. Like I haven't heard that tired line about a million times.

Then, it's on.

I shuffle forward, careful to keep behind boulders and walls whenever possible. The silence is unbearable. Someone could jump out at any moment. My gaze darts around, scanning the landscape for signs of movement.

Suddenly I'm into it, like I really want to win this thing. Seeing Skandar get taken out, I realize that being the weak link might have its advantages. People forget about me, underestimate me.

I venture farther out, keeping an eye on the horizon. A detonator explodes somewhere in front of me, rumbling the walls. It's impossible to tell if it was a hit or a miss. I pray it's not Eva.

Then she answers my prayers. "I got Asha," her voice comes over my earpiece. "Now it's just little Chan, all by himself. Move in for the kill, Fisher."

I stifle a laugh. She takes this crap so seriously. Then again, maybe that's my problem. Maybe I don't take it seriously enough.

Even so, it doesn't change the fact that it's two against one. Forgetting that these are thirteen-year-olds, it still makes me feel pretty accomplished. It's a power position. Finally.

"I'm moving," I mumble into the earpiece, gripping the detonator.

"If he knows he's the last one, he might try something crazy," Eva says. "So don't hesitate."

"Blah, blah, blah, blah, blah. You're like a broken record, you know that?"

"Just trying to save your butt, Fisher. Again."

I grab a second detonator, just in case. If I get the chance,

I'll throw the whole blasted belt at the kid. Even with bad aim, at least one's bound to hit.

I crawl around a steep dune and look to the far wall of the training facility. Eva's head rises from behind another dune, a dark dot in the distance. I look down at the small valley in between us. Chan stands in the center, looking frantically around.

For a moment I feel bad for the kid, up against two Year Nines with belts full of detonators. It must be pretty scary. Then I remember what Captain Alkine always says. No mercy for the enemy. I can't empathize with the kid. I've gotta do what I've gotta do.

So I attack, lunging forward and throwing one detonator after another. They explode well in front of Chan, shooting puffs of sand up from the ground. Mass embarrassing.

Then, two things happen at once. Eva hurls a detonator with laser precision behind the kid and I know it'll hit him square in the back. Unaware of his impending doom, Chan chucks a detonator at me. I try to dart out of the way but it's too quick. I shouldn't have been watching Eva.

The detonator barrels straight for my chest and explodes. I have just enough time to see Chan knocked out of the game before I collapse to the ground and stay there, unmoving.

———

Swirls of green mist cloud around me. At first I'm convinced that Mr. Wilson has changed the training program.

But as I stumble to my feet, I realize that I'm not in the training room at all. I'm not even in a Skyship.

My chest throbs. Whether it's from the detonator or something else I can't tell. I'm not sure I'm awake—or conscious.

A broken city stretches around me. Charred skeletons of skyscrapers disappear into the mist. Empty streets give way to derelict buildings, their windows blown out. Piles of brick litter the ground. There are no people, no cars even. Only the thick, green mist.

I quickly realize that I'm on the Surface, but it's not the same as Syracuse. There's a coarseness to the air. Each passing breeze grates on my skin. The temperature's mild. Cold, even.

I stand alone, as if a giant hand wiped everything away around me. I stagger forward, dizzy. The mist fogs out every detail except for jagged shadows of the buildings. I give into panic for a moment, unsure of how to find my way out.

Then I hear a noise to the right of me, coming from a nearby alleyway. Whispering. Voices.

Eager to find help, I follow it. Even if this is just a dream, I know I don't want to be here. My fingers cut through the mist and I stumble forward to see who's there, but the persistent fog bars my way.

The voices fade. I stop in the middle of the intersection and look down at my chest. A silver key rests on my white shirt.

And then, a shadow.

Something behind me. Someone.

I start to cough as the mist pours down my throat. My legs feel numb, as if they haven't been used in years. My head drops. Dead weight. Then the world becomes a blur and all I can see is green.

———

I wake with a start, lying in a pile of sand in the middle of the training field. My body feels like it's just been stuck in an electric socket, but it's my chest that's the worst. A carefully aimed detonator will do that.

Mr. Wilson kneels at my side. I must've been out long enough for him to come down from the balcony. "Jeez, Fisher." He shakes his head. "It was only a detonator. You've gotta toughen up a little."

Skandar and Eva stand off to the side, staring down at me. The Year Sevens are nowhere to be seen, thank god. Suddenly, the humiliation of the whole situation dawns on me and I bury my face in my hands and fight back tears, which makes the whole thing even more embarrassing. If this had been a real combat mission, I'd probably have been left for dead.

Mr. Wilson pats my shoulder, the first sympathetic move he's made today, and turns to the others. "I want you all in homeroom for debriefing in twenty minutes." He strolls off, leaving the firing squad to assess their fallen comrade.

"Great job, mate." Skandar barely contains his chuckle.

Paulina Sterner pushes him. "He lasted longer than you, didn't he?"

Skandar grunts. "Dumb luck, that's all."

I fold into a fetal position.

Eva crosses her arms. "I gotta hand it to you, Fisher. Even though you missed Chan completely, which is pretty pathetic considering the amount of detonators you threw at him, at least you showed some fighting spirit."

Skandar reaches down to help me up but I push him away. I just wanna lie here. That way I can pretend this never happened. The fact that it feels like a truck's just been driven into my chest doesn't really give me the opportunity.

"Whatever." Skandar withdraws his hand. "I'm gonna go hit the showers." He waves goodbye. Paulina and Manjeet leave too, now that the spectacle's over.

Eva lingers. "You just gonna lie there?"

"Go away," I mutter into the sand. It's better to give up, chalk it up to fate. Even when I *try* not to make a fool of myself, the universe still finds some way to kick me in the butt. Other kids would have family to comfort them, to go on and on about how mass special they were. I've got Eva, standing over me like a disappointed bodyguard.

"You know, you can't keep doing this, acting like a baby when things don't go your way." She waits for a response, but I don't give her one. So with one final disapproving sigh, she walks away, leaving me alone in the middle of the empty battlefield.

9

Two a.m. Any sane person would be asleep by now. I am decidedly *in*sane.

I sit upright in my bed. I gave up on sleep twenty minutes ago. My body wants to droop into the mattress and shut down, but my mind's going 300 miles per hour.

Every time I close my eyes I'm filled with images of that dead, mist-clogged city—the key around my neck, the figure behind me.

I glance around my darkened bedroom. Shadows cover the walls like toothed monsters. The floor's dotted with piles of clothing and junk. It's an obstacle course to get to the bed without stepping on something.

I toss the covers from my legs and throw on the first pair of shorts I can find. Time to roam the corridors until I'm too exhausted to move. Time to fool my body into submission.

Slipping out the doorway, I turn down the hall past dozens of closed doors and make my way to the outside corridor.

Moonlight streams in through the wall of curved windows. The stars are impossibly bright.

I head up the stairway to the fifth level, in search of another night owl whiling away the early morning hours in one of the rec rooms. After clearing the first flight of stairs, I freeze.

Rumbling. Just beyond the entryway to the fourth level, echoing along the hallway. It sounds for a second longer—low, crackling—and stops. Footsteps.

I tiptoe to the entryway and peer around the side of the wall, staring down the empty hallway. Level Four's mostly living quarters, but at its center sits the largest of the Academy's three research laboratories.

Just as I'm about to move, the rumbling returns, softer this time. I step forward, inching down the hallway in pursuit of the sound. For a second I wonder if it's coming from a bedroom. It sounds like snoring, but the dorm walls are much too thick. No one snores *that* loudly.

No, it's coming from the end of the hallway.

The rumbling stops again. I pause and glance around the vacant hallway, expecting someone to jump out and grab me.

Silence.

I venture forward, turn a corner and head deeper into the center of the ship. A lighting tube crackles above my head, burnt out. I listen for the sound, but everything's quiet. Quiet as the stars.

Then I see movement at the end of the corridor. A door

opens. A person steps outside. I flatten against the wall, hoping I won't be seen. But it's too late. The figure takes a few nervous glances around and sneaks down the hallway, right toward me.

There's nowhere to hide, so I step out from the shadows and shove my hands into my pockets, trying to look as nonchalant as possible. The figure freezes as soon as it notices me. It's dark, and the person is too far away to make out facial features.

"Hey," I mutter, hoping that it's a student and not a faculty member. After Alkine's little lecture last night I'm not dying to be alone with a teacher again.

"Jesse?"

I step forward and watch as the figure fumbles with something in her pocket. "Avery?"

Avery comes into view. Her hair's pulled back in a ponytail. There's a smear of black grease on her cheek. "Jesse, what are you doing out here?"

I shrug. "Couldn't sleep. Did you hear that noise?"

"Noise?" She rubs her cheek.

"Yeah. Rumbling. Kinda loud for two in the morning."

Her eyebrows raise. "Could've been the water reprocessor."

"You can hear that all the way up here?"

She frowns. "If everyone's quiet enough, I guess."

I crane my neck around her outline and peer down the hallway. "Where were you? I thought your dorm was on Level Three."

"It is." She rests her hand on her hip. "Um … you know Phoebe, right? She was in my year, back when I was still training. We were friends. Well, kind of … but anyway, she needed to talk about, you know, girl stuff." She glances at her watch. "I guess we got a little carried away."

I look down the row of closed doors. "I didn't know you hung out with Phoebe."

"Uh huh." She runs her hand through her hair. "I can have other friends, you know. They may not be as flaunt as *you*, but still …"

I rub my eyes.

"I thought Year Nines had curfew," she says. "Shouldn't you be in your room?"

"I could ask you the same thing."

She chuckles, pushing past me to the corridor. "You forget. I may not be an agent, but I still work here. I can come and go as I please. I am a god among men. No, strike that. *Goddess*. Tremble in my wake."

"Yeah, yeah." I follow her into the corridor, staring at her moonlit face. "I swear I heard rumbling."

"You've got an active imagination," she replies. "I didn't hear a thing." She pauses, fumbling with her pockets before turning her attention back to me. "Nice shorts."

I look down. They're so baggy that they reach well past my knees. "They were Skandar's once. He likes them … uh … roomy, I guess."

"Right." She yawns. "So what's up? I hardly saw you today."

I lean against the windowpane and push my thumb against the fiberglass. "Oh you know, the usual. Got yelled at in math for talking to Skandar. Got knocked out in Bunker Ball. Mr. Wilson said I had too much sympathy for the enemy, that I hesitated instead of 'stickin it to him.'" I frown. "Wilson's words. Not mine."

Avery crouches at the edge of the corridor, her back to the stars. "Sometimes sympathy's not such a bad thing. Missions aren't easy when feelings are involved. Trust me."

I sit next to her. "What's that supposed to mean?"

She shrugs. "Just saying. Emotion compromises a person. You've gotta choose between your brain and your heart." She smiles. "Heart should always win, I think."

"I wasn't emotional. I wanted to win that stupid game as much as anybody."

"Yeah? Well, I want a flying dog that barks the alphabet backwards. Some things just ain't gonna happen, kiddo."

"Don't call me kiddo," I mutter.

She ignores me. "So what's the real reason you're up so late?"

I play with a loose thread on the bottom of my T-shirt. "Bad dreams, I guess."

Avery nods. "Gotcha. After your little Surface adventure, I'm not surprised you'd have nightmares. Pearlhounds can be pretty scary."

"You've fought them?"

She chuckles. "If running away is considered a form of combat, then yeah. It was my junior year, right after transferring from Mira. I hadn't had much Surface experience so they stuck me with a few of the more promising students in my grade. It wasn't a Fringe trade like you guys did yesterday. A Pearl had fallen outside of Tallahassee ... pretty far from the nearest Chosen, so we thought we could grab it before the Pearlhounds showed up." She smiles. "They swore we'd be able to handle it."

I grin. "I've heard that one before."

She nods. "You guys were lucky to get dropped up north. You wouldn't have believed the bugs, Jesse. Clouds of them. We had face masks, gloves—covered from head to toe. You'd think the insects would have been enough to keep the government at bay, but Madame's people locked onto the Pearl's trail and showed up fifteen minutes after our shuttle landed. We bolted. Sometimes running is the only way to stay alive. Like I said before: there's more to life than Pearls."

"You ran away? You guys didn't even try to fight them for the Pearl?"

"I convinced my crew that it was the best decision. From a tactical standpoint, of course. Really, I was just scared."

I shake my head, laughing. "I bet Alkine was pissed."

She grins. "And did I care? Not really. See, Jesse? You're not Skyship Academy's biggest screw-up. I'll totally own the title. No worries."

I stare at her face. Her green eyes glint in the moonlight. "You've got grease or something on your cheek."

"Do I?" Her brows furrow as she reaches up to rub her face.

"You and Phoebe doing arts and crafts?"

She wipes off the rest of the dark grease with her finger and smears it on her jeans, frowning. "Yeah. Something like that."

"I'm headed to the rec rooms. Wanna watch a movie or something?"

She pulls herself from the ground. "It's late, Jesse. I should be going. You need to sleep."

I sigh. The last thing I want to do is go back to my tiny, messy room and sleep.

Avery stretches and yawns. "See you tomorrow?"

"Sure." I give a slight smile. She starts off along the corridor. Another minute and she's gone.

10

Cassius arrived on Skyship Atlas late the next afternoon. The enormous ship, located directly above the dark ruins of Washington D.C., functioned as the Seps' East Coast stronghold. Their capital city, if one could truly call the flying fortress a city. Madame had piloted them up from the Lodge herself, taking the opportunity to point out Surface landmarks along the way: notable Fringe Towns, the Appalachian colonies.

After landing in Atlas's docking bay, they were ushered through security checks. Madame's bodyguard stayed close to her the entire time, eyeing the scanners as Skyship guards analyzed her briefcase. When they were given clearance to go forward, a guide escorted them through a crowd of barely contained protestors and into the next corridor. Cassius tried to ignore the angry shouts of the Shippers as he passed, keeping his face forward the entire time.

Now the four of them stood inside a spacious elevator, traveling up to the Tribunal Building on Atlas's main level.

From what Cassius had seen earlier from the cruiser

window, Atlas was a vast gray triangle, suspended impossibly in the middle of the sky. Pearl Power kept it aloft. Stolen, no doubt.

The inside corridors were well-maintained, with careful attention to details. Modernized Renaissance columns and arches gave the ship a bizarre, avant-garde aesthetic.

Madame leaned closer to him. "Dramatic, isn't it? These ships were our last great masterstroke before we were forced to refocus our efforts. A pity they were taken over by the Seps."

Their escort flashed Madame a dirty look but stayed quiet, turning away to face the elevator doors. A noticeable tension filled the elevator, the whirring of gears above them the only sound. Cassius fidgeted with the black bag slung over his shoulder. Passport. Pistol. Suit. Somehow it had all made it through security undetected. Madame knew what she was doing.

The elevator came to a stop and the doors pulled open, revealing a large plaza. They marched along the marble stonework at a hurried pace. Madame ignored the guide, taking the lead and sizing up the approaching Tribunal Building like it was an enemy to be defeated. Cassius gazed up at the clear sky. Though he knew there was a large dome stabilizing the air pressure around them, it was invisible from the ground, leaving the air open and uncluttered. No Bio-Net, no chemical smog. He expected to feel dizzy from the altitude. The dome controlled *that* as well.

He caught quick glances at the city as he followed

Madame. Everything hunkered low to the ground. The tallest building he could see was only three levels high. There appeared to be roads, but no cars or chute system like in the Chosen Cities. The only vehicles were small buggies, no bigger than golf carts, that whizzed silently across the plaza. He avoided eye contact with the drivers.

They continued around an impressive, three-tiered fountain and advanced onto a narrow, tree-lined pathway that led to the two-story Tribunal Building. It had been modeled after the White House, of course. A mini version.

"One last security measure," their guide stammered as he regained the lead and ushered them up a staircase. Three bulky security guards patted them down at the top before they were allowed into the building. Cassius winced, convinced that they'd find the disassembled pistol sewn into his pack. But they moved quickly, brushing against the three pieces, assuming they were part of the reinforced corners of the pack. Madame was right. They were easily fooled.

Madame wore a disgusted expression as the guard touched her. Once cleared, she pushed past their escort and stepped into the entryway, heading up a second set of decorative stairs.

Cassius followed her into what looked like an old-fashioned courtroom. In place of a judge's seat, there were three wooden podiums. Behind each sat a member of the Tribunal, their party's icon etched into the wood beneath them. A Democrat, a Republican, and a Libertarian—two men and one woman. All three were older than Madame by at least a decade.

Cassius followed Madame down the aisle between rows of empty seats and to a table directly below the Tribunal's watchful eyes. Madame motioned for her bodyguard to set the briefcase in front of her, then took a seat, clasping her hands and waiting. Cassius pulled up a chair beside her and sized up each Tribunal member.

"Good afternoon, Jessica." Democratic Representative Leone spoke first, rubbing the stubble on his chin. His droopy, glazed eyes gave the impression that he could fall asleep at any moment. "It's nice to see you again."

Cassius glanced over at Madame, expecting to find outrage. Nobody used her real name.

Her expression remained stony. "I would ask you to please honor the title my party has given me during proceedings such as these."

The old man smiled. "Of course. We wouldn't want to humanize things."

Republican Representative Buchanan, a portly woman wearing an expensive red jacket, leaned forward in her center seat and met Cassius's eyes directly. "Is this your son, Madame?" Her voice was thick with a hint of a southern accent.

Cassius gripped the edge of the table, waiting to hear Madame's answer.

"Yes," she responded.

Buchanan smiled, her heavily colored lips prodding full

cheeks. "How beneficial for him to witness the outcome of the Hernandez Treaty firsthand. What are your impressions of Skyship Atlas, boy?"

Madame grabbed his wrist, whispering to him. "You don't have to answer that."

Libertarian Representative Chandler, the youngest of the three, cleared his throat, producing a stack of papers from under his podium. "I believe you'll find all of our reports are in order. Military engagements, energy consumption ... it's all there."

Madame nodded, motioning for her bodyguard to grab the papers. He quickly transported the stack from the Tribunal to the tabletop, then moved behind her once more.

She opened the briefcase, removing an ink pen from a small pouch inside. Cassius knew that she had to read and sign each document in the presence of the Tribunal. The ritual was bound to drag on for a few hours at least. He was counting on it. Boredom was part of the conceit that would allow him to escape.

Madame flipped through the first document, adding her signature to the bottom. "A group of your schoolchildren were seen on the Surface the other day." She spoke without looking up. "Collecting a Pearl from a group of Fringers."

Cassius watched as the members of the Tribunal exchanged furtive glances.

"Impossible," Leone muttered.

Madame smiled as she ran her fingers along the text. "Impossible that they were down there? Or impossible that they were seen? This is in direct violation of clause three of the treaty, as you well know."

Chandler leaned back in his seat, hands clasped. "And you have proof? Photographic, documented proof?"

"Of course not," she responded, flipping through another document. "I don't believe you'd be so careless as to offer us proof. No, I have my suspicions, as always."

"Suspicions won't hold up in a court of law." Buchanan crossed her arms. "Even one as ... unified as yours."

"I just wanted you to know, Representative. Don't get sloppy. We are waiting."

Buchanan shook her head. "I have no idea what you're talking about."

Madame's eyebrows raised as she ran her finger across the top of a page. "I'll have to put on my glasses to read such tiny print. One would think that you were trying to squeeze something past us here."

Leone frowned. "We have no secrets."

"No, of course not." She dug through her jacket pocket and pulled out a pair of spectacles. "That was a lovely little circus downstairs, by the way. I don't remember the crowds being as large last time."

"We can't help the way our people feel."

"No." She finished scanning through the document and signed at the bottom. "I suppose you can't be blamed for the actions of your people. They were contained well enough."

Buchanan glared down at Madame. Cassius watched as the red of her face deepened. "Listen, Madame. People don't like the idea of a dictatorship being allowed to flourish right under their noses."

Madame set the pen down on the table, clasping her hands once more. "It is not a dictatorship."

The woman scoffed. "What is it, then? It's certainly not the three-party democracy the people voted on."

"Your democracy died along with the White House," she replied. "Tragedy unified us. Finally. After years of partisan bickering we were free to get on with it, to unite and preserve our way of life. If you would care to float down from your cloud and visit one of our Chosen Cities, you'd realize that our people are quite happy—and very well taken care of."

Buchanan controlled her expression, taking a deep breath before responding. "Does that include the people outside of the Net? The people in the Fringes?"

"You mean your *friends* down in the Fringes?" Madame smiled.

"No. The people you've forgotten. The people your cities are killing every day."

Madame sighed. "Despite what you may think, we cannot control the human will. It's true, some people opt out of our environmental tax program and choose to stay in the Fringes."

Buchanan laughed. "Poor people, sick people, nonconform—"

"It is a choice," Madame interrupted. "Without the funds collected from the tax, there would be no Bio-Nets."

Chandler held up his hand. "From what I hear, Fringers don't like you very much."

Madame scowled. "I'd be careful what you say, Representative. One might get the impression that you've been spending more time on the Surface than is legally allowed."

"Please." Buchanan sneered. "Why would we want to go down to the Surface? You've ruined it. As if taking care of your so-called terrorists wasn't enough."

Madame grabbed her pen, returning to the stack of papers. "Retaliation was necessary."

"Killing millions of innocent people? When is that ever necessary?"

She signed and dated the next sheet. "Our country was destroyed. They would have done it again."

"Oh, here we go." The lady grabbed the edge of the podium. Her nails matched the red blazer. "Revenge, revenge, revenge. It's always the same with you people."

Cassius shifted in his seat. Madame flipped to the next page.

But Buchanan wouldn't stop. "You know what I think? I think you were all ashamed. All of your anti-terror initiatives weren't enough. After everything you asked the American people to give up, you didn't even see it coming. Nobody did. No terrorist organization ever claimed responsibility for the bombings. You and I both know that."

Madame pushed her chair back, standing up and meeting the Republican head on. "Who else, Representative? What would you have had us do? Wait? Wait until they destroyed the rest of the country? They would have done it again."

"They didn't."

"Because we didn't give them a chance."

Buchanan rested her chin in her hand, smiling. "And now look what you've done. It's karma. The planet's becoming more unlivable by the day. Your Unified Party can hide behind monikers as long as you'd like. But someday soon the people are going to know what you did. And heaven help you then."

Madame sat down, clearing her throat. "We have Pearls now. Nobody need suffer anymore."

"There's no telling how long Pearls will last," Leone replied. "Your control is weakening."

Madame returned to the documents. Cassius knew he wasn't supposed to move on with the plan until halfway through the meeting, but he couldn't stand to sit and watch the Tribunal antagonize her. So he leaned over and whispered in her ear.

She nodded, glancing back up to the three podiums. "My son needs to step out and use the restroom."

"Of course." Chandler motioned to the far door. "There's one down the staircase in the hallway to your right."

Cassius stood, the black pouch clutched tightly at his side. He looked down at Madame, knowing he wouldn't see her again until he'd captured Fisher.

She kept her face forward, ignoring him. "Would it be all right if he stays downstairs for the remainder of the meeting? I don't wish him to be subjected to any more of this."

Buchanan chuckled. "You brought him up here."

"And I regret it."

"Sure." Chandler flashed Cassius a patronizing smile. "There's a waiting room in the same hallway with some old Wi-Fi pads. Make yourself at home."

Cassius nodded, then looked back to Madame. He waited for a show of support. A smile. Something. Her eyes never left the papers in front of her.

Rather than wait around, he turned and walked away, moving down the aisle until he exited the meeting room. Once down the stairs, he found the restroom and darted inside. Although it was empty, he stepped into the nearest stall and locked the door behind him just in case. Then he quickly unbuttoned his jacket and slipped into the plain suit he'd brought with him.

Stuffing his government clothes into the now-empty bag, he quickly checked the skin graft on his right wrist that covered his hexagonal identification socket. If it peeled off during his stay in Skyship Territory, he'd be instantly revealed as a Surface inhabitant.

Next, he ripped the light blue passport from the lining of the bag and placed it in the breast pocket of his suit. He was now Michael Stevens, born and raised on Skyship Orion. His life could depend on remembering that information.

His heart raced as he realized the full ramifications of

what he'd just done. He was no longer an invited guest on Atlas. He was an undercover agent. If he was caught before finding Fisher, he'd be punished like one, thrown into one of the prison ships down south.

Still, what had transpired back in the meeting room made him even more anxious. Madame had often talked about the Tribunal and life after the bombings, but had never offered details outside of what was written in the instructional databases. He'd never seen her so angry before. So angry that she hadn't even paused to pat his shoulder or smile at him.

Forgetting her, he pushed open the stall door and stepped out to check his new appearance in the mirror. He'd have to be careful. He'd be wearing the same clothing until the Academy's Visitation Day and needed to stay presentable.

Satisfied, he left the restroom and turned down the hallway, looking for a subtle, unguarded exit. After a few close calls, he stumbled upon an unmarked side door and snuck outside. Once he felt the sunlight on his skin, he knew he'd made it. Next came a long shuttle ride to Skyship Polaris before he could board the school ship to the Academy the following morning. He darted into the nearest alleyway and headed into the city, keeping his face down. He was ready. Madame wouldn't be disappointed.

11

"Paulina was totally checking me during Bunker Ball yesterday." Skandar reclines in a shady spot under a transplanted oak tree at Lookout Park. A vast green field stretches out beneath us, empty except for a team of students playing soccer in the distance. "Couldn't take her eyes off."

Lying on my back, I toss an antigravity ball up into the air. It hovers aimlessly for a few seconds before whirling around the nearest branch and dropping back into my hands. "There wasn't much else to look at. The view from the bench is pretty boring. I should know."

"Last guy standing." He whacks my shoulder. "Nothing to be ashamed of there. The fainting? Well, that's a different story, isn't it. Now let me see the note you found."

I set the ball on the grass and pull a crumpled note from my pocket. "It was slipped under my door when I came back from breakfast." I hand it over. "It's from Avery."

Skandar unfolds it. "*Jesse Fisher,*" he reads, "*Meet me in the library at six-thirty. I'll kill you if you don't come.*"

I quickly grab it back. "Okay, maybe it's not the most romantic note ever written."

He grins. "Man, she mass wants you."

"Yeah, right."

"I'm not kidding," he continues. "Tonight you've just gotta wait for the right moment and then lay one on her."

"Yeah." I chuckle, trying to imagine the alternate reality where *that* would happen.

"I'm serious. Girls love that kind of stuff. You've gotta take control. How long have you guys been all buddy-buddy?"

"About two and a half years."

"See? You're practically married."

"When we met, I was twelve and she was almost fifteen. I don't think she thinks of me that way."

He shrugs. "All I'm saying is take a chance. What's the worst that could happen?"

I sigh, picking up the antigravity ball and tossing it. "I don't know. I just don't want to look like an idiot. Again."

"Trust me," he replies, "You've got nothing to worry about with *that* girl."

"What's that supposed to mean?"

He scoffs. "She's as spazzy as you are, mate. Did I tell you I saw her outside the training room last week?"

"So?" I chuck the ball over a branch. "She gets bored. She's all over the place."

Skandar reaches over and grabs the ball as it falls, yanking it away. "It was the middle of the night." He pauses to let his little revelation sink in. "She's a weirdo. But hey, you're into weirdos. That's cool."

I glare at him. He grins back.

"You gotta put some more spin on it, mate. Watch." He crouches down and winds up his arm, tossing the ball in a curved pathway around the trunk. It spins up the tree, looping around three branches and back again before returning to his outstretched hand. "It's all about the wind-up."

I sit up. "Hey, that was—"

A soccer ball bashes into the side of my head, knocking me halfway onto the grass. Skandar's first instinct is to laugh. Mine is to groan in pain.

The ball settles at the base of the tree. I rub my head, disoriented.

"Fisher!" A familiar voice cuts through the otherwise silent park. I turn to see August Bergmann jogging up the gentle slope to meet us. I don't make eye contact, hoping that he'll go away. It's been the same since Year Seven. Just because he's a year older than me and a Grade-A specimen of agentdom, he's taken it upon himself to remind everyone exactly how much I pale in comparison to him.

"Fisher," he repeats, closer now. "Hey Fisher, I'm talking to you!"

He stops a few feet away, panting. It's not training time, but he's still in full jock regalia. I think the outfit's permanently affixed to his body. Sweat dampens his buzzed hair.

"So you gonna give me my ball back?" He crosses his chiseled arms, grinning.

Skandar grabs the soccer ball and holds it captive. "You mean the one you chucked into his head?"

He shrugs. "It was an accident."

"Yeah," I mutter. "Sure."

He watches me cradle the side of my head, barely containing his laughter. "Jameson's got one hell of a power kick. I guess you guys shouldn't be sitting here."

"It's a free park," Skandar replies.

August smiles. "Hey, at least you didn't faint this time, right Fisher?"

I keep my eyes fixed on the grass. Bergmann knows about my little training room disaster—just what I need.

He turns back to Skandar, hands on hips. "You gonna give me that ball or not?"

Skandar nudges me. I pull my head up, glancing at him. He tosses the antigravity ball into my lap. I fumble to catch it.

"It's all in the wind-up," he whispers, clutching the soccer ball close to his body.

August rolls his eyes, annoyed. "Five seconds, Harris, or I pry it from your fingers."

Skandar shifts the ball to his left hand, taunting August. I realize what he wants me to do. Retaliation's not really my thing.

But I can make exceptions.

Skandar throws the soccer ball high up into the air and I switch the settings on the side of the antigravity ball to "boomerang." Then I hurl it into the field. It curves to the left, hangs in mid-air for a second, and reverses its path. August looks up to the sky, oblivious. A split-second later the antigravity ball plows into his back, right between the shoulder blades.

He swears. Loudly. It echoes along the transparent fiberglass dome protecting the park.

Skandar slaps my hand. "Payback!"

August lunges straight for me. Panicked, I try to stand up and get away. He's too quick. Before I know it, he's pinned me to the grass, fist held up in front of me ready to punch my face into the dirt. He smells mass disgusting. The soccer ball lands behind him, rolling down the hill.

"Stupid move, Fisher." He glares at me. "You don't throw the first punch if you're not prepared to fight."

I try to squirm away, but he's too big. Too strong. I wanna point out that it was actually him who threw the first punch—or soccer ball—but I know it'll only make him angrier.

"What?" He slaps my face, keeping me pinned down with the other hand. "You gonna fight back? You gonna whip me with those little noodle arms of yours?"

I kick at him, pressing my heel against his thigh, trying to push him off or flip him over or something. But it's like trying to move a slab of concrete.

Skandar leaps from the ground, eager to join the fray, but a hand pushes him away. Then it grabs August's right ear and twists. His face contorts and he forgets about me, yanking his ear free and flipping around to sit on the grass.

Eva stands before us, arms crossed. "Boys." She frowns. "What the hell are you doing?"

"Jeez, Rodriguez." August cradles his burning ear. "What are you, my freaking mother?"

"No," she replies, "But I don't think your mom would be happy to see you picking on a Year Nine."

"Fisher's not a Year Nine." August glowers at me. "He's like … a Year *Two*."

Eva sighs. "Not funny, Bergmann."

He sneers, rubbing his ear. "I was just asking for my ball back." He picks himself off the ground and backs down the hill, mouthing threats in my direction.

I keep an eye on him until he's out of sight, then turn to Eva. "You know, I can take care of myself."

Her eyebrows raise. "Looked like it."

"I *can*." I brush the dirt from my hands, sitting up. "I was just about to push him down the hill."

"Sure you were."

Skandar grabs the antigravity ball, switches it off boomerang, and tosses it from hand to hand. "Where'd you even come from, Eva? I swear, you've got a sixth sense or something."

She sighs. "In case you didn't realize, August Bergmann isn't the most subtle person in the world. They probably heard him cursing all the way down in the library."

I pull myself up, rubbing the side of my head. "Maybe next time you should just stay where you are instead of rushing in to help me. I'm gonna go get some ice."

She grabs my shoulder, stopping me. "Jesse."

"What, Eva? What else do you wanna do to embarrass me?"

"It's not to embarrass you."

I turn around, meeting her face to face. "Then what is it? Because I don't see you stepping in and saving any of the other guys."

"You're not *any of the other guys*," she says.

"Yeah," I reply, "because I've got my own personal baby-sitter. Look, you're a girl. I don't expect you to understand."

"You're my teammate, Jesse."

"August is never gonna let me live this down," I mutter, ignoring her.

"We're responsible for each other."

I shake my head. "Saved by a girl. What a freaking wimp."

She sighs. "You're not a wimp."

"Just... next time, please stay away." I start off toward the field, but three steps in, something stops me. A tug at my consciousness. A sudden awareness.

"Guys," Skandar points at the sky, squinting, "what's that?"

Eva's gaze follows the path of his finger. I raise my head to stare at the blanket of blue beyond our ship. It doesn't take me long to notice it. Something bright above us, and not a star.

"A Pearl," Eva says, a grim frown on her face. "It's falling. Fast."

We run down the hill to get a better look. I keep my eyes focused on the green dot, growing bigger and bigger with each second that it hurtles toward Earth. "Can you tell what direction it's headed?"

Before anybody can answer, a dull alarm sounds around the park, followed by three clear warning chimes. Everybody in the Academy knows the drill. We practice it each semester.

"It's heading right for the park," Eva says. "It'll smash through the dome as soon as it hits." She takes off through the field, shouting back at us. "Emergency tunnels. Now!"

Skandar and I sprint behind her, heading to a darker patch of grass beside a plot of flowers. Eva digs between the blades, finding the handle of an invisible trapdoor. "Skandar, help me with this."

Skandar moves to her side, grabbing hold of the handle and pulling. The alarms sound again, followed by three more chimes.

I spin around and stare up at the Pearl. It hurtles down at us like an out-of-control bowling ball. Two years ago, one came three feet away from smashing into the top of the Central Tower. This one's headed straight for the dome, and there's no changing a Pearl's course once it gets started.

"Jesse!" Eva shouts behind me, tugging my arm. "Get in the tunnel!"

I ignore her, transfixed by the bright jewel in the sky. Skandar jumps through the trapdoor. Eva positions herself halfway down, pulling at my ankle. "Jesse, the oxygen will disperse if it hits!"

Her words are muted by a ringing in my ears—not from

the alarms, but from the Pearl itself. It's like I can hear it piercing the atmosphere as it draws closer. My heartbeat increases, thumping faster and faster the nearer it falls.

I stretch out my arm, pointing two fingers and shutting one eye until I've framed the Pearl between my fingernails. My hand buzzes with static. The hair on my arm stands on end.

I blink.

The Pearl rockets to the side, shoved off course by some invisible force. I watch as it shoots to the left and disappears beyond the row of trees bordering Lookout Park.

Seconds later, the alarms shut off. I drop my arm to my side.

Eva crawls out onto the grass, scanning the skies and muttering something in Spanish. "What were you doing?" She swallows, whispering to herself. "Pearls don't change course." I rub my fingers. The electricity leaves my arm.

She's right. Pearls aren't like antigravity balls. I've never once seen one move even the slightest inch from its prede-termined path.

Eva shakes her head, blinking twice before breaking from her stunned trance. "I don't ... I ... " She pauses. "I'm going to the library." She lays a hand on my shoulder before heading to the nearest staircase. Skandar's already retreated to the emergency bunker below the grass, along with every-one else. An uncomfortable silence falls over the park as I stand in the middle of the field, alone.

I sit down, cross-legged, and pick at the grass. Every

once in a while I glance up at the sky, wondering if I imagined the whole thing. After a few minutes, people start filtering back up to the park—August and his friends, a group of adults jogging along the outer perimeter. I trace the lines on my palm, feeling for anything out of the ordinary. It's a coincidence, that's all. I just happened to blink when the Pearl shifted course. Yeah.

Could happen to anybody.

12

Clutching Avery's well-worn note, I punch in the six-digit code to unlock the transparent door to the library. It's secured after six o'clock, but now that I'm an official trainee I can get in whenever I need to for studying. Not that there's going to be any studying going on tonight. I hope.

I think back to what Skandar said at Lookout. She's gotta have a reason for wanting me up here so badly. Considering all of the different possibilities kept me going through Dr. Hemming's two-hour *History of Pearls* lecture in astronomy this afternoon.

Half of the lights inside the circular room are turned off. A few adult agents huddle around a table by the computers playing chess. They glance up as I enter, probably wondering why a kid would want to spend his evening in the library.

I walk past a display of black-and-white Surface photographs. Heavy wooden tables sit neatly arranged on the main floor in front of me. Circular staircases hug the walls, leading up to the second and third levels, the highest of which juts up into Lookout Park like a secret underground house. They poured a lot of money into this place. Too bad I get mass distracted whenever I come in here to work. Maybe if they forced me to study in a white room with no windows or furniture or anything I'd actually get something done and ace a test for once.

I peer down the rows of bookshelves, looking for Avery. Other than the group of agents, the place is deserted.

Someone grabs my shoulder and spins me around.

"There you are, stranger." Avery grins.

I stare at her in silence for a moment before holding up the piece of paper. "I got your note."

"Crumpled." She smiles. "Is that what you think of me, Fisher?"

"No, no." I lay it against my knee and attempt to straighten it out. Instead, I end up ripping off the corner. "Oops."

"Cute."

I wince, stuffing the pieces back into my pocket. "Where did you come out from? I didn't even see you."

She shrugs. "I was hiding behind a shelf. Thought I'd sneak up on you."

I try to keep a straight face but it's hard. She's too weird. "Okay, then."

She grabs my hand, sending sparks through my skin up to my chest where they explode like fireworks. "Come on. Let's get going."

"Where are you taking me?"

"Oh, just wait. Tonight's the best yet. I've got something to show you."

I sigh. During the past year, Avery and I have covered every inch of the Academy together. She loves sticking her head where it shouldn't be. And she asks more questions than any person I've ever known. No wonder they didn't make her a bonafide agent.

She pulls me through the library over to the glass doors. Her death grip doesn't ease up until we're out in the hallway. Not that I'm complaining.

"Did you hear about the Pearl that almost smashed into us this afternoon?" she whispers as we walk out toward the canteen.

"I was there."

"You were at Lookout?"

"Yeah, it happened right after August Bergmann almost pounded my face into the ground."

"What a creep. We should've done the chili thing last night." She shakes her head. "Don't worry about him. Remember, being the big, flaunt agent is overrated."

I shrug. "After today, I'd rate it a million percent."

She rolls her eyes. "I don't think you can go over a hundred." She leads me through the canteen, grabbing an apple from a basket on the counter as we go. "They said it was a false alarm. The Pearl, I mean."

"I think they're lying."

"Wouldn't be the first time," she mutters. "You saw it, then?"

"It was headed straight for us, definitely. Then all of a sudden it changed course, curved to the side."

She spins around, pulling me closer and blocking the exit. "Changed course? You been falling asleep during Dr. Hemming's lectures again, Fisher?"

I shrug. "Yes, actually. But it happened, I swear. I was standing right in front of it."

She flashes me an inquisitive look. "Do you have a death wish or something?"

"No." I sigh. "It's not that. It was just … interesting."

She turns around, leading me out into the curved hallway along the perimeter of the ship toward the staircase. "Sure. Interesting until it smashes into you."

The last remnants of daylight stream up through the windows, creating a soft glow around Avery's face. I can't help but stare. Luckily she doesn't notice, too busy chomping on the apple.

"So tell me where we're going," I say. "I can't get in trouble again."

She swings her arm around my shoulder. "You won't get in trouble. Promise." She bites into the apple. "I've made an amazing discovery and tonight's the night to test it out."

"Why tonight?"

She pulls her head closer to whisper. "Alkine's having one of his closed-door staff meetings."

"So? They always do that before Visitation."

"We're gonna bash those doors down."

I look around to see if anyone's listening. "That sounds dangerous."

"Nah," she says. "Not with my discovery."

"Let me guess. You invented an invisibility potion."

"Nope." She bounds down the stairs and pushes me into a hallway leading back toward the center of the ship. We make our way past dozens of closed doors and two befuddled-looking agents before stopping outside Room 514.

"Isn't this just a maintenance room?" I try the door-knob. "And it's locked, anyways."

She tosses the apple core into a nearby trash chute and digs in her pocket, pulling out a small pointed key. "Bam!" She shoves it in my face.

"Shh!" I look around the empty hallway. "Someone will hear you."

"Yeah, right." She crouches toward the door, sliding the key into the hole and turning. "Now spot me, Fisher! I'm going in."

I keep my eyes on both sides of the hallway, waiting for someone to show up and drag me away to Mr. Wilson's office. Or worse, Alkine's.

Thankfully, nobody does.

Avery conquers the lock and grabs the back of my shirt, yanking me into the room with her and slamming the door behind us.

One thing she forgot to do was turn on the freaking light. It's pitch black now. Like, beyond black.

She giggles. "Oops, where's the switch?"

Panicked, I grope around the room looking for a button. Any button. A couple of minutes in here and I'll go insane. Tight spaces are bad enough. Tight spaces in the dark are hell.

In my quest for the lights I trip over something—a broom, maybe—and land on the floor with an agonizing thud. Avery stops laughing and crawls over me, flipping a switch next to the door. Fluorescent light flickers on above us, casting a spotlight on me doing my best impression of a puddle.

I pull myself to a sitting position and rub my shoulder. The closet's tiny. Stacks of buckets sit next to boxes of mechanical junk and dried-out, still-dirty mops. A row of brightly colored bottles line the shelf along the far wall. A wide metal tube in the corner stretches from the floor to the ceiling.

Avery rests her hands on her hips. "You like?"

I'd like it better if we were in here to do something other than snoop around, but things are never that simple with Avery.

"So we're in a maintenance room." I stand up. "This is really blowing my mind."

Ignoring me, she heads over to the far wall and lifts herself onto a wooden crate.

I walk over to her. "What are you doing?"

She struggles with a square grate on the ceiling, yanking at the corners until they pop out from the panel and reveal an open air vent. "Think of this as our own little portal." She bends down and leans the grate against the wall.

I stare at the dark hole in the ceiling. "A portal to where? The trash chutes?"

"Of course not." She rubs her dirty hands on the front of her jeans. "This is how we're gonna spy on Alkine."

"Oh, no." I take a few steps back. "I'm not going up there, if that's what you're thinking."

"Relax." She crouches to a sitting position, the heels of her feet kicking the crate. "I'll go up first. All you've gotta do is follow. It's safe, I promise. And you'll kill yourself if you don't go."

I cross my arms. "Now why would I do that?"

"Because this meeting, Jesse Fisher, is about you." She pauses. "They're going to talk about *you* in there."

"No they're not."

"Yeah. They are. And you wanna know how I know that?" She points to the hole in the ceiling. "Because I was up there in that vent a week ago when Alkine announced it."

"No way." I picture the faculty sitting around some fancy table arguing over reasons to throw me off the ship. "Why would they be talking about me?" I think back to my weird conversation with Captain Alkine the other night and suddenly it's not so hard to believe.

"Trust me, Jesse. Have I ever lied to you?"

"I guess not."

"And do you really think I'd drag you up into some vent for nothing?"

I take a moment to consider it. "Yes."

She laughs. "Okay, maybe I would, but you're still coming up with me."

My arms drop to my sides and I give a defeated shrug. She's impossible to argue with.

She beams. "Good enough for me."

Without wasting another moment, she stands and grabs onto the ceiling panel. Her shirt rises, revealing an inch of midriff. If her words weren't enough to get me up into the vent, that'll sure do it.

Then she lifts herself into the hole. She's definitely done this before. I bet she's a pro.

Once she's all the way through and has a second to turn herself around, I crawl onto the crate and grab her outstretched hands. She helps me up until I'm halfway in. I scoot toward her and turn to look back at the closet. I'm gonna regret this. I just know it.

13

With each room we pass over, grids of light stream through the metal grates below us. It's never completely dark. Of course, it doesn't change the fact that I'm wedged inside an air vent. I'm glad I'm skinny.

Avery doesn't seem to mind. She crawls through the narrow spaces with ease, contorting around corners with lightning speed. I follow dutifully behind, convinced that the entire system's going to give way and drop us right into the middle of a classroom. Or fill with hot air, or poisonous gas, or some equally unpleasant substance.

Again, Avery doesn't seem to share my concerns.

"Shh!" She waves her arm behind her. I do my best to tread lightly, careful to stay as silent as possible.

Then I hear it. Alkine's voice in the distance, coming from somewhere below us.

Avery slows her crawl, sliding along the thin sheet of metal without a sound. I copy her. The farther we slide, the more clearly Alkine's voice flows up into the vent. I can't believe I'm doing this. Sneaking around empty rooms is one thing. Spying on people from air vents is mass different. It feels wrong.

Avery intersects the bars of light shining up through the nearest grate and cautiously spins around so that she's on one side of the opening and I'm on the other. We lean our heads down, peering through the empty slots.

Captain Alkine stands at the head of an oval table. Before him sit the head teachers for Year Seven and up—all six of them. Mr. Wilson reclines in a chair closest to us. His bald spot glints with the reflection of the overhead lights. It could be blinding at the right angle.

Each teacher jots notes on a circular memo-pad in front of them, but I'm too far away to read the writing. From the amount of scribbles on each, the meeting must have already been going for a while.

"Our stats this month are looking very good," Alkine booms, his voice echoing through the vent. "Three Pearls taken from the Surface and transported to the Tribunal— two Fringe trades and one from Richard Harris's team down in Boston. That makes a total of twenty-one collected from all eight agent facilities." He smiles. "The Tribunal is satiated."

"Well, thank heavens for that," Mrs. Higgins, head of Year Seven, replies. The teachers laugh.

"Richard Harris is Skandar's dad," I whisper to Avery. "Poor guy's been on the Surface for months now." Surface work is the worst, and the most dangerous. I can't imagine being stationed down there for longer than a day. Skandar never talks about it, but I know it's hard for him, not knowing what's happening.

"Then there's Visitation Day," Alkine continues. "I know you all heard my spiel at assembly today, but I just want to give you one last heads up. It's your job to secure everything that needs to be secured by eleven o'clock tomorrow morning. It's a pain, but I'd like us to all be aware of our surroundings. I know I don't need to remind you about what nearly happened in the level five training room two terms ago." He pauses, taking a seat. "Now, if there's no further housekeeping to take care of, I'd like us to focus on the boy."

Avery tilts her head and meets my eyes. Neither of us says a word. Alkine doesn't even have to say my name. Somehow I just know he's talking about me. Avery was right.

Alkine sighs. "It's no secret that I'd hoped he'd be in a better position right now. The good news is, we've still got time. He's only just entered the program and I believe that if we focus our attention and work as a team there's hope for him yet."

I lean my face closer to the grate, forgetting that any of the teachers could look up at the ceiling and see me.

"I spoke with Fisher when he came back from the Surface," Alkine continues. "Incoherently, I'm sure. You all know that I'm no good with kids. Anyways, I let him know what my expectations were, that he should come to me with any concerns."

Mr. Wilson shifts in his seat. "Sending him down to the Surface without an escort was a big mistake. What if the Unified Party had found him and not just some punk kid?"

Alkine holds up a finger. "If we hadn't sent him down, he would have wondered why he was the only one in his year without Surface training. And he did have an escort."

Wilson slouches forward, resting his head on his hand. "Rodriguez doesn't count."

I glance at Avery. "Eva?"

Alkine sighs. "Doug, you of all people should be able to appreciate Rodriguez's considerable skills. Plus, she has a direct line to me. If anything had happened, I'd have been down there myself. Syracuse is a deserted town, miles from the nearest Chosen City. We know what we're doing. We've managed to keep him off the Tribunal's radar well enough, haven't we?"

Wilson shakes his head. "Another mistake, if you ask me. Sometimes I think it would have been better to turn him in the day we found him, spare us all this trouble."

I bristle at the tone of Wilson's voice. My fingers wrap around the grate.

Mrs. Dembo, head of Year Ten, sets down her pen and scratches the back of her dark, shaved head. "What trouble? He's a normal boy."

Alkine crosses his arms. "I'm afraid that may no longer be true." He presses a button underneath the table and the door buzzes. My shoulder jerks. Avery grabs it, silencing me.

I watch as someone new enters the room. At first I

don't recognize her from above, but as she takes a seat beside Alkine I spot the uncomfortable scowl on Eva's face. Suddenly this nightmare meeting turns into full reality.

"Evening, Rodriguez," Alkine glances in her direction. "Tell everyone what happened two days ago."

Eva nods, shifting nervously in her seat. "Okay. Well, I didn't exactly see it myself, but piecing together what Jesse said it seems that he ... I don't really know how to say this ... but he survived a twelve-story freefall. On pavement."

Mr. Wilson snorts. "That's impossible."

"I know," she replies, her eyes fixed on the table. "That's what I told him. I thought maybe he was kidding around. You know, being stupid. But I know he was up there on that rooftop, and the only way to get down to the street as fast as he did was to go through the hotel lobby. Harris was there the whole time and he swears Fisher never came down the stairs. The only other explanation is that he fell. Unless they're both pulling one over on me."

I frown, wishing I hadn't told her anything. Hearing her recite all this brings the memory flooding back. I'd been trying to repress it.

Mr. Kennewick, head of Year Twelve, clasps his hands. "You're saying he became invincible?"

She nods, meeting the faculty's eyes for the first time. "*Became*, yes—but not for long. When I found him, there was a gang of Fringers beating up on him pretty bad. It doesn't make any sense. Survive a fall like that only to be brought down by three teenagers?"

Mrs. Dembo jots something down on her memo-pad. "And he confided in you? About the fall and everything?"

"Yeah," she replies. "I just told him he was being stupid. You said not to respond if anything weird came up."

Alkine nods. "You did just as I asked."

Her brows furrow. "But what's going on? Why am I looking after someone who's apparently invincible? Why isn't he protecting *me*?"

A chill runs down my spine at the word *invincible*. That's a superhero word, not a Jesse Fisher word. And the fact that Eva's telling Alkine anything is enough to make me wanna drop down and punch her in the face. But I can't even move.

"He's not invincible," Alkine says. "It must have been some sort of anomaly." He turns his attention back to the teachers. "Has anybody noticed anything different lately?"

I peer around from teacher head to teacher head, fuming inside. It's all I can do to keep from shouting through the grate. What right do they have to be talking about me like this?

Mr. Wilson sighs. "He conked out during a round of Bunker Ball the other morning, but that's hardly different."

"He does seem more unfocused than usual," Mrs. Dembo adds. "I kept catching him daydreaming this morning in class."

Mrs. Higgins rests her hand on her chin. "Could it be some sort of residual effect from the chemicals?"

Alkine shakes his head. "No, no. We've tested his chemical levels each year since the day we found him. It was amazing he was alive at all, down in Seattle so soon after the bombings. It's barely safe now, and it's been decades."

Avery's face darts up again and she flashes me a concerned frown. "Seattle?" she whispers.

I meet her eyes for half a second, but my mind's spinning so fast that words don't register at normal speed. My hand slips against the grate, squeaking. For a second I'm sure they're going to notice us, but nobody at the table seems to hear.

"Well," Eva starts, "personally, I think it's time you told him everything you know. The poor guy's gonna develop a complex."

Alkine clears his throat and takes a sip of water from a glass beside him. "I'm beginning to think the same thing. I wanted to keep him safe, to give him as normal a childhood as we were capable of up here, but he's growing up. He needs to know the truth about his past before the Tribunal, or worse yet, the Unified Party, finds out."

I frown. The Tribunal *and* the Unified Party? Neither should have a reason to care about me. I keep waiting for everyone to look up and yell "gotcha" like in one of those stupid prank shows on the e-feed. But somehow I don't thing that's gonna happen.

"Bring him the key," Mrs. Dembo starts. "Tell him it belonged to his parents."

The word echoes through the vent. *Parents*. The teachers never talk about my parents.

"We don't know that for sure," Alkine responds. "And I'm hesitant to broach the subject with him until we know more. I've sent team after team down to Seattle but there's got to be something we're missing. There's a connection here, with the bombings, with Fisher . . . I just can't work my head around it."

Eva straightens up in her chair. "You think Jesse had something to do with the Scarlet Bombings? He wasn't even born yet."

Alkine nods. "Yes, but we found him in Seattle on the tenth anniversary of its destruction. He didn't know who or where he was, but he was completely immune to the chemicals around him." He pauses. "There we were, faces strapped up with gas masks. Meanwhile, this three-year-old child is wandering around in the middle of the apocalypse—dazed, but otherwise healthy."

My mind flashes back to the dream, the mist-covered city and the key hanging around my neck. The shadow behind me. Alkine's shadow.

Avery grips my wrist. "Maybe we should go."

I shake my head, keeping my face down. There's no way I'm leaving until I hear everything they have to say.

Eva leans forward, drumming her fingers nervously on the edge of the table. "Do you think he remembers any of it?"

"Doesn't seem to," Alkine replies. "He was so young. We've never given him a reason to trigger the memories."

Suddenly everything falls into place. I slot Alkine's words into the jigsaw puzzle that was my childhood. Orphan. Birth certificate destroyed. "Routine" medical tests. I guess when you grow up like that, you end up not even questioning it. Skyship Academy's always been my home. It's all I remember.

Alkine clears his throat. "Maybe I'll head down to Seattle myself before talking with him. There's got to be something we overlooked. Children don't appear out of thin air, especially in the middle of a war zone."

Mr. Kennewick crosses his arms. "Meanwhile what are we supposed to do if the kid starts flying around the room or shooting laser beams from his eyes?"

"He's not some sort of mutant," Mrs. Higgins responds. "He's our student. We'll take care of him."

"Take care of him by telling him the truth," Mr. Sorensen adds. "He has a right to know. What are you so worried about, Jeremiah?"

Alkine sighs, shifting in his chair. "I'm worried that if we tell him, that if he finds out we've been covering this for all these years, he'll end up doing something stupid and wind up in the hands of the government. They have to know he was down in Seattle that day. Madame herself was there, remember? What if she knows something we don't? She's a very charismatic woman. If Fisher's angry with us it will only weaken his judgment. He could go running right into her arms."

The pit in my stomach grows larger. Madame. The crown jewel of the elaborate story they're spinning below me. The cherry on top.

Mr. Kennewick clasps his hands together. "You speak as if you suspect an attack."

"Rumblings," Alkine replies, "as always. It'll happen. We've known that since day one. The only question is which side will fire first. Throw this miracle kid into the equation and you've got a catalyst, something for the Skyships and the Unified Party to fight over."

"Besides Pearls," Kennewick adds.

"Besides Pearls," Alkine echoes, pausing in thought. "I'm going down there one last time with the key to see what I can find before talking to the boy. We have to know what we're dealing with before we rush into things. Keep a close eye on him. If anything happens, I should be the first to know. But please be discreet about it. I don't want him to know that he's being watched."

Eva sighs, continuing to fidget in her seat. "It's getting harder, sir, to make it look natural. I can't always be there."

"I know. It's a hell of a position we put you in, but if everything goes the way I hope it will, you won't have to watch over him in secret much longer." He pauses. "We crack Fisher, we'll crack everything. That's what my gut tells me. Thank you all for hearing me out on this. Give me a week. If I haven't found anything, we'll brainstorm how best to approach the boy."

"A week." Wilson nods reluctantly.

"Fantastic." Alkine pushes back his chair. "Now if there's nothing else, I need to head up to the Tower and look over some files before tomorrow morning. It's a busy day." He stands and stretches, waiting for any responses. "Very well. Remember to get those rooms secure, people. I'm counting on you."

Without a goodbye, he leaves the table and heads out the door. Eva's the next to go, darting from the meeting room without making eye contact with the teachers. Everyone else shuts off their memo-pad and chats quietly. I only pick up the occasional phrase. It doesn't matter.

Avery lets go of my wrist. "Seattle," she whispers. "They found you in Seattle?"

I shake my head, unable to form words. I feel like I'm gonna puke right over the vent so it'll fall on top of the so-called "teachers." The lying teachers.

My air vent fueled claustrophobia disappears as a bazillion questions attack my brain. Seattle. Chemicals. Bombings. Key.

"Jesse?" Avery scoots closer. "Are you okay? Look, maybe this wasn't such a good idea."

I close my eyes—really shut them hard—and clench my jaw, hoping to snap myself out of this bad dream. But when I open them again, I'm still in the vent. The teachers are still in the meeting room, whispering about me. I shake my head and turn around, motioning for Avery to follow me back to the closet.

I drop down into the maintenance room first, and move to grab the doorknob. Avery lays her hand on my shoulder.

"Do you want to talk about it?"

I shake my head, keeping my eyes fixed on the door.

"Look," she starts, "I'm sorry if it was too much to hear."

"It's not your fault," I mutter.

"But I—"

I open the door and leave before she can finish her sentence. She doesn't try to follow me. I spend the rest of the night in my room, replaying Alkine's words over and over in my head until my body finally surrenders and I fall into a fitful sleep.

14

Cassius awoke on Skyship Polaris pressed against a hard, springy mattress on the second floor of the Shangri-La Inn, a garish building resembling a miniature version of the Taj Mahal. Why people needed to pretend they were sleeping in a palace when they were actually staying in a cheap, dirty hotel, he'd never understand. He left the establishment as soon as check-out would allow him.

The sun had barely risen, perched somewhere below the ship as he stepped out onto Polaris's empty, faux-cobblestone pathways. He stopped to take a glance at the ship's outer perimeter—an unobstructed view of the stars. Bundles of light hung in the distance from Skyships far away, like tiny galaxies nested in the darkness.

It had been a relatively short trip across the country to Polaris, plagued by a crying baby in the seat directly behind him. Twice he'd been tempted to reassemble the pistol and fire it right into the thing's head. Cold-hearted, sure, but the thought alone gave him some satisfaction.

He stepped into the city, which seemed to be modeled after some grotesque theme park. An electronic brochure on the shuttle ride over had proudly described the top level as "six square miles of nonstop action!" In reality, Polaris had expanded to its limit. The Shippers were running out of room to add more junk. If it wasn't for Pearls, the entire ship would have come crashing down years ago. Skyships were designed to run on solar power and biomass. Pearls had allowed them to expand without consequence.

He weaved through Saturn Market, a crowded area of street vendors and performers erected at the northeastern corner of the ship, and the best place to buy illegal Serenity in the Skyship Community. Or so he'd heard. Everyone was still asleep, the stalls and tents boarded up until late morning when the market would be packed once again. He passed by an old man dozing on a stool, a ramshackle sign strung around his neck with an arrow pointing up to the heavens and the words "keep your eyes on the stars" scrolled in messy black ink. A member of Heaven's Rain, most likely. Even the crazies were sleeping.

Surrounding the market on all sides were bizarre, decadent structures that sprung from the ground like neon monsters. Last night he had stopped to marvel at the flashing glitz of the casinos. The largest one, a fake castle christened "Fortunato," sat in the very center of the ship. He could see the tips of the flagpoles from where he stood now. The cobblestone pathways below his feet echoed the medieval theme, though it was more like gaudy, electric castle-land than a historically accurate depiction of the Middle Ages.

He exited the market and walked under a wire structure designed to resemble the Eiffel Tower. The town had an odd, ghostly feel at such an early hour. He expected to find fog settling across the streets, but had to remind himself that he was *above* the clouds now. He wasn't technically outside, either, though the environment had been created to fool his senses into thinking he was.

It took several minutes to find the nearest entrance to the elevators. He stepped inside the open chamber and descended to a curved corridor at the bottom level, joined by a handful of quiet travelers. He suspected the rush didn't start until late morning.

He'd be traveling by school-chartered sky taxi to the Academy, set to depart from Docking Bay Seven. If he had taken the right elevator, it'd be just around the corner.

He checked his suit's inside pocket for the small pouch containing the three pills Madame had given him back at the infirmary. As if he didn't have enough to worry about, he had to consider the possibility that the incident in his dorm room would repeat itself, that coming close to Jesse Fisher would trigger the fires again. It was a possibility he couldn't risk.

He passed Bay Six and continued until he came upon the next open door. Confirming he was in the right place, he entered and looked around for the school shuttle. Last night, the parking area had been abuzz with activity. It had been almost impossible to move. This morning, the shuttles lay silent in rows before him—a graveyard of commuter vehicles.

Then he spotted it. Alone in the far left-hand corner, framed by a blanket of early morning sky, stood the school taxi. Letters on the side of its long, thin body read *SkyWave 557*. Smooth and flat, it was little more than a giant white rectangle with landing gear—built for simplicity rather than power. It was probably cramped inside too. He wondered how long the ride would be. And if any babies would be onboard.

He trudged toward it, careful to act like a normal, clueless student. A few kids had already gathered around the front end of the taxi with their parents. A man in a navy, buttoned-up uniform stood next to the entrance with a clipboard.

Cassius felt several pairs of eyes latch onto him as he approached. He had to remind himself that nothing about him stood out. Nobody knew he was from the Surface. Still, he kept his face low as he walked. When he was within striking distance, the driver glanced up from the clipboard.

"Morning," he yawned. "Identification, please?"

Cassius nearly thrust his hand forward to show the man his Surface ID code, but caught himself and removed the doctored passport instead.

The driver flipped the passport open, comparing the picture on the inside cover to the boy standing before him. After a moment of consideration, he nodded and returned it.

"So you're Michael, our late registration." He checked

off a box on his clipboard. "No parents, siblings, or relatives with you today?"

"No," Cassius responded. "No parents."

"Very well. I'll take your bag and you can have a seat with the others while we wait for everyone to show up."

Cassius gripped tightly to the strap of the pouch. "Is it okay if I take it on with me? It's just a small school bag. There's some reading I want to go over on the way."

The driver frowned, then craned his neck to glance behind Cassius's shoulder. "Fine. It'll fit below the seat. You're okay."

"Thank you."

Relieved, he stepped to the side of the shuttle and moved toward a red-headed boy. The kid was engrossed in a book held inches in front of his face. Only four students had shown up so far. One girl and three boys, counting Cassius. He kept the bag close to his body as he sat on the ground next to the kid, avoiding eye contact.

The boy shut the book immediately. "I'm Colin."

Cassius groaned inwardly. He should have brought earplugs.

Colin scooted closer. "You just registered, yeah?"

He nodded, looking at the ground.

"So'd you just find out about the Horizon College recently or something?"

"Yeah," he whispered.

"What's your focus?"

He turned around and met the kid's eyes for the first time. "My what?"

"You know, what are you into? Philosophy? Literature? Art criticism?"

"Oh," he started. "Philosophy, I guess."

"Me too!" Colin grinned. "I hear Horizon's the best. So as a fellow academic, I've gotta ask, who's your favorite?"

Cassius stared at the kid's pasty, overeager face, wondering if he should even attempt a response. Philosophy was one of the Wasted Subjects on the Surface. Didn't do anybody any good.

Colin leaned closer. "Sartre? Descartes? Hypatia?"

He could have been making up words for all Cassius knew, but he realized he had to play along. "Yeah," he started. "He's good."

"Who? Hypatia?"

"Sure."

"Hypatia's a woman." Colin frowned.

Cassius cursed mentally, but didn't miss a beat, summoning the best fake smile he could. "Of course she is. It's a joke."

"Oh." Colin scratched the back of his head. "Funny."

Cassius bowed his head, sighing. He had a suspicion the entire flight was going to be "funny." He hoped he wouldn't be tempted to use the pistol in his bag before landing.

"Hey," Colin grinned. "We should be seat partners."

Cassius sighed. The pistol was sounding pretty good right about now.

15

I wake with a sharp yelp as something hits the back of my head. In a panic, I realize that I'm sitting at my desk in the middle of Mrs. Dembo's class. She pauses her lecture mid-sentence as everyone turns to stare at me. Did I really just yelp in the middle of class?

Barely concealed snickering spreads from the back of the room as Mrs. Dembo's dark eyes latch onto me. I keep my head inches from the top of the desk. Teacher stares are the creepiest things ever. The longer they do it, the creepier it feels. This stare is like a marathon.

After thoroughly inspecting me, she throws a death glare at the gigglers in the back of the room and continues her lesson.

It's not like she can blame me for falling asleep. After all, it's her fault that I didn't get any quality shut-eye last night. Her and the other teachers.

When Dembo's not looking, I spin around to meet August Bergmann's smirking face. He sits at the desk behind me, a rubber band spinning around his finger. Congratulations, moron. You managed to humiliate me for the umpteenth time.

"No girls around to protect you now," he whispers.

I glare at him, though it's not like I'm gonna do anything. I'd just get in trouble. After all, he's not the one who fell asleep in the middle of class. He's not the one all the teachers are secretly watching. "Leave me alone."

He shoots me an I'm-so-much-better-than-you-times-a-million look. "You and me Fisher, tonight outside the rec room."

"Wait," I smirk, "you asking me out on a date?"

"You come alone," he sneers. "We'll see how tough you are without Rodriguez there to save you."

I turn and lay my head on the desk. It's the first time the two of us agree on something. Eva Rodriguez is officially banned from being my friend, if she ever was in the first place.

They've got thirty of us crammed in here. Normally we're in smaller pull-out groups, spread around the Academy, but today we have to look all prestigious for Visitation. That's why I'm wearing this irritating, too-tight-in-the-shoulders suit and the whole classroom's decorated with artsy posters and fake writing assignments and schedules. All of us kids are crammed onto the sixth floor while the adult agents get to lounge around in the lower levels. Our visitors won't see any more of the Academy than Alkine wants. Of course the way I'm feeling right now, I might just jump on my desk and holler like a madman. "We steal Pearls from the government, kids! Come join our top secret organization—so secret that the teachers will lie to *you*, too!"

That'd show Alkine.

I fight to keep my eyes open. It gets harder with each endless word that spills from Dembo's mouth.

"Please open your textbooks to page 276," she says.

I groan, lifting the heavy textbook from under my desk and halfheartedly flipping through the pages. It's ridiculous. We never use textbooks, especially ones about "the use of predicate logic." As far as I know, the Academy's only got one set of books for each class, dragged out unceremoniously each Visitation Day.

Eva—a.k.a. traitor friend—sits to the side of me, diligently running her fingers through the pages of her textbook. She stops only to flash me quick, disapproving glances as if to say, "Can't you just *try*, Jesse Fisher?"

After what Avery and I found out last night, I'm not sure I see the point in trying to be the perfect Skyship student.

Avery met me outside my room this morning, still mass apologetic for dragging me up into the vent. I told her I wasn't mad. Not at her.

"Jesse." Mrs. Dembo shifts her attention straight to me. "Care to start us off?"

I glance over to Eva's book to see what page we're on before looking up to Mrs. Dembo.

She frowns. "The text, Jesse. Read us a few paragraphs aloud."

I nod through clenched teeth. We don't usually do a lot of reading out loud here, especially in classes with this many people. With August sitting right behind me it's just asking for trouble.

I labor through, clearing the first paragraph well enough, understanding next to nothing. But just as I'm starting to feel pretty confident, the words run together on the page. I stumble on the next sentence. August chuckles.

My vision blurs. I blink, shaking my head and trying again.

The words won't come out.

Then something explodes inside my chest. Like, literally, explodes.

The jolt of pain stops me cold. I freeze, staring at the front of the room, eyes wide, mouth hanging open. Lightning bolts spread from my chest, coursing through my body with the force of an electric chair.

"Jesse?" Mrs. Dembo approaches me. "What's the matter? Are you all right?"

I can't speak. I close my eyes and focus on breathing. Inhale. Exhale. Inhale. Exhale.

I've gotta get out of here—escape the pain.

Inhale. Exhale.

I try to stand, but topple back onto my seat. The electricity turns mass cold, like I've been shot with a freeze ray.

"Jesse!" Mrs. Dembo rushes to my side, kneeling beside me. The room falls silent. Every last eye is focused on me.

I start to shake. So cold.

"Somebody call the medical staff," Mrs. Dembo shouts. Eva bolts from her desk and runs to the door, ripping a communicator from the wall.

"Get it out," I mutter, too quiet for anyone but Dembo to hear. There's a polar icecap growing in my stomach. Before too long I'm gonna be frozen from the inside out.

She grabs my wrist. "Get *what* out? What's happening, Jesse?"

I clutch my chest, mouth open.

Mrs. Dembo squeezes my arm. "Tell me what's happening."

I shake my head. Inhale. Exhale. All I can do is breathe and hope the pain goes away.

Then, relief. My arm goes limp in Dembo's grip. As suddenly as it had started, the insanity snaps away. My body temperature stabilizes. The shaking stops.

Mrs. Dembo lets go and motions for Eva to put the communicator back. I sit up in my desk. The entire class crowds around me. Nobody says a word.

My breathing's staggered. I keep my eyes peeled on the front of the room, wishing I could disappear.

"What was that about, Jesse?" Mrs. Dembo whispers.

I rub my chest, debating what to tell her. If I say what really happened she'll tell Alkine, and who knows what he'll do. So I lie.

"I'm fine," I mumble. "I didn't get much sleep last night."

"You don't look fine," she responds. "I think we should send you to the infirmary."

"No." I meet her eyes, pleading. "No, I'm good."

She sighs, clearly not buying it. She stares at me another moment before speaking. "Okay, here's our deal, then. You stay here for now, but if you start feeling ill it's straight to the medics. And I'm going to march you down there as soon as our visitors leave."

"Fine," I mutter. "Can I finish up the reading, then?"

She shoots me one final, disapproving glance and stands to motion for the rest of the class to get back to their books.

I continue the paragraph, making sure not to look at a single person in the room. Nobody pays attention to the words coming out of my mouth. I feel their eyes on me. I hear the whispers. I'm a walking canister of toxic waste. Even August Bergmann won't dare hit me with a rubber band now.

16

Cassius's sky taxi pulled into Horizon College's docking bay, landing smoothly on the ground as the overhead seatbelt lights flickered off.

Cassius undid his belt, thankful that the trip had taken under an hour. Colin had managed to find a seat next to him and rattle off questions the entire way, concerning everything from life on Skyship Orion to Cassius's views on the Unified Party. Cassius had supplied mostly single-word answers. Halfway through the journey, he wondered if Madame had secretly sent the boy up to test him. It certainly wasn't beyond her.

Luckily the taxi's cabin was reasonably spacious, and newer than it looked from outside. Cassius had taken the window seat so he could stare at the clouds while Colin blathered on. His mind raced from thought to thought, mostly regarding his meeting with Madame in the infirmary. The shiny black cube. Fisher could open it, she'd said. He had some sort of key. Why he'd have anything to do with it at all was beyond Cassius. And why hadn't Madame mentioned the cube before? If it really belonged to his mother, then he had a right to know about it.

When the last of the onboard lights turned off, the driver shut down the power and moved down the ship's walkway.

"All right, kids. In a moment I'm going to ask you to quietly file out using the side exits—two in the front and two at the back. There'll be folks at the far end of the docking bay to meet you and let you know where to go next. I'll be onboard waiting for departure, so if you need to leave anything behind, that'll be all right."

With that, he walked back to the driver's seat and pushed the button to open the doors. Those nearest to the exits stood, stretched, and filtered off the ship.

Cassius waited a moment for the cabin to clear, allowing Colin a head start before leaving the ship himself. As he stepped into the docking bay, a shiver ran down his spine. This was it. No turning back now. He cleared his dry throat and took a deep breath, trying to keep his hands steady. He couldn't let his anxiety show.

Once ready, he followed the group to the far side of the bay. It didn't take long. Compared to Atlas and Polaris, the Academy was nothing.

At the arched entrance to the bottom level stood two adults. Mr. Sorenson and Ms. Gray, senior teachers who would be showing Cassius and the others around the Academy. Cassius wondered what they really did. If Madame's intelligence was correct, he was looking at a pair of secret agents.

The teachers distributed a pair of pamphlets and went over the rules of the day: stay with your guide at all times, don't get lost, don't head into the students' quarters. With any luck, they'd be taking him right to his target. Maybe things weren't going to be so difficult after all.

Then they were split into two groups. Cassius ended up in Ms. Gray's. Colin, thankfully, was put into the other group. That would make things easier.

Ms. Gray took a quick head count and Cassius's group left the bay, traveling to the elevators. All the while, Cassius considered ways to separate himself. First he had to find Fisher, which meant playing along a little while longer.

Soon they arrived in the center of a meandering hallway on Level Six. Posters, artwork, and faded maps hung along the curved walls. The gray carpet was noticeably stained. Ms. Gray wrangled them together in a huddle, keeping her voice low. "We're heading by some of the classrooms on our way to the canteen so I need you all to be quiet, especially around open doors. The teachers are expecting you, but we don't want to interrupt lessons."

She turned and started off down the hallway. Cassius lingered by the elevators and stayed on the outskirts of the group in case he needed to make a quick escape. He closed his eyes for a moment, calming his racing nerves.

Then they wound down the most randomly designed corridor Cassius had ever walked through. What could have been a straight shot devolved into a series of twists and turns, alcoves and walls. Terribly impractical, but it would make hiding easier. He made a note of it.

They passed several closed, numbered doors before arriving at the entrance to a library. Cassius peered through a large glass window in the wall before traveling around the perimeter into another hallway. Several doors hung open before them. Ms. Gray raised her finger to her lips and moved forward.

As they passed the first open door, he hid behind a tall Asian boy and caught a quick glance of the room. Empty except for a few old desks shoved into the corner. Same with the next room. Where were all the students?

Then his chest tightened. Heat.

Not again.

He loosened his tie, struggling to block out the pain. His breathing shortened as he considered the worst possible scenario. Fire. Explosions.

Remembering the medication, he reached into his jacket and felt around for the pills. When he was sure no one was looking, he slipped the tiny white capsule from the packet and tossed it into his mouth.

They arrived outside the third door. His heart did a back-flip. The pain remained steady. A woman's voice came from inside the room. Ms. Gray held out her hand to stop the visitation group and stepped through the open door.

Cassius gripped his chest, forcing the fire back inside

of him. He was not going to let this happen. Not when he was so close.

Ms. Gray emerged from the room and ushered the group of eager students closer. They surged through the entrance. Cassius stayed back. He couldn't risk any of the Shippers he'd met in Syracuse recognizing him. He settled just outside the doorway, ducking behind the group.

The teacher, a short African woman with a bright smile, stood facing them, going on about the merits of the college's academic programs. Cassius tuned her out. The heat pounded through his torso but he held it at bay, peeping through cracks in the group. His eyes searched every row of the classroom, up and down, looking for Fisher.

In the fourth row from the doorway, two seats back, he found him—the same pathetic runt he'd met only days earlier on the rooftop, head resting sluggishly in his hand.

Cassius fought back a smile. He ducked away and detached himself from the group, tiptoeing to the next open doorway.

He slipped inside the empty room and darted behind a shelf, pulling the bag from his shoulder and unzipping it. He removed the pieces of the pistol from inside and attached them, hooking it onto the belt underneath his jacket. Just in case.

He leaned against the wall and controlled his breathing. The thudding in his heart grew fainter. The medication had begun to take effect.

17

"All right, folks." Mrs. Dembo closes her textbook. "Excellent job today. Time to head to next period. Monday will be infinitely more interesting, I promise."

I shut my book with a satisfying thud and shove it under the desk as the rest of the class shuffles out the door. Only two more periods of this left. Hopefully I can make it. And given what's happened already, I mean that literally.

I stand and stretch, walking through the row of desks to the door. Just as I'm about to leave, Mrs. Dembo holds out her arm to stop me.

"Not so fast, Jesse." She positions herself between me and the exit. The remaining students pass around her until it's just the two of us.

She frowns, arms crossed. "What was all that about today? You looked horrible."

I focus on the wall, hands in pockets. "I told you. I didn't sleep very well."

"Lack of sleep doesn't cause seizures, Jesse."

"Maybe I ate some bad chicken." I shrug, knowing what's really going through her mind. "You should check with the cooks."

Her eyes narrow. "If we didn't have visitors today, I'd have sent you down to the infirmary without question. As it stands, we're going to get you checked out tonight."

"But, I—"

"If it happens again today, you're to get help immediately, even if there's a whole group of visitors in the classroom at the time. Do you understand?"

"It was just a stomachache."

"We're not arguing about this, Jesse."

"Whatever," I mutter, and try to push my way past her.

Her arm stays steady, a bar across the doorway. "Was it just a stomachache, then?"

I glare at her. "What else would it be?"

She shakes her head, but doesn't respond. I push past her. She lets me go. I leave the room without looking back. She knows full well that there's something wrong with me, but won't come out and say it. Nobody will.

I storm down the hallway, but I don't get more than a few feet before an arm juts out and curls around my neck, choking me from behind as it yanks me into an empty classroom.

The door shuts and locks in front of me. My captor's arm tightens around my neck, drawing me closer. "Don't make a sound," a voice whispers in my right ear, "or it's over."

I gasp for air and reach up to my neck.

The arm loosens and pushes me to the ground, face first. I flip around, just as my captor pulls a gun from underneath his jacket.

I look up. Even without the Unified Party badge I recognize him immediately. It's the guy from the rooftop. Cassius Stevenson.

He aims a pistol at my face, looking down at me with the same arrogant expression as last time. And I thought my day couldn't get any worse.

"What are you—" I don't finish the question, realizing how senseless it'd be. He's here. End of story.

"Shh." He takes a step forward. "I told you to be quiet. Next time I fire."

"How did you get up here?" I whisper, not expecting an answer. I comb my memory for mistakes I made back on the Surface, breadcrumbs that could have led him back to the Academy. But even if he'd found the ship, security would've taken him out before he reached the sixth level. He shouldn't be here. A Pearlhound like him shouldn't think twice about someone like me.

Cassius eyes the room for a moment before returning his attention to me. "This is what's gonna happen, Fisher. You're gonna help me out here, all right? We need to get down to a shuttle and head for the Surface. You're going to take me to the elevators, and you're gonna to do it in silence. This pistol is loaded with Pearl energy. You want it fired into your heart?"

"I'm not taking you anywhere." I push the pistol away from my face.

He crouches and grabs me by the collar, forcing the tip of the pistol into my chest. "All right, then."

"No, no!" I panic. Sweat pools inside my school suit. "Don't shoot!"

He drops me, standing but keeping his finger on the trigger. "I could've killed you easily a few days ago," he starts. "I can do it again, so don't play games with me."

I nod and bring my knees to my chest. "You ... you wanna get off of the Skyship?"

"That's what I said," Cassius responds, "and I'm taking you with me."

"No way."

He sighs, a flash of anger in his eyes. "You go where I tell you to go, Fisher. Now get up and check the hallways. And no screaming for help or you'll be dead before anyone arrives."

I lift myself off the ground and head to the closed door, hoping there'll be someone in the hallway. Mrs. Dembo could still be in the classroom.

Cassius follows inches behind me, concealing the weapon but keeping it at the ready. I unlock the bolt and twist the doorknob, hands wet with sweat. Cracking open the door, I peer out into the hallway.

Cassius pokes the tip of the gun into my back. "This isn't a time to play around. Get going."

I open the door and step outside. Cassius stays close.

The hallway's empty. Anyone who could actually help me is hiding down on the lower levels because of Visitation. Students and teachers are in the classrooms pretending to study liberal arts. Whether Cassius planned this or not, it couldn't possibly be a better set-up for him.

"What do you want from—"

"Shh." He nudges me in the back. There are so many other people onboard that the Unified Party could kidnap. So many stronger, more important people. This has to be a mistake.

I turn right and head down the hallway, hoping that the door to Dembo's room will still be open. But when we pass by her classroom, I realize that I'm doomed. The door's shut. She's left already. If I shout down the hallway, Cassius'll shoot.

So I head forward. Cassius shifts to my side, walking casually like we're old buddies or something.

"Don't go out to the main corridor," he whispers. "Stick to the inner hallways."

I nod, scanning each open door for a sign of movement.

We pass around the backside of the library. I crane my neck to see in through the windows. There's a Visitation group bunched together inside, backs turned in our direction. I look around for Avery. She should be in the stacks, working. If I could get her attention, she'd know what to do.

"Face forward." Cassius pushes me to speed up.

Before I know it we arrive in the final corridor, steps

away from the elevators. They're deserted. Hope shrivels inside of me. If I'm going to make my move, it's gotta be now. But I'm unarmed. Cassius is stronger.

I slow to a crawl, stepping forward with legs of concrete.

"Faster." Cassius pushes me again. I nearly topple to the ground before catching myself.

We arrive at the elevators and Cassius moves to press the request button. The doors slide open right away. He forces me inside and follows.

The doors slide shut. We're alone.

"Why are you taking me to the Surface?" I blurt as Cassius presses the button on the wall.

He ignores me. "These elevators bugged?"

"Why would I tell you that?"

He scans the upper corners before responding. "You did something. To me."

"You're the one who had me dangling off a building."

"And then you did something."

"Yeah, I fell."

"You're lying." He shakes his head. "When we get to the bottom level, you're gonna get us into a shuttle so that we can head down to the Lodge."

"I'm not authorized to pilot a shuttle," I reply, like it really matters.

"You let me worry about that." He moves to the front of the elevator. "I just need you to get us in."

I'm about to argue when the elevator doors open to

reveal the ground level. Cassius sticks his head into the corridor, then grabs my wrist and attempts to pull me out.

I latch onto the metal bar at the far end with my free hand. Cassius struggles to break my grip, but before he can yank me into the corridor, a girl darts out from around the corner and tackles him to the ground. His fingers slip from my wrist. I turn in panic. Avery leaps from the floor and grabs my hand. Cassius lies in a heap on the ground, flummoxed.

"Hurry!" She pulls me across the corridor into the docking bay. We fly through the entrance as Cassius lifts himself off of the floor.

My heart ticks like a time bomb as we race through the docking bay. I don't know how Avery knew to attack when she did, but I'd be dead without her.

"Stop or I shoot!" Cassius yells from behind us. Avery keeps running. I pull her back and spin around to see Cassius gaining ground, pistol raised.

"Don't move another inch." He approaches, glancing around the empty bay. The visitation taxi rests in the corner across from a line of empty Academy shuttles.

"I don't know who you are," Cassius glares at Avery, "but you better move out of the way and let me take what I need. My trigger finger's itching for some action."

Avery stands behind me, clutching my shoulders. Neither of us moves.

Cassius takes several more steps in our direction before stopping. A figure approaches behind him at the entrance to the bay. As the silhouette nears us, I notice the familiar bald spot. It's Mr. Wilson.

I look back at Cassius. So far he's oblivious.

"Last chance," Cassius says. "Step away from Fisher."

Avery stays close. Cassius cocks the pistol, preparing to shoot. But before he can pull the trigger, Wilson sneaks up and yanks his arm to the side.

"Run!" Wilson bellows. Avery and I turn and bolt to the nearest waiting shuttle.

Cassius reacts immediately, kneeing Mr. Wilson in the gut and breaking free of his grip.

Avery and I dart behind the shuttle.

"Your code!" she urges.

I frantically plug the numbers into the keypad and wait for the door to open. The moment it does, we jump inside.

Cassius swears, stumbling away from Mr. Wilson and raising the pistol. Wilson lunges at him—misses.

Avery fires up the shuttle. Cassius pulls the trigger.

A blinding green beam erupts from the pistol, hitting Mr. Wilson in the chest and burrowing through his body until it pokes out the other side and dissipates into the air. Wilson collapses face-first onto the ground with an echoing thud.

"No!" I stare out the window in horror. Mr. Wilson lies still, a willing sacrifice. For me. He took the bullet for me.

He didn't even like me.

Cassius winces for a moment, then turns to come after us. He's too late. We hover off the ground. Our landing gear rises and Avery takes the pilot's seat, steering us through the docking bay.

I watch as Cassius barrels toward us, gripping the pistol. He could shoot if he wanted, but he doesn't. Instead, he stops halfway and heads for the row of empty shuttles.

I turn to Avery. "He's gonna follow us."

She keeps her attention on the sky outside the docking bay. "He'll have a tough time without an access code."

But as I watch Cassius struggle with the shuttle locks, pounding his fists on the door, I know he's gonna find a way to break in. All we can do is put as much distance between us and him as possible.

18

"He shot Mr. Wilson!" I gape out the back of the shuttle as we pull away from the Academy. "Avery, he shot him!"

"I heard you the first time," she replies, gripping the steering wheel. "Get up here and flip on the radar."

I stumble to the cockpit, heart pounding out of time. "He kept saying that he'd shoot me. I didn't believe him, but now I—"

"Jesse," she grabs my shoulder. "Calm down. We've got more important things to worry about."

"But, Avery. He actually shot him."

"I know." She sighs. "Why do you think I tackled the bastard? Be thankful it was Mr. Wilson and not you."

"But he could be—"

"We're going down." She takes the shuttle into a nose-dive, cutting through the clouds until we're in clear air again. The Surface fills the window—a panoramic brown blanket meeting the Pacific Ocean in a wobbly line to our left.

I stare at the desolate landscape, trying to slow my breathing. Avery straightens us out again.

"Wait." I grip the control panel. "Where are we going?"

"Where do you think?" she answers. "Down."

"But that's where Cassius wanted to take me!"

"Well, he's not in this shuttle, is he?" She lays on the accelerator.

"But...but we could go to another Skyship!"

Her eyes close and her head jolts to the side. Her fingers tense up on the wheel.

"Avery?"

"Seattle." She grits her teeth and glances over to me. "They found you in Seattle, not in 'another Skyship.'"

I stare at her face. She's trying to control her expression, I can tell. "Is something wrong?"

She blinks. Her mouth relaxes. "A killer chased you from the Academy. I'd say something's wrong."

"No. I mean, with you."

She keeps her eyes on the scenery in front of her. "Right as rain. Now I can turn around and head to Atlas if you want. You can file this all with the Tribunal, but you're better off investigating things yourself. Trust me."

"Is there something you're not telling me?"

Avery opens her mouth to speak. Before she can get a word out, our shuttle rocks violently back and forth. I grip onto my seat to avoid falling.

"What was that?" I cock my head around the cabin.

Avery frowns. "Unified Party."

"No way." I scan the radar screen, ignoring the meaningless lines and numbers and focusing on the two red dots closing in on our shuttle.

"It's Madame." Avery sighs.

I crane my neck to see out the rear window. Two government cruisers cut through the sky behind us like a pair of enormous bats.

Avery shakes her head. "They were waiting, ready to pounce as soon as we crossed the Skyline."

I wince. "It couldn't be Madame. Madame wouldn't care about us."

"The hell she wouldn't," Avery mutters as she guns it.

The cruisers barrel down with insane speed, equipped with enough firepower to blow our shuttle apart. They blot out the sun behind us. A missile whizzes by above us, missing the roof by inches.

"What do we do?" I spin back to the control panel, wishing I had my flying permit. It's lucky Avery's here. She may not have graduated, but at least she knows what the shuttle's buttons do.

"Buckle up," she starts. "We're changing course."

"I'm not so sure that's a good idea." Our shuttle lurches to the side as a second missile scrapes the bottom.

"Hold onto something, Jesse." Avery pulls back on the wheel. The shuttle does a ninety-degree turn and rockets up into the cloudbank. We disappear into a puff of white.

My whole body's thrown against the back of the seat. My stomach feels like it's about to pour out of my mouth.

Struggling to move my head, I glance at the radar. "They followed us into the clouds."

"So much for losing them in Skyship Territory." Avery frowns. "Is your seatbelt on?"

I nod, but double check anyway. We pierce the top layer of clouds and Avery flips the shuttle upside down.

The belt cuts into my chest and waist, but the centrifugal force keeps me from falling onto the ceiling and splatting like a bug. My stomach spins in circles. My neck feels like it's about to snap.

We make a tight U-turn and plunge down through the clouds with reckless speed. Whiteness overtakes the windows until two dark shapes cut through beside us, devouring the clouds as they head up. Our shuttle wobbles in their wake.

Avery steers us straight down. I wait for the shuttle to break apart and disintegrate in the air. These things are not made for maneuvers like this.

Avery scowls. "We've gotta get to the Surface while we can."

"What if Cassius follows us?"

"One problem at a time."

Our first problem comes back big time. Both cruisers emerge from the cloudbank, splitting apart to surround us.

"Frag it!" Avery pounds her fist against the console and makes a sharp dive. The Surface blots out the window again. Only this time it's not barren and brown. This time we're heading straight into a Chosen City. Portland, from the looks of our coordinates.

Two massive black crosses float into view on either side of our shuttle. Bio-Net connectors, affixed to their positions in the air by a system of magnets. Together with their thousand or so companions, they form an upside-down butterfly net around the city—a man-made ozone layer responsible for filtering sunlight, absorbing Fringe chemicals, and programming weather inside. All powered by Pearls.

"You've gotta pull up!" I shout.

Avery shakes her head. "They won't fire if we're in range of a city. It's our only chance."

"But we can't go through the Bio-Net."

"Who says?"

I look out my window at the nearest connector. A double-barreled cannon rests on the side, waiting to destroy anything that threatens the city below. I open my mouth to warn Avery, but before I know it we shoot past. A monstrous, x-shaped shadow blankets our shuttle. No explosions.

The government cruisers split off course and shoot away from the city in opposite directions.

Our shuttle shakes as we pass through the invisible Bio-Net field. Avery speeds up, even though we're about to crash in the middle of a Chosen. A yellow light flashes maniacally above her head, sounding a dull alarm through the cockpit.

"The solar panels are failing," I say.

She presses a button to the side of the steering console. "Filtered sunlight. Guess I forgot."

"Do we have any reserve power left?"

She frowns. "I burned it up trying to get away from those cruisers. We've got twenty-five minutes left, tops. The Net's freaking this old junker out."

My eyes dart from window to window, watching as the tops of skyscrapers reach out all around us. This isn't like the Fringes, where there'd be plenty of open space to attempt a crash landing. This is a mousetrap, an endless labyrinth of arches, sky bridges, balconies, and towers. And we're heading down. Fast.

"Jesse?"

I break away from the window. "Yeah?"

"You know how you survived that fall back in Syracuse? Now would be the time to pull something like that out of your hat."

I take a deep breath, shaking my head. "I've got nothing."

She grits her teeth, gripping the wheel tight. "Then brace yourself for impact. This isn't going to be pretty."

19

After taking over the chartered sky taxi, Cassius blasted off from the docking bay. Reinforcements barged in to stop him, but they were too late.

Piloting such a lengthy ship felt unnatural, but he'd always been a quick study. Though his trajectory was wobbly, he dipped beneath the clouds until the Surface came into view. No sign of Fisher's shuttle. He cursed. They'd gotten a head start.

Fisher was off the Skyship, but he could have headed anywhere... even to Atlas. He could have alerted the Tribunal.

Cassius fumbled with the control deck, searching for a radar or tracer or anything that would allow him to pinpoint the shuttle.

The com-pad on his belt beeped. He removed it and held it before his face, grimacing as he read the code on the screen. It was Madame.

He toyed with the idea of ignoring it. A failure like this could derail him entirely, and he couldn't afford disappointing her. She knew more than she was letting on. She knew about his parents.

Still, ignoring her would be worse. She'd be angry. Anger was more dangerous than disappointment.

As much as it pained him to do it, he pressed the touch screen. "Hello?" His hand shook as he waited for her response.

"Cassius," her cold voice filled the cockpit, "tell me where you are."

He considered lying, but didn't. "I'm in a sky taxi heading away from the Academy."

"And Fisher? Is he with you?"

"Uh—no, Madame. He's on another shuttle." He paused. "I took down one of their teachers."

The truth was, he hadn't meant to. He hadn't *wanted* to, but the old man had gotten in the way. Cassius had acted on instinct and pulled the trigger. Before he knew it, the guy was dead.

He gritted his teeth, waiting for Madame's response. After an agonizing silence, her voice continued, steady as ever. "I appreciate your honesty, Cassius. I stationed two of my cruisers beneath the Academy in case something like this were to happen. They've driven Fisher's shuttle to Portland, Oregon—a short distance from your coordinates. I've put a hold on the city's defense canons. I'd like you to follow him. Contact me when you land. I'll be waiting to hear from you."

"Yes, Madame." He barely got the words out before she hung up. He stared at the blank screen. "Hello?"

He held it to his ear, wondering if he'd accidentally silenced it himself. She was gone. No "Good job" or "Did you run into any trouble on Polaris?" or anything. Not that he had expected warm congratulations, but she hadn't even seemed to care.

He brushed the thought away, eager to land on the Surface.

Folding the CP and attaching it to his belt, he charted a course for Portland at double speed.

20

Avery yanks on the steering console to bring us level as we rush past a 200-plus story building. The hull of our shuttle scrapes the corner. Eventually we're gonna make a wrong turn and head straight through an office building.

Chosen cities are built *up*, not out, giving us no air space to maneuver. Towers stretch like spires around us.

"Watch out for the sky bridge!" I point at a rapidly approaching overpass. The people inside notice us, freezing and pointing in terror as we hurtle toward them.

"I see it." Avery swoops beneath the bridge just in time. It's like some insane obstacle course out here.

Something beneath us pops and the shuttle vibrates. The yellow warning light continues to flash. Avery swats a button on the wall and the cockpit goes dark. "Sorry, but we need every drop of power we can get."

"What are you planning to do?" I watch as the energy meter drops from nearly full to a red stump.

"Land in a pillow factory," she replies through gritted

teeth, right before flipping the shuttle sideways and darting through a narrow space between buildings. We take out a balcony railing as we plow through the air. It's lucky no one was standing outside.

I jostle in my seat, still feeling like I'm gonna puke. Avery straightens the shuttle as we arrive over a wide plaza—the first bit of open air so far.

"Crank the emergency brakes," she motions. "Blue switches to your right."

"All three of them?"

She nods. "Quickly, Jesse."

I reach over to the switches, pulling them down and listening as the backside of the shuttle opens up outside. We look like an airborne flower now, with metallic petals spread out behind us for air resistance.

Another building looms before us, its fiberglass siding quickly blotting out our view. Coiled tracks stretch out at different angles and elevations. Slick egg-like train carts dart along each, disappearing into the city. Chute Transport, no doubt. Under safer circumstances I might be impressed. Right now, it's just a bigger-than-usual roadblock.

Avery takes a hard left, whirling between two pieces of track to keep us from smashing into the station. With no time to catch our breath, she pulls up to avoid hitting a rooftop park on the next street. I watch a group of children pause below us, pointing up from the pristine playground as we tear by. We probably look pretty flaunt to them.

But we can't keep this up forever. Eventually we're gonna hit the ground.

We pass safely through the next street before flying over a brick square, yards from smashing into the heads of the travelers beneath us. Water shoots up from a fountain below, smacking our underbelly and shoving the already frantic shuttle sideways.

There's no use pretending we're anonymous anymore. People run to move out of danger, falling to the ground seconds before we'd hit them. Others point. I hear muffled screams through the window. Sirens. They're everywhere.

And then it happens.

We plow directly into the bottom floor of a residential building. Avery tries to change our course, but it's not enough. The shuttle's airbag punches me back into my seat.

We hit the side of the building with earthquake-sized force, driving right through the siding, through the windows, and into the nearest room. I can't see anything beyond the expanded airbag, but I hear it all—the twisting of metal, shattered glass, and the screams of the crowd behind us.

We smash into the ground, then lift up again before landing with a tooth-chattering thud. My body jerks back, twisting awkwardly in the seat.

Our shuttle slows as its nose crumples up like an aluminum can. Windows blow out. Sideways raindrops of metal and plastic explode around us. I try to shield my face, but with all the scrap flying around, it's useless. Some pieces whiz by, others lodge themselves in my skin. If it wasn't for the mind-numbing pain, I'd be thinking about how much it's going to hurt when these things get pulled out later.

Chaos spins around us for what seems like minutes. Then everything stops. The front end quits caving in and the air clears.

We sit—bloody and battered—for a few moments before either of us speaks.

Alarms blare around us, breaking me from my crash-induced trance. Though we're both in horrible pain, we know we can't stay here.

Avery stumbles to a standing position, staggering to the door and pulling it open. It detaches from the shuttle and crashes to the ground. I lift myself carefully from the copilot's seat and grab onto her hand, shaking.

A shallow scratch runs the length of her cheek. Her arms are torn up, but she's standing. I glance over to see a triangular piece of glass lodged through the arm of my jacket just below the shoulder. My body feels like it's been put through five hours of torture.

I almost died.

The thought strikes me as we limp out the doorway, nearly tripping on the jagged metal. It wasn't even because of some super-heroic mission. We were chased. We ran. We almost *died*.

I shake the idea from my head as we jump down onto the rubble-strewn carpet outside. A couch sits in two separate pieces beside the shuttle's front window. Splinters of wood litter the ground—remnants of pulverized furniture. Food falls out of what's left of a refrigerator in the corner. This was somebody's home.

I search around for bodies. Thankfully, we're alone.

Not so outside. A crowd of onlookers from the square converge behind our shuttle, drawn from all angles by the alarms. A few of the more reckless ones start to climb through the hole in the outside wall, probably hoping for some sort of citizen's arrest. We've got no choice but to split.

I take off first, looping around the front of the shuttle and sprinting through a smaller hole that leads farther into the building. Avery follows, grabbing onto my shoulder. "Are you all right?" She leads me around a chair to the exit door.

"I'll be fine," I wheeze, though I really doubt it. Blood trickles down my arm from the glass shard. If I don't stop to take care of it soon, I won't be running long before I pass out.

Avery pulls open the door. I follow her into a narrow hallway, lit with artificial sunlight from flat ceiling panels above. Corridors stretch out on both sides of us—no clear exit in either direction.

Avery leans against the door, breathing hard. "Left or right?"

"Left." I bolt away, sprinting down the corridor as fast as my throbbing body will let me. I try to ignore the blood as it spills down my sleeve and drips onto the white flooring below, leaving a dark trail.

Our footsteps echo down the length of the hallway as the alarms fade behind us. We turn a corner. A glass exit comes into view.

We run faster until the glass door slides open and lets

us out into the city. The temperature-controlled air hits me immediately, revitalizing my parched lungs. It's so fresh I can almost taste it, and for a moment it dulls the pain. But only for a moment.

We arrive in a wide marble passageway between buildings. Decorative birch trees stand in small square plots of dirt placed evenly down the center of the street. People funnel around us, eyes shifting uneasily in our direction. A woman grabs her daughter's hand and speeds up as she passes by. Avery and I huddle close together in the shade of the building.

"Where do we go?" I whisper.

She shakes her head. "They're everywhere. We have to find a place to hide."

I glance down the street and see four men in government uniforms hurry around the corner of the smashed-up residential building. They're not running. Yet.

Avery notices them too, and grabs onto my good arm. "Come with me. Just walk."

We cross the street halfway and dip behind a bunch of trees coiled in the center. To our right lies a narrow alleyway, burrowing between two lofty skyscrapers. We pause. I watch as a young man runs down the street and seizes the shoulder of the nearest policeman, whirling him around and pointing back at us. The officer cranes his neck in our direction, motioning for the others to follow him.

Avery swears silently. We count to three, then tear through

the crowd of people beside us, fighting our way into the alley. It's like swimming upstream. Mass difficult.

The cops start to shout. Everybody notices us now. Two teenagers try to play hero, grabbing the back of my jacket and yanking me into the crowd. I punch the closest guy in the side of the face, breaking free from his grip. Avery pushes another as she grasps my hand and pulls me through. We bust into the alley, dwarfed on all sides by walls that stretch up as far as I can see. A pair of dumpsters block our path halfway down. We grab onto the handles and climb up over them. The smell of garbage rises from beneath our feet.

Assisted by the crowd, the cops gain ground on us quickly. Before we've even cleared the dumpsters, they're right behind us.

A gunshot rattles the entryway. Something sharp hits the back of my neck, clinging onto my skin. I reach back frantically and claw at the small device.

A second shot hits Avery square in the back. We stop in our tracks, struggling to pull at the devices. Once it's clear that they're not coming off, I jump down from the dumpster, desperate to get away from the police any way I can.

Moments later, the devices activate, propelling a shockwave of electricity through our bodies. At first all it does is stop us. But as the current increases, it forces us to the ground. My body convulses. Details black out around me. The walls close in. My arms lie limp on the pavement. And then it's over.

21

Cassius landed the stolen sky taxi at Portland's southern border, on the outskirts of the wide lot reserved for public shuttles. Switching off the power, he watched a small band of security personnel gather around the side of his ship, no doubt curious as to why a Skyship vehicle had made an unplanned, illegal landing.

He scooped up his bag from beside the captain's seat, threw it over his shoulder, and flipped the controls to open the doorway. Hands in the air, he exited the craft and jumped down onto the granite pavement. All five security guards paused, waiting for something more than a fifteen-year-old to emerge from within. They kept their guns pointed straight at him.

"Relax." Cassius reached up to his right hand, wincing as he tore off the skin graft and revealed his identification code. "I'm Unified Party."

The men exchanged curious looks. The one nearest Cassius lowered his gun, removed a handheld scanner from his belt, and scanned Cassius's wrist. The blue laser caught the inside of the ID socket and the guard nodded, turning to the others. "He's telling the truth."

Cassius sighed, pulling at the neck of his shirt. Even the residual effect from the nearby Bio-Net wasn't enough to counter the sweltering heat.

The guards lowered their weapons. Another strode forward, hands on his hips. "Where did you find this ship?"

Cassius sighed, glancing over to the Bio-Net entrance. "Consider it a gift."

Then, without waiting for any more questions, he turned and made his way toward the city, passing long rows of shuttles glistening in the hazy sunshine. When he was out of the guards' sight, he flipped open his com-pad and entered Madame's secret number.

It rang two times before she picked up. "Cassius."

"I've landed outside Portland."

"Fantastic," she replied. "I've just had word of a crashed shuttle inside the city. That will be Fisher. No doubt the authorities have already captured him. I'd like you to head to the Security Center and find out where he's being held. Make sure he is not transferred."

"And what then?"

"I will rendezvous with you in Portland as soon as I can. Something has come up and I'm afraid I may be delayed. Don't let Fisher out of the city, Cassius."

"I won't."

"If he escapes, he'll head to Seattle."

He frowned. "Why would he head to Seattle? It's deserted."

"Trust me, Cassius. That's where he'll go. Don't let it happen."

"Okay," he replied.

"Excellent," she said. "I will be in touch."

The line went dead.

He stared at the com-pad before clipping it back onto his belt. *Something had come up*, she'd said. From the urgency in her voice back in the infirmary, he had assumed this mission was priority number one. Not to mention the destruction he had caused in the Lodge. But after two frustratingly brief conversations, he began to wonder if he was being intentionally kept in the dark. He wasn't in the habit of questioning the government, but questioning Madame was something different entirely.

As he approached Portland's southern gate, he toyed with the idea of interrogating Fisher himself. If Madame was going to take her time, he might as well use the opportunity to his advantage. Maybe he could find out what had happened back on the rooftop. She wouldn't even have to know.

Two government officials stood at the entrance gate in front of him, positioned between ground-level Bio-Net connectors. Whirring spheres of Pearl energy spun in the center of each, weaving the force field that rocketed up to the floating black crosses. He remembered the group of

Fringers destroyed at the entrance to Rochester. A chill ran down his spine.

A large screen hung above the entrance, displaying temperatures both inside and outside the Net. Seventy-two versus one-hundred and sixteen. Cassius couldn't wait to feel the difference after stepping inside.

The officials scanned Cassius's wrist with a dark gray wand as he passed Portland's entrance sign. He straightened his tie, making sure he looked presentable before preceding.

Nodding to the guards, he stepped up a gentle ramp and into the city. First stop, the Security Center. Then he'd find Fisher. And answers.

22

A woman grips my hand and leads me down a darkened hallway, dozens of closed metal doors on either side of us. One lies halfway open at the end. Beyond is a laboratory. I know this. I've been here before. Light bulbs string overhead, flickering on and off. We're underground.

Flashes of green light illuminate the small circular window at the top of the lab doorway, coupled with muffled explosions from inside. Thunder and lightning. Flash. Bang.

I dig my heels into the ground, pulling back on the woman's hand. She leans down and whispers something in my ear that convinces me to keep walking. The flashes grow more intense. The banging gets louder.

We slip through the doorway and arrive inside the laboratory. I pull away from the woman, covering my ears.

A tall man in a lab coat turns to face us. He says something to her, but his voice is too soft to be heard beyond the muted explosions through my fingers. Behind him, a computer devours the entire wall. To me it looks like a monster—all shiny knobs and coils.

The woman runs over to him and the two embrace, leaving me in the center of the room. A glowing tube crackles and hisses in the corner, filling almost a quarter of the small laboratory. Dark green flames quiver in a transparent box on top, surrounded by swirls of mist that spill out from inside and fog up the ceiling. It's like an out-of-commission elevator, plopped down with nowhere to go. Instead of moving up or down it just sits there, grumbling like it's hungry for something.

The man whispers into the woman's ear. I look up at her and realize that she's crying. She's been crying the entire time. I step forward to comfort her. The man breaks away, stumbling back to the computer and opening a drawer behind him.

I watch as he removes a vial of clear liquid from inside. Giving it a shake, he pulls a syringe from another drawer and fills it with the liquid. For the first time, he looks at me.

I grab onto the woman's leg, but the man's fast. He's at my side before I can do anything to stop him.

Suddenly we hear footsteps echoing in the hallway beyond the door. The man frowns, preparing to insert the needle into my arm.

The woman grabs his shoulder, stopping him. The footsteps grow louder—closer.

She digs in her pocket and removes a chain, spinning me around and looping it over my neck. I look down at the silver key resting on top of my white shirt. While I'm distracted, the man jabs the needle into my arm. "This won't hurt a bit," he promises. But it does.

The liquid enters my bloodstream and I start to go numb. First my arm, then my chest, and finally my legs. My body gives up.

The man tosses the syringe aside and reaches down to catch me before I collapse to the floor. He cradles me in his arms and carries me toward the machine. At first I want to shout, to run as far away from the banging and hissing as I can. But my fear disappears, like somebody pressed an off switch deep inside of me.

The laboratory door bursts open and three soldiers barge through, guns at the ready. Before they can get to me, the man lays my body inside the tube-shaped machine and everything fades to green. The whirring energy around me obscures my vision of the laboratory. I think I hear screams—shouting—but it's impossible to tell.

Numbness is replaced by incredible warmth, awareness replaced with nothing.

I am nothing.

23

Avery smacks my shoulder and I bolt up, awake. It was a dream. Lifelike, sure, but just a dream.

I feel my face for a blindfold, but nothing's there. My eyes quickly adjust to the darkness and I begin to make out the stars outside our slit of a window. The two of us are crammed into a cell that would make a dog kennel seem luxurious. A beam of meager light streams in from outside. It's not enough to see by.

The one upside to our current predicament? It forces Avery and me to squeeze together.

"I've been jabbing you for fifteen minutes now," she says. "Took you long enough to wake up."

I reach around to the back of my neck. The shocker device is gone. No silver key, either. No laboratory. No soldiers. It felt so real.

Also gone are the fragments of shrapnel from our crash landing. A thick bandage wraps around my shoulder. They fixed us up before chucking us in here. Makes me wonder what else they did.

"Where are we?" I rub my eyes, hoping that things will become clearer.

Nope. Still dark.

"I don't know for sure," she replies, "but I can guess."

"Security Center?"

"Yep."

I sigh. "We almost made it, too."

"I guess this is what we get for crashing a shuttle into a residential building."

I lean back against the wall. "How long have you been awake?"

"About twenty minutes. Were you dreaming?"

"Why?"

She moves closer, pressing against me. "You were just making funny noises, that's all."

"Oh." I turn away from her. I should be mass worried about being locked up in a cell in the middle of a Chosen City right now, but having Avery Wicksen hear me make funny dreaming noises is even worse. "Yeah," I start. "It was weird. I was a kid, maybe three years old at the most. There was this machine ... this light coming from inside. And there were soldiers."

"Soldiers?"

"There was a key around my neck, too."

Her head darts up. "Like the one Mrs. Dembo mentioned at the meeting?"

I nod. "It isn't the first time, either. There was another dream, a couple of days ago after Bunker Ball. I was in a city. Seattle, I think. The key was around my neck."

"I knew it! We're definitely going now," she says.

"It was only a dream."

Her eyes narrow. "Do you normally dream about demolished cities?"

I sigh. "No, I guess not. Not until after the rooftop."

"Exactly."

I fall silent, eager to change the subject. "How are we gonna get out of here?"

"Beats me." She kicks the wall. "Honestly, I don't even know which side's the door."

I glance around from wall to wall, trying to get my bearings but finding it next to impossible. My breathing tightens. The thought that I'm stuck in here, with no way out, is almost too much. Confinement. Never been a fan, even when I was a kid. I try to suppress my reaction, but Avery notices.

"What's the matter?"

"You know," I mutter through labored breaths, "I'm just not a fan of tight spaces."

She puts her arm around my shoulders and pulls me closer until my head touches her cheek. "You're quite the hero, you know that?"

"You're being sarcastic."

"Not really. You know, I wouldn't have crashed into a Chosen City for just anybody."

Her skin presses against mine and suddenly I forget where I am. I block out the whole horrible situation until it's just the two of us, sitting alone together in the dark. I consider leaning over and kissing her, but just as I'm about to work up the nerve, she pulls away, hugging her knees.

"You trust me, right Jesse?"

I smirk. It's the most obvious answer in the world. "Of course."

She sighs. "You shouldn't."

"What do you mean? You saved me back at the Academy."

"Yeah," she replies, "Right place at the right time, huh? It's almost like I knew Cassius was up there."

"Sixth sense, I guess."

"I *knew* Cassius was up there, Jesse." She turns, analyzing my expression in the darkness.

Her words don't settle with me at first. Instead they whiz right by. My ears refuse to let them in. "Very funny, Avery."

She lays the back of her head on the wall, eyes drifting to the ceiling. "God, I didn't want to tell you this."

"Tell me what?"

"But we're stuck in a cage," she mutters to herself. "It's not like you could go anywhere."

I stare at her for a second. She's serious. A lot of people don't get Avery, but I can always tell when she's being funny. I swallow. My voice comes out a whisper. "Avery—"

She glances over at me. "There's something you should know ... something I've been keeping from you. And now that we're down here it's gonna come out sooner or later. Better to hear it from me." She sighs. "You're gonna think I'm such a hypocrite."

"No, Avery."

She pats her knees, taking a deep breath before speaking. "The thing is ... I've ... I've been working for the Unified Party."

My heart drops. It's a delayed reaction again, and when the statement finally catches up to me, it's like a round of bullets straight through the chest.

"I wasn't transferred from Skyship Mira," she continues. "My parents didn't die. I was born on the Surface."

I chuckle at the absurdity of it. I don't want to, but it's all I can do.

"I'm serious," she responds. "The Unified Party enrolled me at the Academy under a false background three years ago. I've been funneling down information ever since. Schematics, training procedures ... observations. Madame's got all the Intel she needs for a full-scale assault, but the President won't let her make a move. Doesn't want a war."

I clutch my arm, trying to keep from being sick. I stopped listening halfway through.

Avery notices. "Jesse?" She pauses, waiting for a response. "Do you understand? Are you hearing what—"

"All this time?" My voice comes out choked and small.

She nods. "That's how I knew those were Madame's cruisers back there. But it's not what you think, Jesse. I'm not like them. I was young. I was just doing what they told me. I didn't know any better."

I shake my head. The ability to form coherent sentences fails me. "The Unified Party?"

"Didn't you think it was strange that I was so interested in snooping around?"

"You were curious."

"I *had* to do it, Jesse."

I bury my face in my knees. All the events of the day catch up to me. I close my eyes, refusing to cry. "First Eva, now you?"

"No." She grabs my shoulder, then drops her hand to her side. "Oh god, Jesse. I'm so sorry."

"What is it?" I look up, gritting my teeth. "What have you told them?"

"Not a lot," she whispers. "When I first arrived at the Academy I overheard Alkine talking about you. I mentioned it to Madame, that's all. She asked me to keep an eye on you."

"You're friends with me because Madame told you to be?"

"No." She groans. "This is coming out all wrong." She leans her head back. "This is why I didn't want to tell you. It sounds so sinister."

"Maybe because it *is*." My brain catalogs the past few days. "Wait. That night, when you said you were talking with Phoebe... the mark on your cheek. You were spying, weren't you?"

"Yes," she says, "but it's not as bad as it sounds. This past year, I've been trying to throw Madame off. At first it was business, but then I got to know you, Jesse. Emotion, it...compromised things. I regretted telling her anything. Whenever she asked about you, I played dumb."

"Madame asked about *me*?"

Avery nods. "I don't know what she wants. I didn't give her any specifics, Jesse. I swear. I didn't know that they found you in Seattle until last night. I just knew you were the guy all the higher-ups were talking about. They were concerned about you, like it was so important that you were strong enough to take care of yourself. Out of all the students, it was always *you*. I thought it was strange, so I relayed it to Madame. She wanted to know your family history...your age. I didn't know why she was so interested. I still don't."

"Pearls," I sigh. "That's all the Unified Party cares about."

"Pearls and Jesse Fisher," Avery replies. "Mentioning you was my biggest mistake."

I scoff. "But you have no problem selling out Alkine and the Academy."

"It's not an easy position—"

"Yeah. I bet it's not."

"It's *not*," she counters. "Both Skyship and the Surface have their problems. You know that. There are spies everywhere. Take Skandar's dad, right? You're not mad at him for spying on the Unified Party."

"Because we're the good guys!" The words come out louder than I mean them to.

Avery shakes her head. "It's never that simple."

"Tell that to those government cruisers trying to shoot us out of the sky."

She frowns. "They'll be shooting at me too, after what I've done. Cassius was supposed to take you to the Lodge today. I couldn't let that happen."

I grimace. "How do I know that you're not in on it too?"

"I can't—" She stops and reaches up to her forehead. Her eyes shut in pain.

"Avery?"

"Headache," she whispers. "Ever since we left the Academy." She rubs her temple for a moment before opening her eyes. "It's gone."

I look down at the floor, tracing circles with my finger in the dirt-stained concrete. "You didn't have to work for the government," I mutter.

She sighs. "It was my job."

"You can change jobs."

She lays her hand on her knee, bowing her head. "Not some."

A silence fills the tight room. Someone thumps against the far wall, followed by muttering from the neighboring cell. More prisoners. Probably Fringers caught trading with Skyship.

"Look," Avery starts. "I know it's going to be hard for you to trust me. It should be. But I'm on your side now. I wanted you to spy on Alkine's meeting so that you'd know the truth. Anything you want me to do, just tell me. I want to help."

I shake my head, mumbling. "I think you've done enough already."

"I can help," she replies. "If I hadn't had contact with Madame I wouldn't have known about Cassius today. I wouldn't have been able to stop him."

A silence fills the chamber. Then I ask the question that's eating away at my mind, though I'm not sure I really want to hear the answer. "Does she want me dead?"

She shrugs. "I don't know, but she could've blown us out of the sky back there and she didn't."

I frown. "Then she knows where we are."

"Maybe," Avery starts. "I'm off-grid. I haven't spoken with her for over twenty-four hours."

I cringe at the thought of Avery speaking with Madame. "I can't believe I was so stupid," I mutter. "All this time. I thought maybe you actually . . . " I trail off.

"What, Jesse?" She reaches her hand over to me.

I pull away. "Nothing. It's nothing important."

She kicks the wall, shaking her head. "You know I—"

A reverberating click from outside interrupts her.

Her head darts up. "What was that?"

I peer at the wall to our left. A crack of light streams in as the cell door slides open. The light widens into a blinding rectangle until it overtakes the darkness.

A figure stands in the doorway. I squint to make out details. It takes a second before I recognize who it is.

I knew he'd find a way down here.

"Evening, Fisher," Cassius Stevenson smiles. "I've been looking for you."

24

Something bursts inside me and I jump to my feet and lunge at the guy. I don't think about it. I just attack.

I catch him off guard, reaching under his jacket and grabbing the pistol. Cassius stumbles to the ground.

Avery stands behind me. "Wow."

I point the gun down at him, hands shaking.

Cassius gives an awkward grin as he pulls himself to a sitting position. The three of us are in an empty hallway, dimly lit by cheap overhead lights. The brown linoleum floor's sticky. I guess Security Centers are the one part of Chosen Cities that don't get the obsessive-compulsive scrub-down.

He stares at me, smiling. "Bravo. Looks like you got me."

Dang right I did. And it's the first thing I've done right this entire time.

I feel the trigger against my finger, the same one responsible for shooting Mr. Wilson. "Stand up."

Cassius's smile falls to a sneer as he lifts himself to a standing position.

"Finally grew a pair, huh?" He leans against the wall. "Good for you. And that must be your girlfriend. That's twice in one week you've been saved by a girl."

"Shut up."

Cassius shakes his head. "You're just delaying the inevitable. We both know you're not going to shoot."

"I thought this was between me and you."

"Who said it wasn't?"

Before I can respond, Avery steps forward and grabs him by the jacket. "Where's Madame?"

Cassius squirms in her grip. "Who the hell are you?"

Avery ignores him. "I know she's pulling the strings. If you—"

I glare at her. "Stay out of this, Avery."

After a moment's pause, she lets go and moves behind me without a word.

"Whoa." Cassius grins. "Guess things aren't as rosy in the happy little sky community as I thought."

I ignore him. "Ever since I met you things haven't been right. Something inside me went crazy today ... like a heart attack."

His eyes widen for a second before he can control his expression.

"Jesse," Avery whispers behind me, "if we're gonna escape we need to do it now."

"Quiet." I keep my eyes pinned to Cassius. "What happened on the rooftop?"

He shakes his head. "You ... you don't know? Madame said—"

"Answer me. Or I'll shoot."

His expression softens. He shakes his head again, saying nothing.

Avery pushes me out of the way and grabs the pistol, keeping it pointed at Cassius. "Get in the cell!" She prods him forward. "Sorry Jesse, but we've gotta get out of here before the guards arrive."

I sigh, watching Cassius move cautiously toward the cell door. "You heard her."

Avery backs away from him, keeping the pistol out of reach.

Once he's inside, I slam the door and turn the dead-bolt, sealing him in darkness.

"Here." Avery forces the pistol back into my hand. "I wouldn't want you to think I'd use it on you."

She takes off down the hallway. I stare at the weapon for a moment before following her, keeping an eye out for any movement. I'm not sure what I'd do if we ran across a guard. This isn't a stunner I'm holding. It's made to kill.

We tiptoe down the long, barren corridor, past a dozen cells just like the one we came from. A plain wooden door blocks our way at the end. There's no telling what's outside. Could be freedom, could be guards. I'm kinda doubting it's freedom.

Avery leans her head against the door, listening for sounds on the other side. She glances at me with a doubtful look, but it's the only way out. On the count of three, we yank it open and make a run for it—right into the belly of a security guard.

The guy grabs my wrist impossibly fast and sends the pistol flying to the ground. I cry out in pain. So much for the tough guy act.

Luckily, Avery's on it, with a swift knee to the poor guy's crotch. He loosens his grip, giving us the opening we need.

We push past him and careen through the small office, winding up on a rickety metal platform hugging the outside of the building. The night air's cool on my skin. The city skyline surrounds us, window-shaped lights shining like a bright yellow checkerboard. The buildings stretch up too far to see the sky.

Below us zigzag several levels of equally rickety, rusty metal stairs. There's no way they meet government standards, but the only way out is down. Cautious of the guy in the office, we wind our way down the steps, clearing two or three at a time.

When we arrive on the next landing, a squad of security guards pool around the ground level of the building. Several surround the bottom of the staircase. From two stories up they look like insects. Insects with guns.

Shining heavy-duty beams in our direction, the guards notice us and raise their weapons to shoot. We stop at the landing and squeeze together in the spotlight.

A voice bellows from below. I can't tell which soldier's speaking, but it's mass loud. Magnified. "All you're doing is making things worse for yourselves. You won't escape, and even if you did you wouldn't get through the Net. Give yourselves up before we're forced to shoot."

I look over to Avery. She shakes her head, muttering something to herself. It would be easy for her to turn me in, show her true colors and let the guards take me to Madame. I wait for her to do it, to betray me like everyone else.

"Thirty seconds," the guard warns.

Then, picking the absolute worst time in the history of the world, my chest goes insane. It's pain like back in Mrs. Dembo's classroom. This time it forces me to my knees.

I sink to a crouching position, holding my burning chest. Low alarms blare somewhere off in the distance. I'm so disoriented, I can't tell if we triggered them or if they're sounding for a different reason.

"Don't move!" the guard orders. I can barely hear him. I open my mouth wide, hoping to puke or scream or something to stop the throbbing. The alarms aren't helping.

"Jesse!" Avery sinks down to my side, gripping my shoulders. I can't feel her.

I shut my eyes, exhaling—pushing everything out of my system. But it's not like back at the Academy. It doesn't help.

And then, a flash of light.

My eyes dart open and I force my head up to look at the skies. A ball of energy hurtles down from the stars, lighting up the sides of buildings as it crashes down. Past the Bio-Net. Past security.

A Pearl, and it's headed straight toward me.

25

I take a deep breath and push myself to a standing position. It's like moving through syrup, muscles howling in pain as I watch the Pearl plummet closer and closer to the Surface. Avery and the guards notice it too. They pull back, dropping their weapons.

The alleyway glows a brilliant green as the Pearl's light reflects along the windows of the towers. Its path stays fixed on me.

"Back up." Avery grabs my arm, trying to pull me away. "Jesse! It'll kill you!"

I keep my eyes on the Pearl, ignoring her. My feet are cemented in place, every bit of me hypnotized by the glowing ball of light speeding to the ground.

I reach out my arms, hands open.

One thousand feet.

My eyes widen. The pain shoots from my core and meets the Pearl head on, pulling it forward.

Five hundred.

"Jesse!" Avery screams behind me, pressed against the railing at the back of the landing.

Fifty.

My fingers tingle with electricity as the Pearl rockets toward them.

Then I catch it. I don't even stumble backward. It lands right in my hands like it was always meant to be there.

I hold it out in front of my face, gazing at the swirling chaos within—an entire universe before my eyes. It should have burned right through me. I should be dead. Instead, I feel mass complete, like a part of me I never even knew was missing has returned.

I glance down at the dumbfounded expressions on the faces of the guards, illuminated in soft green.

"What did you just do?" Avery whispers from behind me, approaching carefully.

The pain is gone, absorbed by the Pearl in my hands. Without realizing what I'm doing, I push it away from my skin. It floats off into the night until it hovers inches before my fingers.

My senses buzz, on overload.

I ball my hands into fists.

The Pearl explodes, sending a shockwave of energy in all directions. The guards topple over into a heap. My body deflects the energy, sparing Avery and me. The alleyway cracks and hisses. Street lamps and windows shatter, raining shards of glass onto the ground. Everything beams a brilliant green for a second, so intense that I have to shield my eyes.

As this happens, a figure emerges from the top of the Pearl, shooting up into the sky like an arrow until it's well out of sight. It was humanoid, I think, but too blurry to tell—like it hadn't quite flickered to life yet. I'm not sure anybody else saw it against the blinding energy. I'm not even sure if it was real, myself.

The Pearl energy finds a home in the circuits and transformers throughout the area, and soon we're left with nothing. No more Pearl—just empty air and stillness.

The night is quiet once more, with one big difference. The guards below us lie in piles, unconscious in the alleyway. I hope they're breathing.

I survey the scene around me—the blanket of broken glass, the blown-out windows—and realize what I've just done.

My fingers hum with residual energy. The hair on the back of my neck stands on end.

Avery starts off down the remaining steps, stunned into silence. I follow close behind, eager to escape the alleyway and get away from the bodies. Too much damage. Too easy for them to find us again.

As I take the final step into the alleyway, Avery grabs my shoulder and pulls me close to her, hugging me tightly. "You're amazing," she whispers.

I keep my arms at my sides, breathing hard. When she releases me, the shock of what just happened begins to sink in. I crane my neck upward, looking between the two buildings at the narrow strip of stars so far away. The alarms continue to rumble through the city.

"I don't know what I am," I whisper back, shaking my still-buzzing hand in the cool night air. "Let's get out of here."

She nods. We take off running through the corridor, leaving the chaos of the alleyway behind us.

26

Cassius balanced on the tips of his toes, peering out the slit of a window at the top of the cell. He couldn't see much beyond the siding of the closest building. There was a street below. From his vantage point he could only make out the very edge.

Alarms rumbled along his ribcage. The Pearl Warning System. He recognized it immediately, though there was no telling how close the thing was to the city.

He'd been stupid and careless, allowing Fisher to get the jump on him. Part of him conceded that he deserved to be in the cell after underestimating the guy, but that didn't mean that he was about to surrender. He'd contacted the head of security seconds after being locked up. They were taking their time.

He knew he had to stop Fisher and the girl from heading out of the city. If Madame found out that their escape was his fault, there would be consequences. He'd seen it before—confident trainees reduced to whimpering children after a meeting with Madame. What she said or did to them was a mystery, but the results spoke for themselves. No, he could not let Fisher and the girl get away.

He frowned. The *girl*.

She'd made an already complicated mission even more treacherous. She'd known to stop him at the elevators back in the Academy. And the way she'd looked at him in the hallway … it was as if she knew who he was. Cassius had never seen her before. He'd need to be careful.

Footsteps echoed in the hallway outside, nearing the cell door. Good. They were coming.

He rested his heels back on the ground and turned away from the window. But something caught his eye outside, stopping him.

He recognized it immediately, the reason for the warning alarm.

Like a falling star, the Pearl plunged toward the building. Its radiance grew stronger the nearer it came.

He analyzed its descent, amazed. With all the empty Fringe space, Pearls didn't often fall inside Chosen Cities. It was considered a good luck omen when they did, though a dangerous one. Worse yet, this Pearl seemed to be heading straight for the security building.

Cassius watched as it grew in size, unable to turn away from the window even though he knew the danger of staying close.

Then the Pearl made an unusual change in direction,

curving past his cell and down to the street below. He'd never seen a Pearl curve before. Something was wrong.

He grabbed onto the thin windowsill and craned his neck to look down at the alley, but couldn't find an angle where he could discern anything of note.

So he waited, impatient. There was nothing worse than a fallen Pearl with nobody to capture it. He longed to hold it, to be the first to touch it.

The lock slid open behind him and a guard pulled on the cell door. Before he could get it completely open, an explosion from outside rattled the building.

A blinding green energy coursed through the rectangle window, throwing Cassius backward into the guard's legs. The guard stumbled into the hallway, crashing against the wall.

The energy lingered only a second before disappearing into the air. All was still once more.

Cassius rubbed his neck and waited for his breath to come back before standing up and returning to the window.

Two figures darted off to the left. Fisher and the girl. They'd be heading to the Chute, probably. Quickest way out.

He dusted off his jacket and prepared for a sprint. He'd need to be fast.

On his way out of the cell, he stepped over the guard. "You were late," he muttered before racing full-speed down the hallway and out the open door of the emergency exit.

27

"Move it, Jesse!" Avery shouts back as we bound up a short flight of stairs to the Chute Station. I don't know where she gets off throwing orders around after what happened in the cell, but right now my number one goal is to get out of this city. The two of us will talk later.

As I join her on the waiting platform, I watch the Chute crawl toward us, a thin white monorail approaching like a snake. They say these things can travel up to 150 miles an hour when they get out of the city. It's a good thing, too. The speedier, the better.

Finding the nearest station had been a hassle in itself. Tight alleyways gave way to tighter streets, while monolithic buildings stood watch on all sides like sentinels. I don't see how people know where they're going around here.

The Chute blows my hair to the side as its front end passes by and stops beside the platform. Circular doors on each car whoosh open and crowds of people pour out, rushing past us to the exit queues. I spin around to see government officials scanning the wrists of the passengers as they exit the station and head into the city.

"You don't have some fancy ID code, do you?" I whisper to Avery.

She shakes her head. "They removed it before I came up to the Academy."

I groan. Without codes we've got no credit. This is gonna be a stolen ride.

A crowd of waiting passengers fills in around us. We stay in the center and join the current, hands in pockets. Boarding this thing probably isn't the safest plan ever, but we don't have a lot of options.

When the car empties, a pair of scanner guns pop out from inside. Travelers push their way onto the Chute, wrists up to display their ID sockets. Blue lasers brush over codes with a series of electronic beeps. Avery and I deliberately keep our hands in our pockets as we squeeze in between passengers, hoping that there aren't any security cameras watching.

If they don't catch us coming on, they'll get us for sure when we exit. We might be able to fool a laser. A government official won't be so easy.

We board the Chute without setting off any alarms and find two corner seats in the back. I slump next to the window, making myself as invisible as possible. I peer out at the city, focusing on the third-floor window of a neighboring office building. Rows of desks stretch beyond the glass. Late night workers plug away at computer boards inside. Mass joyless—kinda like Visitation Day.

An elderly woman takes a seat across from us as the circular door slides shut. The Chute remains still, waiting for the rest of the cars to fill up.

"Hey, Jesse," Avery points at a small screen affixed to the front end of the car, "this one heads to Spokane."

I look over to the screen. Sure enough, bright yellow letters flash *Northwest District Line: Spokane - #46*. I allow myself a sliver of hope. "That's near Seattle, right?"

"Not really," she says, "but at least it gets us out of the city. It's better than heading south."

I nod. South is no good. I don't feel like being eaten alive by mosquitoes.

A pounding on the door causes everyone to turn. I crane my neck to see a face pressed against the window, inspecting the travelers around me.

It's Cassius. How did he find us so quickly?

I try to duck out of the way but he spots me almost immediately.

He pounds his fists on the side of the car. The passengers stare at him in annoyance, especially the elderly woman.

"Frag it." Avery flattens against her seat. "Persistent little bugger, isn't he?"

I ignore her, wondering how he could have escaped the cell. This is getting ridiculous. It's like trying to crush a cockroach.

A man in a government uniform grabs Cassius's shoulder and spins him around, away from the door. I watch as Cassius motions with his arms for the guy to let him in, but the officer shakes his head and points toward the open cars at the back of the Chute.

Cassius digs through his jacket, searching for something. Before he can pull it out, the engine whirs to life and speakers around the perimeter of the Chute begin to beep.

With a frustrated glance at the officer, Cassius gives up and turns around, sprinting to the back of the Chute.

"He'll get on," I whisper.

Avery sighs. "I don't doubt it. Just be glad he can't get between the cars."

"Unless we stop," I remind her.

"There isn't another Chosen between here and Spokane. It's a straight shot. Relax."

I recline in my seat. I could be lying in bed right now, safe and sound back at the Academy. Instead, I'm heading for a city I've never been to. On the run, chased by some psycho teenaged Pearlhound—and maybe even Madame. And Avery wants me to relax?

The speakers inside the cabin hiss to life, followed by a woman's calming voice. "Welcome aboard this Northwest District Line to Spokane, city number forty-six. This is a non-stop journey with an arrival time estimated at eleven twenty-five."

I glance at the digital clock beside the screen. About two hours from now. Two hours without any running.

"We hope your journey with us is a comfortable one,"

the overhead voice continues, impossibly cheerful. "Our automated cabin crew is always available if you have any questions or concerns."

The Chute begins to pull forward, slowly at first, but building speed until we're rocketing along the track. The rapidly passing scenery outside is the only clue that we're moving at all. Motion control.

The skyscrapers blur into a tapestry of fuzzy lights until we pass through the Bio-Net. Then nothing. No lights, no movement, just darkness staining every window.

The temperature control hums to life and stabilizes the air inside. During the night, it can easily stay above 100 degrees out here. And it's not even summer yet. I hear it's killer in the summer. Surface Tan turns to Surface Stroke. No wonder Fringers try to break into Chosens.

I stare out the window. The Chute dips forward until the tracks touch the ground. Dust kicks up from underneath our car, clouding the air before dissipating back into the blackness. We've officially entered the Fringes. Dustbowl territory.

"We made it." Avery lays her hand on my knee. "Look, about what I told you back at the Security Center—"

I turn to her. "I don't wanna talk about it. I don't know what side you're on, but I don't want to do this alone. Not after what just happened."

She leans closer, whispering. "It should have burned right through you, Jesse. You should be dead right now."

I nod. It's everyone's worst fear. Even the crazy members of Heaven's Rain wouldn't want to be standing in front of an oncoming Pearl. But I've done it.

I pause in thought. I've done it twice.

The words spill out of my mouth before I even know what I'm saying. "When the Pearl almost smashed into Lookout Park, I stopped it. I caused it to veer off course somehow. It was me. I knew it wasn't just a coincidence."

"You think you can control them?"

"Or destroy them," I reply, "like back in the alley."

She nods. "It's something you're meant to do. They did something to you back in Seattle when you were little, didn't they?"

I press my fingers against the glass, staring out into the nothingness. "A laboratory, with green energy. Pearl energy, like in my dream."

"And a key," she adds. "Maybe this lab's in Seattle. Maybe that's what Alkine's key is meant to open."

I frown, pulling my hand off the glass and sinking farther into the seat. "I need to trust you, Avery, if we're gonna do this."

"I don't know what I can say … "

"If I can really control Pearls, the government's gonna want me. The Tribunal's gonna want me. It's just like Alkine said. They'd start a war over this."

She leans closer, keeping her voice low. "I've burnt bridges on both sides, Jesse. For you. I can't go back to the Academy *or* to Madame. I don't know what else I can say to convince you." She reaches up and rubs her forehead.

"Headache again?"

She nods, shutting her eyes. "Wouldn't happen to have an aspirin, would you?"

I shake my head, turning back to the window and the thick darkness outside. The Chute lurches to the left. I turn my head to see the tail end of the train curving out behind us. Cassius is back there somewhere, planning his next move. He could be calling Madame at this very moment, letting her know where to pick us up.

My heart sinks. We escaped the city, but this Chute is a moving prison—a serpentine gift box wrapped up just for Madame. If the Unified Party's anywhere near as organized as everyone says they are, they're going to pounce on us as soon as we get to Spokane.

I face forward. Avery's eyes flutter closed, exhausted. Rather than broach the subject, I keep the panicked thought to myself, searching my mind for a game plan as we tear through the Northwestern wasteland.

28

Cassius squeezed into the one remaining seat at the tail end of the Chute, between an overweight man in a business suit and a teenaged girl with dark blue hair. As soon as he was settled, he buried his face in his hands, cursing silently.

The automated "welcome aboard" announcement came over the speakers but he tuned it out, smacking his fist against his forehead. Stupid. Stupid. Stupid.

The blue-haired girl noticed, raising the headphone on her earpiece. Her frenetic music formed a tinny symphony above his head. "You okay, man?"

He sat up, glaring at her. She backed off, flipping the headphone and turning her attention to the window.

He wasn't okay. First he'd lost Fisher on the Sky-ship, then he'd lost him on the Surface. Worse yet, when Madame finally arrived in Portland expecting to find him, all she'd get was an empty prison cell and a bunch of beaten-up guards. Then Cassius would never have a chance of opening the black cube and discovering what was inside.

What's more, Fisher seemed utterly clueless about what had actually happened back on the rooftop. Madame had seemed convinced that the guy was responsible for his combustion, but looking into Fisher's eyes, listening to his panicked voice, Cassius wasn't so sure anymore. Madame lied to others. Maybe she was lying to him now.

The windows filled with the sprawling darkness of the Fringes. The cabin lights flickered off for a brief moment as the temperature control kicked in. He felt a vibration in his pocket. His com-pad beeped.

He reached for it, glancing down at the front screen. Madame's code flashed in tiny numbers, on and off in rhythm with the beeping.

Don't let them transfer Fisher, she'd said. He was pretty sure escaping on the Chute was worse than being transferred.

He hit the button on the side of the com-pad to silence it, staring at the numbers as they flashed noiselessly. If he didn't answer, she'd know there was trouble. If he did, he'd have to explain the situation. Or lie. She'd see through a lie.

Before he had a chance to make up his mind, the numbers disappeared and the screen went dead. He took a deep breath, realizing what he'd just done. If she wanted to track him, it'd be easy enough to activate the microchip inside of the device. She'd probably already done so.

He wasn't scared of her. He couldn't be. She was like a mother to him. *Like* a mother, but not really.

No, she was a member of the Unified Party first and

foremost. He'd seen a glimpse of it back on Atlas, a peek into the things she didn't talk about ... the choices the country had been forced to make after the bombings. He couldn't deal with her right now—not while he still needed to capture Fisher. Let her call him when he had some good news. Talking would only complicate things—cause him to second-guess himself.

He couldn't face her empty-handed.

He put the com-pad back in his pocket, forgetting it.

Two hours—two hours to think of something, some way to capture Fisher without getting the government involved.

He glanced over to the blue-haired girl, bobbing her head to the music, eyes shut. So unaware.

He loosened his collar, cursing himself once more before reclining in the seat and closing his eyes. Focusing.

29

The girl I've been in love with for almost three years is working for the enemy.

An hour into our journey, I pass the time by slowly unraveling a thread from a hole in the arm of my school suit. Then I start to play with the gauze around my shoulder. It itches. I decide to take it off and stuff it into my pocket. Underneath, my skin is as smooth as it ever was. Weird.

Whatever they did to us before chucking us into the cell certainly did the trick.

Avery's slumped over, fast asleep with her head on my shoulder. Normally I'd be mass psyched about this little turn of events, but not now. Not with so much to think about.

She's working for the enemy, the Unified Party—the group everyone's warned me about since I was a kid.

She's clever, that's for sure. She fooled the faculty. She fooled me. Yet somehow I don't think it's all an act. Maybe with the rest of them, but not with me.

My mind rockets back to the day we first met. I was at

Lookout Park, hiding behind the thickest tree I could find, pressed up against the protective dome. August Bergmann and his cronies had threatened to stuff me into one of the supply lockers and rig it shut. I'd slipped away after class, pressing through the crowd of students into the elevators before they could come after me. I spent the next period squeezed behind the tree. Not my proudest moment.

Then I heard her. "Hey kid," she'd said. I looked up and there she was, perched in the branches like some crazy animal. I'd never seen a girl like her before. Turned out she was skipping class too, though not for the same reason as me. We spent the next hour talking. She seemed to understand it all—the big picture. She knew everything I was going through.

Now I understand it. She'd been spying on me before that conversation. She *did* know everything about me, maybe more than I knew myself. Still, it doesn't change the fact that she'd cared enough to comfort me. Nobody else had.

Before meeting Avery, I'd had to make do with my teammates. Skandar's cool, but never really understood things like she did. And Eva ... Eva obviously had ulterior motives.

I do my best not to move, taking light breaths so I won't wake her. Most of the passengers in our car have fallen asleep, too. I don't blame them. There's nothing to see outside beyond the darkness. Twice we've passed tiny Fringe Towns with one or two makeshift lanterns perched on tall wooden posts. The lights whipped by so fast that I barely noticed them. It's better that way. After what happened back in Syracuse, I'm not too eager to try my luck again in the Fringes.

Then something hits the window on the far end of our cabin, breaking the stillness. My shoulder jerks back into the seat. The poor old woman across from us pops up with a start, looking around.

Avery shifts in her seat. I freeze, hoping that she won't wake up. Too late.

Another microsecond and the noise rattles the window once more. Then again. Again.

A volley of rocks batter the outside of the Chute like maniacal, heavy rain, pelting the windows. The cabin jostles, waking up those who weren't already alert. Muted shouts of anger echo outside.

A second later and it's gone.

Avery's head darts up from my shoulder. She looks at me with groggy eyes. "What's happening?"

"Fringers," I respond, "I think. Throwing rocks."

"Oh," she yawns. "I woke up for that?"

"Probably their goal," I say. "I mean, it's not like they were going to stop the Chute."

She glances over to my shoulder. "Did I—I mean—"

"Yeah," I reply.

The captain's voice comes over the intercom, letting us know that everything's going to be okay, that we just experienced a bit of Fringe turbulence. People chuckle. Me, not so much.

Being forced into a burning brick wall by a trio of bloodthirsty teenagers? Now that's Fringe turbulence.

30

Focus gave way to exhaustion as Cassius's eyes struggled to stay open. He was about to drift into sleep when the pain hit him again. Same as the Lodge and the Academy, like an eighteen-wheeler was being driven through his chest.

His eyes darted open automatically. His thoughts lagged behind, more annoyed than concerned.

Now? Just when he was about to get some sleep?

But as his sleep-addled mind began to clear, annoyance turned to panic. *Now? On this train with nowhere else to go?*

The medication had kept him safe up to this point. Its effects must have expired. Tightening his lips to keep any noise in, he felt around in his pocket for the small envelope of pills Madame had given him. He found it almost immediately, pressed tightly against his warming body. Only two left.

Realizing he needed water, he fought through the pain and stood up, staggering through the length of the cabin toward the bathroom door on the opposite side. The light above shone green. It was unoccupied.

Pushing into the bathroom, he shut the door behind him and leaned against it, breathing hard. His heart leapt out of his chest, speeding up with every second, trying to break free. Soon it would match the pace of the Chute. Not again. Not now.

He stumbled to the miniature silver sink in the corner and poured the two white pills from the envelope, cradling them in his palm.

Out of nowhere the room began to shake. Something pelted the outside of the wall. Rain? No, it was impossible. It hardly ever rained in the Fringes.

The noises grew louder. Something heavy rocked the right wall of the bathroom, tilting the ground up beneath his feet. Before he could prevent it, his hand flew into the air. The pills scattered, landing in the sink. Clank. Clank.

He panicked, watching as they danced around the outline of the drain before disappearing into the dark hole.

Body on fire, he reached down to try to retrieve them, but the drain was deep and narrow. His fingers only went so far. No pipe to unscrew. No pills.

He kicked the wall, tears forming in his eyes before they evaporated into the air.

He did what he could.

Crouching on the floor, he huddled in the corner and gripped his chest, focusing on breathing. Desperate to inhale cool, temperature-controlled air and exhale the heat, he imagined snow. Ice cubes. Freezers.

Dropping his head down between his legs, he gritted his teeth, struggling against the growing pain. He'd conquered worse in his life. He could do it.

He removed his jacket and threw it to the floor, unfastening the top buttons of his shirt. He chest felt tied up with rubber bands. His skin was wet with sweat.

He grabbed the com-pad from his pocket, dialing Madame's number. She knew what was wrong. She could help him.

There was a ring on the other end. No one picked up.

Another ring. Still no answer.

After five, he cursed and threw the com-pad to the other side of the bathroom. Madame said she'd be in constant contact. Why not now, when he needed her?

The tiny chamber steamed up as fire erupted inside of him. He knew he wouldn't be able to control it much longer. He thought about running back into the cabin and forcing the door open—jumping outside. But he didn't have the strength. He couldn't even stand.

So he cowered like a baby, waiting for it to happen, wishing someone would come and take away the pain.

But there was no one. He'd ignored Madame. His real parents were gone. Nobody on the Chute knew him. Even if they did, they wouldn't be able to help.

At 10:08 p.m., halfway between Portland and Spokane, car number fourteen exploded in a great ball of fire, lighting up the darkness for miles around. The flames quickly spread to the reserve engine in the back and shut down the entire Chute.

Knocked off course by the blast and unable to control its breakneck speed, the Chute's front end plunged into the rocky abyss of the Fringes, zigzagging through the dust until it flipped sideways, carrying the rest of the train with it. Many up front died instantly, including the engineer.

The Unified Party would later blame the accident on a Pearl power surge, though the Fringers would somehow convince themselves that they were responsible. Nobody would believe the truth, that a fifteen-year-old boy had taken down a Chute carrying more than 500 passengers without as much as a weapon. The country was in dire straits, for sure, but something like that was just ridiculous.

31

I peel my body off the window, feeling my face for blood. Avery's toppled over beside me. Her arm lies limp against my back. She's breathing, and her eyes are open. That's all that matters.

I inch myself along the glass, careful not to rub against the spider web cracks of jagged windowpane. Pulling myself to a crouching position, I look around the cabin.

Most everyone's spilled over to the windows, which are now the floor. Some moan in pain. Others don't move at all. I see a guy over in the corner, blood pouring from a gash on his forehead. I turn away, feeling sick. The old woman who sat across from me moments ago now lies in a twisted heap, her limbs all jumbled up like she's made of clay. Her face is turned away from us. I don't wanna see it.

Avery lifts herself from the ground beside me, rubbing the back of her head. "What was that?" she mumbles before looking around the cabin. Her mouth falls open as she takes it all in.

I try to answer, but nothing comes out. My voice has disappeared. I wish my body could do the same.

One moment we were speeding along the track. Then, shortly after the Fringers threw their rocks, the Chute went crazy. I tried to buckle my seat belt, but before I knew it the entire cabin flipped over on its side and everyone fell to the window like rag dolls.

Two times in one day.

Two times in one day, we've crashed. The first one was expected—controlled, even. This wasn't, which makes it a thousand times more horrifying.

People start to scream as they realize what's happened. Avery and I stay quiet. The ceiling lights to our side flicker on and off, then off completely. A horrible choking stench flows into the cabin. It takes me a second to realize it's smoke. As my eyes adjust to the darkness, I notice a faint light flickering from somewhere outside.

Fire. The Chute's on fire.

"You okay?" Avery asks.

"We gotta get out of here. There's a fire."

"What about Cassius?"

"Isn't time." I crane my neck up to the ceiling—the right-side windows now framing the stars overhead. The circular entrance door lies slightly ajar, busted open from the force of the crash. Getting to it might be a problem, but it's our only way out. The firelight advances in the distance.

Avery lays her hand on my shoulder. "Over and out?"

I nod, wondering exactly how we're gonna get up there.

But Avery's on it, pulling herself up onto the armrest of the nearest seat and standing across what used to be the center aisle. Pressed against the flooring, she grabs onto the next closest armrest and uses it to pull herself into the top row of seats. She crouches for a moment before making the final push.

I look up at her, perched in the sideways chair like she's climbing a tree. This is going to be much harder than she just made it look. It's like doing pull-ups, and I hate doing pull-ups. Can't do more than ten. Luckily I've only gotta do two to get up and out of the car. Come on, arms. Don't wimp out on me now.

Before I totally psych myself out, I move to the nearest seat and grab onto the armrest a few feet above my head.

Then I pull mass hard, trying to pretend like this is just another skill test. My muscles strain as I press my feet against the bottom armrest and launch myself upward.

After clearing the first pair of seats, I yank myself over the aisle and into the final top seats. Avery bends down and grabs the edge of the opening, letting her body go limp until she's hanging in the air directly below the doorway. I sit on the armrest and watch her pull herself up onto the side of the train. Seconds later, she spins around and drops her arms through the opening.

"Just like climbing up into the vent," she smiles down like the most beautiful monkey I've ever seen.

I flash a worried smile and grab onto her waiting hands,

pressing my feet against the back of the seat so I can push out.

With Avery's help, I lift myself out from the cabin and into the steaming-hot night air.

We stand on the curved siding of the Chute, careful not to slip. I look to the right: nothing but zigzagging train cars stretching on into the darkness. Then I turn around and see the flames spreading from the back. The very last car stands attached to the track, though just barely.

The Good Samaritan in me screams to head back down into the car and help some of the other passengers, but then I remember that Avery and I are fugitives, that we stole this ride. The longer we stay here, the greater chance the government will find us. Or maybe even Cassius. Avery steps to the edge of the car, sitting with her legs hanging over the side.

I move to join her. "What now?"

"We can't stay here, obviously."

I nod. "There was a Fringe Town a ways back."

She shakes her head. "They're hostile. We'll head in the opposite direction. Northwest."

I stare into the unknown. Shadowy rock formations jut out in the distance. Maybe they're not rocks at all. "It's dark. We'll get lost out there."

Avery pushes herself from the train, landing with a thud on the dusty ground below. "The stars, Jesse. You've seen 'em enough. They're just a little farther away, that's all."

I follow, landing in an undignified heap beside her. My ankles rattle with a buzzing pain.

"I know the Surface," she continues, "ever since I was a little girl. I know what to do if we get lost." She grabs my hand and pulls me into the night. Even with the fire behind us, the darkness swallows us quickly.

After a minute of running, we stop and turn to survey the wreckage. The fire's gobbled up a quarter of the Chute already, but it doesn't seem so threatening all of a sudden, like it's not even real. I feel a pang of guilt as we turn and walk away. The emergency fire systems are probably starting to kick in. It won't be long until the flames are put out completely and a government squad is summoned. We made the right choice.

I repeat this mantra in my head, but it still doesn't feel right.

"Keep your eyes peeled for lights," Avery says.

I shake my head. "I wasn't serious about heading into a Fringe Town, you know."

"I know, but we need a place to sleep. Windstorms are common in this area. Towns will have shelter."

"They'll also have Fringers," I reply. "Or have you forgotten that fun little mark on the side of my face a few days ago?"

"We'll pretend we're one of them," she says, climbing up a gentle hill. "We're certainly filthy enough."

"Nomads," I suggest.

She nods.

"And we're ... we're desperate for water and shelter for the night," I continue, "and we'll be gone by morning."

"*If* we run into trouble," she says. "Most of these towns are deserted."

"I've heard *that* one before." I pause. "Avery?"

She turns, looking at me. "What is it?"

"You were serious back in Portland, right? About being on my side?"

She stumbles forward, grabbing me up in her arms and hugging me. This time I hug her back.

"I've never been so serious about something in my life," she whispers. "Look at all we've survived so far. I'm not letting you down, Jesse."

I rest my head on her shoulder, hands pressed against her back. "I think I believe you."

She lets go, stepping away. "We need to get as far away from the Chute as possible." She scans the flat expanse around us, pointing. "That way."

I nod and we take off through the darkness, guided by little more than the moonlight.

32

Cassius regained consciousness just as the flame retardant foam began to blanket the inside of the cabin. It wasn't going to help anyone around him. They'd been burned to a crisp long before the system switched on. The car itself was reduced to a metal shell, heated up until it stung to touch it.

Unlike everything around him, Cassius wasn't burned. He lay in the middle of a bed of flames, but they passed through him, ignoring his tender skin. His senses were alert, his mind sharp and refreshed. If his insides weren't all raw and bruised, he'd think he had suddenly become invincible. It was the most painful form of invincibility he could imagine.

He pulled himself from the bathroom floor, searching for clothing to cover his naked body before heading out into the night. Most everything had already been mutilated by fire. Retardant foam buried what managed to survive.

He paused a moment to stare at the bodies—the blue-haired girl lying still in the corner, the businessman crumpled in a heap below his chair. The force of the explosion had killed most of them before the flames could do anything.

He had done this. Whether he had meant to or not didn't make any difference. This wasn't a killing in the name of the Unified Party. This wasn't part of a mission. This was a massacre.

Glancing around the cabin, he found a body lying in the corner of the room least ravaged by the fire. Like all the others, the man was dead, but the foam had reached him before the fire had a chance to completely destroy his body. Most of his clothing remained intact, despite many scuffs and burn marks.

Cassius began the unpleasant job of stripping off the man's jeans and pulling them over his own legs. They were much too loose, but he was able to tighten the belt to an acceptable length. With great difficulty, he yanked off the man's shirt, tearing it at the shoulder as he tried to work it around the guy's limp arms. It was horrifying work, pulling the clothes off a dead body, but he didn't have any other choice. The guy was already gone. Cassius needed it more than he did.

Stumbling into the night air, he turned to survey the wreckage he had caused. The train cars curved into the darkness beyond him. As he stared at the fallen Chute, his frustration with Madame began to turn to doubt.

Twice now this had happened, and she knew why. Yet she wouldn't tell him. Not without a price. Not without Fisher.

It was a game. They were pinballs, him and Fisher. Pinballs filled with gun powder. The more they ran into each other, the worse things got. And she didn't seem to care.

He wiped tears from his eyes and allowed himself to break down for a moment. He wasn't a killer, not like this. Not when it was a Chute full of innocent people just trying to get from one city to another.

After giving in to his emotions, he regained control of his breathing and realized that he had to go on, not only to prove that he could do it, but also because he had to know.

He had to know what was happening to him, who his parents were, and what Jesse Fisher had to do with it.

But he didn't need Madame's help anymore. Now he was going to do it his way. His com-pad was lost in the fire, his link with Madame gone. He was going to find Fisher, and he was going to find answers. With or without her.

And if he had to set the whole world on fire to find out what was wrong with him, then so be it.

33

Dawn.

After walking for hours last night, we took refuge in a chewed-up fortress at a broken-down playground on the edge of the nearest Fringe Town. Sleeping in a park—classy. Avery and I took turns keeping guard, on constant lookout for any movement. There was nothing all night; most Fringers have migrated to the uninfected parts of the coast. Landlocked's the worst. Landlocked will kill you.

As the sun starts to heat our little play castle to triple-digit level, we wipe the sleep from our eyes and step down the hot metal ladder to the brown grass below. My empty stomach rumbles. My throat's about as dry as the environment out here. I'd pay a million dollars for a glass of water.

"Keep an eye out," Avery warns as we exit the tiny park and step along a cracked-up street on our way to the center of town.

My feet drag. If I don't get some fluids in me soon this

march to Seattle is gonna be over before it starts. "How's your headache?"

"Down to a dull throb," she replies. "Don't worry. I can manage it."

I nod. "Tell me why we're heading into a Fringe Town again?"

She avoids a wide crack in the pavement, leaping over to the other side. "Water, food. You know, things we kinda need to survive."

A hot gust of wind shoves my face as I walk into it. Waves of dust swirl around in the air. I swallow mouthfuls of sandy air. It's impossible not to.

We walk by lines of old-fashioned homesteads, boarded up and beaten to the ground. In another time, this place could have been one of those picket-fence-type neighborhoods people write poems about. The trees are leafless—dark, decaying silhouettes on an ever-flat background. Weeds survive, a darker shade of brown than the grass. I've heard that areas like this were hardest hit after the government cut power because they were already borderline-desert before the bombings.

So far, it's all empty and silent. Score one for us, because in addition to traveling through a dangerous Fringe Town, we've still got Cassius to worry about.

Avery kicks at a dirt clod as we continue down the center of the vacant, pothole-ridden road. "Makes you miss the comforts of a Security Center jail cell, huh? It's like the Old West."

"The Old, *Old* West," I reply, shirt sticking to my body with sweat. "Are we even close to Seattle?"

"Depends on what you mean by *close*." She points at the pavement behind my feet. "Ooh, watch it."

I turn around to see a snake slither across the roadway, inches from my heel. I jump forward, keeping my eye on the brown creature as it hisses past. "Oh god, I thought those things were only in movies!"

Avery watches it disappear into a crack in the pavement. "It's gone."

We walk in silence for a few minutes. I keep my eyes on the ground, cautious of any more creatures we might stumble across.

Once the coast is clear, I glance at Avery. "So I've been wondering. If you weren't born on a Skyship, where *were* you born?"

"Don't know," she replies. "Look, I wasn't lying about being an orphan. I've never met my parents. They're probably dead."

"Where did you live before the Academy, then?"

"The Lodge."

"*The* Lodge? Like, Pearlhound central?"

She nods. "Madame picked me up from the workhouses when I was little—five years old, I think. She tried to pretend she was my mother, at least for a little while."

"And then she just sent you away to spy on us?"

Avery sighs. "You don't see it as a child. You're so glad to have *someone* act like they care. But as I got older, I realized what she really was. She wasn't my mother. She was using me, and I'm not the only one."

"That's crazy."

"Yeah, but think about it. She's got this idea that the Unified Party needs to strike against the Skyships...that she and she alone recognizes a threat that nobody else does. Rather than go through official lines and risk humiliating herself, she picks up these kids...gains their trust so they'd do anything for her. And then she uses us to gain information...to build her case." She shakes her head. "She's really done a number on Cassius, that's for sure."

"Wait." I grab her arm, stopping her. "Did you know Cassius? I mean, before..."

She shrugs. "I've seen him. I don't think he knows me, though. By the time he was old enough to remember, I was sneaking away from that place as much as possible. Besides, Madame likes to keep her 'children' separate. She really took an interest in him, though. Enough to send me away."

"That's why she sent you to the Academy? To get rid of you?"

"Don't know for sure," she replies. "But I was happy for the opportunity. That place is sick, Jesse. *She's* sick— wracked with guilt from the government's reaction to the bombings. By the time I arrived at the Academy, I was done with it all. To tell you the truth, I was planning to book it on outta there a couple of months after I arrived...find refuge on another Skyship or something, maybe head to the

Commonwealth. I wasn't so keen on snooping around. All I really wanted was to break free of her grip."

It's hard to picture Avery on the Surface, living at the Lodge. I just always assumed her life started when she met me, that she didn't really have a past. I could kick myself now for not questioning it earlier.

I jump over a crack in the pavement. "Then why didn't you leave?"

She shrugs. "I told you. I overheard a meeting. I heard about *you*. I was curious. I don't know what I expected to find when I met this so-called 'miracle kid,' but you surprised me, Jesse. Not many people surprise me." She pauses. "Maybe it was the way they treated you up there, maybe it was because you were alone, like me. Either way, you seemed to get it. You seemed to see past this stupid rivalry between the Surface and the Skyships and just *get it*. You weren't a drone like so many of the others up there. You were different. I guess I kinda saw a part of me in you. We clicked." She sighs. "Once I knew that Madame was interested in you, I knew I couldn't leave you alone."

"You were protecting me?"

"I was being your friend," she replies. "I *am* your friend. Of course, staying at the Academy meant that I had to continue to give Madame enough information to keep her happy. I've seen what she does to those who disappoint her, Jesse. It's not pretty."

I frown, sticking my hands in my pockets as we continue down the street. "We would've kept you safe. You could have graduated and been one of us."

"One of you?" She kicks a rock down the faded white line in the center of the pavement. "Didn't you hear what I just said? I'm not interested in digging up Pearls for either side. As far as I'm concerned, it's all a big distraction. I mean, think of what we could have done without them. There wouldn't be any Fringes without the Chosen Cities. Without the Skyships we wouldn't have to look over our shoulders all the time, afraid of some crazy war. I mean, the Polar Cities run all right without Pearls."

"That's because the Polar Cities are up in the arctic. It's not 500 freaking degrees." I pause. "You fed her information, Avery. Information that could hurt us."

"I know." She nods. "I was stupid, and scared. I wouldn't expect you to understand." She grabs my shoulder. "But that's over now. I'm not going to let her ruin your life, too."

We cross the next street. I notice dull splashes of color in the distance, once-bright signs for fast food restaurants. "Hey," I point in their direction, "do you think that's the—"

A dust-caked, fire-engine red car interrupts me, racing across the next intersection and out of sight behind a cluster of buildings. Avery and I freeze.

After a moment of shock-addled silence, she smiles. "They've got a generator."

"You don't know that for sure."

"Yeah, I do. How else would they get electricity for the

car after all this time? It's not like they're leeching from a Chosen."

"If they had a generator, why would they be using it to power some stupid car?"

"I don't know." She grabs my hand. "But maybe that means they have food. And maybe even a way to Seattle."

We hustle, nearly running through the street now. As we pass the intersection into the fast food restaurant graveyard, I get this weird feeling that we're being watched from every boarded-up window. A billboard to our right reads *len b rg: Pop 786*, though it's clear that some of the letters have been knocked out. *Lenbrg*, I guess. Across the street sits an old gas station with actual pumps, shut down and boarded up before the switch to electric three decades ago.

We keep up a frenzied pace, so much so that we don't hear the footsteps behind us until it's too late. I pull back on Avery's hand, spinning her around.

There are four of them, each one bigger than us, wearing navy blue bandanas over their dark, shaved heads. I'm not sure if the color's supposed to mean anything, but they'd be intimidating with or without them. They're stockier than most Fringers, with muscles the size of grapefruits.

"Hey!" The one in the front steps forward, loose white T-shirt rippling in the wind. "Not so fast, there. Ain't never seen you around." His words echo along the empty road.

Avery and I huddle close together. These guys are twice as big as the ones back in Syracuse. For the first time, I actually wish Eva was down here with us.

Avery steps forward, trying to be diplomatic. "Is this your town?"

"Hell no." The guy chuckles, slapping hands with his friend. "We're from down south, beautiful. And you ain't from around here either."

"No we *ain't*," she counters. "We're wanderers. Just looking for water."

The guy smiles, advancing on us. "Well, come over here and I'll give you a little something."

"Avery," I whisper, "we should run."

"Too many of 'em," she whispers back. "I can handle this."

"What would possibly give you that idea?"

"Shh!" She steps in front of me, crossing her arms.

"Aw, don't be scared," the Fringe leader coaxes. "We ain't gonna hurt you. Just come over here a second."

Avery scowls. "In your dreams, maybe."

I grab her arm, pulling her back. The last thing she needs to do right now is antagonize them.

She digs her heels into the ground, staying put.

The guy grins, rubbing his hands together. "We got a feisty one here, don't we? I like feisty."

Then, his grin turns to a frown as he notices something behind us.

"Stand back, Horatio!" A voice rings through the street. I spin around to see a gangly figure wearing a sweat-stained gray tank top and baggy jeans. The kid looks no older than me.

He stares down a crossbow too heavy for his stringy

arms. A silver arrow glints in the sunlight, pointed in our direction. I can't see beyond his circular goggles, but his mouth curls up in a confident smile at odds with his less-than-threatening build.

"Back up," he yells. "They're mine!"

34

On one side of us, four burly Fringers. On the other, one nasty-looking crossbow. An hour of peace, that's all I ask for.

Horatio and his buddies laugh, wiping the sweat from their brows. "What the hell's that supposed to be, Henderson?"

"Antique," the kid replies, "but these arrows are still mighty sharp. What do you want?"

"We're here to talk to your pops," Horatio responds. "Business proposition."

"Yeah? Don't think he'll like that."

The Fringers continue to advance, slower but no less menacing. "Don't think we care," Horatio grins. "You looking for a fight, Henderson?"

The boy steps back, curving around us until he has a lock on the gang. "Head over to Uni. Now. Or I put a shish-kabob right through each one of you."

Horatio chuckles, hands in the air.

"I said now!"

Horatio nudges his friend, whispering something to him before focusing back on the boy. "One of these days when you're not looking, I'm gonna smear your head all over the pavement."

The boy grins. "I'm a biter. You get near my face and you'll lose an ear."

Horatio shakes his head, amused, and motions for the gang to follow him into the town. With one final nod in our direction, they skirt down the street and out of sight. The boy keeps the crossbow pointed at us, jaw clenched with one hand on the trigger. Then, satisfied that the other Fringers are really gone, he drops it to his side.

"Yo." He holds out his hand like we're actually gonna go over and shake it. It's filthy, like the rest of him. A tuft of dark hair sticks out from underneath a backward baseball cap. His dampened clothing is riddled with holes. "Buncha chickens back there," he mutters, pointing down the street. "Thing doesn't even shoot right."

We stare at him for at least five seconds, utterly silent.

He pulls back his hand. "Guess we're not gonna be shakin'. What's the matter? You ain't city folk, are you?"

"No," I stammer. "We're ... uh ... wanderers." It comes out more like a question than a statement.

The kid flashes an *are-you-stupid* grin, which quickly develops into a full-bellied laugh. "Wanderers? Not out here you ain't. Closest town's thirty miles away. That wanderer crap may fly in the East, but not here. Unless you've got a secret camel hump behind you." He crosses his arms. "So where you really from? Survivors of the train wreck?"

Avery nods.

With lightning-fast reflexes, the kid raises the crossbow again, ready to shoot.

"No, wait!" She holds out her hand. "We're Skyship."

His head tilts, but he keeps the weapon pointed forward. "Prove it."

Avery rolls her eyes. "You said that crossbow doesn't work."

"Works all right."

She sighs, stepping toward him.

"Avery!" I pull on her arm to stop her. She ignores me and grabs the front of the bow, yanking it from the kid's grip and tossing it behind her. It crashes on the pavement, much to the kid's dismay.

She glares at him. "Why would anybody from a Chosen come running all the way out here?"

"City Salesmen." The kid rubs his gloved hand, annoyed. "Couple of 'em wandered in two weeks ago, trying to drag us into the Chosens and make us pay that pretty little tax of theirs. Chuck us out and reel us in ... that's how they do it."

"Do we look like City Salesmen?"

He frowns. "Guess not."

"Who were those guys?" I motion down the street.

"Wannabe gang lords." He lifts his goggles, revealing a pair of inquisitive blue eyes. "Don't know how they keep winding up around here. They're from down south, trying to make a name for themselves. Not tough enough to do it back in YakTown so they mosey up here, I guess."

Avery crosses her arms. "How did you know about the train crash?"

"Big news," he says. "Good thing you left when you did. Twenty miles north of YakTown ain't nothing. Gangs'll be on it like ants on a carcass—druggies looking to cash in on whatever's left."

My mind flashes back to the exploded Chute. I wonder if the government will send help if it means risking a stand-off with Fringers.

"Name's Bobby." The boy removes his cap, rustling his hair. "You guys looking for a Pearl? That it?"

"No," Avery starts. "Actually, we're looking for food. We haven't eaten since yesterday."

He nods, repositioning the cap on his head. "Never seen Shippers 'round these parts before. Ain't there laws against that?"

I glance over at him. "We aren't exactly legal."

He shrugs. "An enemy of the Unified Party is a friend to me. I guess I don't have to kill you or nothing."

"We're just passing through," Avery says. "All we need is food. We can pay you."

Bobby chuckles, crouching down to inspect the busted crossbow. "With what? Skyship credit ain't good down here. Unless you got a packet of Serenity to trade with Horatio and his goons, I'm not interested."

"Rations," she replies. "We can get you rations after all this is over."

"*All this is over?*" He stands. "Where you two think you're going?"

"Seattle," I answer.

He shakes his head, grinning. "Seattle? *Sunken City* Seattle? You really think the Cascade Colony's gonna let you through?"

I hold my hand up to block the blinding sun. "The Cascade what?"

"The Colony." He motions for us to follow him, cutting through a vacant parking lot in front of the gutted shell of a supermarket. "The Cascadians. Old George Barkley's been heading over there twice a month ever since the smog lifted. Gotta pay the toll, though. They trust him." He pauses. "Don't trust nobody else."

Avery speeds up to walk by his side. "There are people living in the mountains?"

"Of course there are people living in the mountains," he replies. "It's cooler up there. Not by much, but there's shade. Trees." He jumps a curb, leading us through a patch of scratchy grass until we're back on another road.

I step over a large crack fracturing the center of the street. "How does this Barkley guy get over there?"

"Moving van," Bobby answers. "Fills it up with trinkets from the city. Stuff to trade. Stuff to tinker with. What's got you folks so interested?"

Avery glances at me, but keeps quiet.

"We're looking for something," I mutter.

"Good luck finding it. Barkley's about picked the place clean."

We cross the street and head into what was once a residential neighborhood. I stare at the vacant, country-style houses on either side of us, trying to picture them as they once were, with mass green lawns and bright new paint jobs. "Has he ever seen anything weird?"

Bobby laughs. "Weird? The whole city's a graveyard, buddy. Ain't nothing to see, weird or otherwise."

Avery tugs at the front of her damp shirt. "Any chance we could catch a ride with this guy?"

"George Barkley? He takes off this afternoon. I can introduce you, but good luck." He heads for an alleyway between two particularly scummy houses. "Never did catch your names."

"Oh." She grabs my shoulder as we follow him out onto the next street. "I'm Avery. And this is Jesse."

"And you came all the way down from Skyship to Lenbrg so you could hitch a ride to Seattle?"

"It's a long story," I reply.

He stops suddenly, pointing at a group of well-maintained brick buildings stretching up a few streets in front of us. "That's Uni. Main part of town. I'll take you there, see what we can do."

Avery smiles. "Fantastic."

He turns around to look at us before covering his eyes with the goggles again. "Don't get too excited. Lots of folks around here aren't too crazy about Shippers. Sure, you ain't government, but you ain't Fringe either. Maybe you're better off with that lame wanderer story after all."

Avery and I exchange glances. The last thing we need is another fight.

"C'mon." He takes off down the road. "I'll keep an eye out for you. Don't worry."

I sigh. Says the kid with the broken crossbow.

35

Cassius dragged his weakening body through the barren desert landscape, trying to pretend that the sun wasn't slowly killing him.

He cursed himself for following the Chute's tracks northeast. Madame had said Fisher would head to Seattle, not Spokane. In all the confusion and horror of the night before, the details of their brief conversation had slipped his mind. Now he'd wasted precious time. He was lost.

With the morning light, the hazy outlines of the mountains came into view far off in the distance. He knew little about Washington's geography, except that Seattle was on the other side, away from the desert. But at the rate he was traveling now, it would take him days—weeks, even—to get there.

Squat brown bushes surrounded him on all sides, the only type of vegetation that could thrive in an environment crying out for rain. He'd wandered into a hilly area, though each hill was identically brown and covered with the same ugly bushes—pockmarks on an already unsightly planet.

His plan was to find a Fringe Town. He knew the locals wouldn't be kind to him, but he'd sneak in, grab what he could, and be out before they could do anything. If he didn't find civilization in the next day or so, he'd be out of luck. Not only could he die of dehydration, but Fisher would escape him. After the incident on the Chute, he wasn't sure which was worse.

He kicked the dirt, swearing to himself. Part of him wondered if this was punishment for striking out on his own, for trying to show Madame that he wasn't going to play her game anymore. No com-pad, no weapons. He'd gotten his wish. He was completely on his own.

The sun pummeled him with each step—a constant enemy, impossible to outrun. He longed for shade, for the shadow of a tree or an old telephone pole. The sky was a pool of blue, so clear that he could see the Northwestern Skyships, tiny dots in the vast abyss.

The land was flat and lifeless, except for the snakes. He'd already run across two, and though they mostly ignored him, he remained cautious. Cassius didn't like snakes, especially ones that weren't part of a Chosen City zoo.

Another twenty minutes passed before he stumbled upon an old roadway, cutting through the desert and disappearing into a dumpy bunch of hills in the east.

He stepped onto the cracked pavement, eager for a sign of movement. His borrowed shoes were too big for him, and worn at the heel. Running his fingers through his sweat-drenched hair, he decided to sit for a few minutes, even though he knew it would make getting back up again infinitely more difficult. He closed his eyes, trying to block out the harsh sunlight. A warm breeze tugged at his tattered shirt.

He opened his eyes to expansive nothingness. Everything was quiet—no people rushing around like in the city. No bells or advertisements or announcements. He couldn't stand it.

Then, a noise.

At first he thought he had imagined it, that he was going crazy from exhaustion. But the more he paid attention, the louder it became. Holding up his hand to block the sun, he looked to the west.

A small red dot approached him, kicking up a cloud of dust as it sped along the road. In his fatigued state, it took a few seconds for him to realize that the dot was in fact a car. An old-fashioned electric car!

Immediately, he gathered what energy remained and stood to wave his arms in the air, jumping up and down in the middle of the road.

As the car drew closer it slowed down, pulling to a stop a few yards in front of him.

It was an old junker for sure. Most of the color had faded, covered in so much dust and dirt. But the novelty of seeing an actual car was enough to completely fascinate him. They were obsolete inside the Chosen Cities.

He approached the driver-side window carefully but quickly. The vehicle shuddered as the engine struggled in the heat.

The driver slid down the window and appraised him.

He was an older man with an abundance of facial hair. Just looking at his bushy brown beard made Cassius sweat.

The man removed his sunglasses and rubbed his eyes as if he was staring at a mirage. "What the hell are you doing out here?" His voice was gritty and loud.

"Thank god," Cassius wheezed. "I'm stranded. I didn't think I'd make it until—"

"Calm down." The man held out a hand to silence him. "I can tell you're stranded. Ain't no reason to be all the way out here if you weren't. Thing is, I've been through these parts hundreds of times and I've never seen someone out on their own between towns, especially a kid like you. Folks are talkin' about some sort of train explosion down south. You're not from the city, are you?"

Cassius took a second to concoct a convincing story, careful to conceal his ID socket—a dead giveaway.

A believable lie would require a certain level of emotion. Luckily, after hours alone in the desert Cassius was already panicked. He wouldn't need to put on much of an act. "I don't know what you're talking about, sir. My dad and I were traveling east and our car ran out of power a few miles down. My father... he didn't..." He paused, looking down at the ground. "The heat was too much. I've been out here ever since and you're the first person I've seen."

The driver drummed his fingers on the car door. "East, eh? I've got family out east. Fact, that's where I'm headed now." He sighed, staring at Cassius's desperate face. "You got someone back there waiting for you?"

"My mother," Cassius responded.

The man nodded, thinking it over for a moment. "You can hop in the back if you want, but keep quiet. I like my space while I'm driving."

"That's all right." Cassius smiled, though east wasn't the direction he needed to go. "There's just one thing. I left my bag over by the bushes." He pointed off to the side of the road, hoping that the driver wasn't paying much attention. "It's got water and rations and stuff. You know, what I could take from the car. It's the only reason I've been able to keep going."

The man frowned. "So go get it."

"It's heavy," Cassius continued, slumping over to look as pathetic as possible. "If you could just help me drag it to the car, I'll let you take what you want. The sun has made me so weak I can barely stand."

It wasn't entirely a lie, but he hoped he'd have enough energy left for one quick attack. All he needed was for the guy to get out of the car.

The man appraised him for a second before giving a great sigh and turning off the engine. He pushed open the driver-side door, shaking his head as he stepped onto the road, no doubt craving rations as much as Cassius was.

He was nearly a foot taller than Cassius, but fairly thin and clearly not expecting a fight. Cassius gritted his teeth. If he didn't do this right the first time, it was over.

The man rubbed the back of his neck, scanning the landscape. "Now where's this bag of yours?"

Cassius pointed off to the side of the road and the man stepped forward, turning his back to him.

As soon as he did, Cassius punched the Fringer right behind the ear, quickly and with enough force to send him slumping over sideways onto the ground. The guy struggled for a few seconds as he slid to the pavement, then stopped moving altogether.

Cassius toyed with the idea of taking the keys and leaving the man out in the open. Less trouble that way. But he couldn't bring himself to do it. He'd already been responsible for so many deaths. The thought of one more, especially one so pointless, sickened him. He wasn't the bad guy.

So he pried the keys from the man's hand and walked to the back of the car, unlocking the trunk. With the energy he had left, he grabbed the guy's ankles and pulled him along the road and up into the trunk. His muscles strained with the weight. As soon as he stuffed the last limp arm inside, he closed the hatch and made his way to the front.

Sitting in the driver's seat, he realized he'd never had the chance to drive an actual automobile before. He couldn't imagine it was very hard, especially in such a barren landscape.

He tried two keys before finding the right one. The engine buzzed to life and he discovered how to shift the vehicle into drive. Spinning the wheel, he made a sharp U-turn and barreled down the empty road, pushing the old junker to its limit.

36

The three of us stand before a cobbled-together, twenty-first century castle. At least that's what it reminds me of. A high brick wall connects dozens of mismatched buildings, forming an almost impenetrable complex. *Almost* impenetrable. Half of the buildings look like they're about to collapse onto the ground.

Bobby leads us across a wide, empty street. "After the electricity shut off, folks that stayed behind started gathering at the old university. Easier to power than the whole city."

We approach the nearest building. Avery runs her fingers across a cracked pillar propping up a wide portico. "Do you have a generator?"

"Nah." He darts up a wide staircase. "Those things bit the dust ages ago. Uni Power comes from the wind field at the north end of town. Kept us going longer than I've been alive."

"Wait," I follow him onto a concrete landing beside the

doorway. "You power this whole city with a bunch of turbines?"

"Just Uni." He yanks open the heavy door. "The blades aren't strong enough for the whole town. It's no worry, though. We don't have none of those fancy gizmos like the rest of you. Just the basics. Temperature control. Light. They used to call Lenbrg the windy city of the west. Turbines were here way before the bombings."

We slip inside, shutting away the heat. Clean, cool air swirls around me. I take a deep breath, easing my scratchy throat. Temperature control: gotta love it.

Staircases border the tight rectangular entryway on both sides. The lights are switched off, leaving the room dim and shadowy. Beams of sunlight stream through patched-up windows above us.

Bobby heads to a nearby bench and climbs on top, standing to read an old-fashioned manual clock hung high on the wall. After pausing for a moment in thought, he slips down and takes a seat. "Community lunch in twenty. Barkley'll be there before taking off for the mountains."

Avery nods. "And that Fringe gang?"

"Aw, don't worry about them. They'll be long gone. Just antsy, that's all." He drums his heels against the bench. "Comin' up on the anniversary of the Chosens. Everybody's antsy."

I shove my hands in my pockets, trying to look casual. "Why's that?"

Bobby shrugs. "People here don't care much. But down

in YakTown? I hear they wanna send a message. Big Fringe revolt or something." He sighs. "They won't get it together, though. Too unorganized." He wipes the sweat from his brow. "There're tons of criminals down there, you know? Ever since the government started chucking 'em outside the Net. Sometimes they come up to Uni. That's why we've built the wall." He stands and motions for us to follow him through the building. We make it three steps before a man's voice stops us.

"Bobby Henderson," the voice bellows from somewhere above us like an angry spirit. I spin around, searching the room. A man steps out from the shadows and clomps down the staircase on the left.

When he reaches the bottom I breathe a sigh of relief. It's not some mass intimidating soldier or Fringe gang leader. In fact, the guy looks a lot like Bobby—tank top, dark trousers. He's much older. Cleaner, too. A roughed-up bowler hat sits on top of his curly hair. He glares at Bobby. "What in god's name have you been up to this morning?"

"Nothing, Pops." Bobby tiptoes back to join us.

The guy's eyebrows raise. "That's not what Horatio said. A crossbow, Bobby? Really?"

He shrugs. "Just something I found. Those guys are bad news."

"Damn right they are. That's why *I* handle them, not you. I've told you a million times not to travel to the south side alone." He pauses, as if noticing us for the first time. "Who're they?"

Bobby twitches and glances over at us.

Realizing he's not going to get an answer, the man faces us, arms crossed. "Who are you? You ain't Fringe, that's for sure."

"They're Shippers," Bobby replies. "I rescued 'em."

The man's eyes narrow as he looks us up and down. "Since when do Shippers need rescuing?"

Avery steps forward, hands clasped behind her back. "We're just passing through, sir."

He frowns. "Is this about Pearls? Because there hasn't been a landing near Lenbrg since last July so don't start thinkin'—"

"It's not about Pearls," she says.

I move forward and stand beside her. "This is … uh … a mass nice place you've got here."

The guy shoots me a look like I've just attempted the worst joke in the history of the world. "Bobby, over here. I need to have a word with you."

Bobby slumps over to the staircase. The second he's close enough, his dad grabs him by the back of his tank top and spins him around, speaking in an annoyed murmur.

I tug at Avery's sleeve and whisper. "Maybe we should leave."

"Just wait."

After a minute of hushed conversation, Bobby and his father turn back to face us.

"I'm sorry if my son has given you any ideas," the man says. "Things come outta his mouth before he thinks them through, don't they boy?"

Bobby nods, his father's hand gripping his right shoulder.

"I'm not without heart," he continues, "and I can't forget how your type have helped us in the past. They'll be serving lunch over at the canteen. Grab a meal if you'd like, but after that I'm gonna have to ask you folks to leave. It's nothing personal. We just can't afford to get involved with things."

"I think you're misunderstanding," Avery interjects.

"No, I think I understand perfectly," he counters. "You're heading to Seattle. Sounds like Tribunal business to me."

"It's not," I reply. "It's ... personal."

He crosses his arms. "From the looks of your clothing, you've been banged up already. Tribunal or not, you're illegal. We've got enough problems with the Unified Party as is, folks comin' in and accusing us of Pearl trading. If they find out we helped you, they'll make me disappear for good. Just the way it is. I'm sorry."

Bobby rolls his eyes.

His father doesn't notice. His grip on his son's shoulder loosens. "Why don't you take 'em to the cafeteria, Bobby? Point them out west when they've finished eating. Don't follow." He glances at us, his expression softening. "We're peaceful folks, here. It's not in my nature to turn people away, but I've gotta think of my town. That train crash last night didn't help things." He sighs. "I need to go work on a letter to send back with Horatio. Straight to lunch, Bobby. Please." He pushes past us and starts up the steps. Halfway up he pauses and looks over his shoulder. "Nice to meet you both."

We nod in response. Then he's gone.

Bobby slinks over, motioning down the hallway. "Sorry about that. He's grumpy, that's all."

I shrug. "Hey, I'm just happy he's not trying to kill me."

Bobby grimaces. "Give him time, man." He starts off down the hallway toward a glass door. "Follow me."

As soon as he pulls open the door, a wall of smothering heat smacks into us. We walk down the steps onto a gravel pathway. Mounds of dirt and crispy grass surround us on all sides. As we cut across the expansive courtyard, Bobby talks about the city. How it used to be called Ellensburg before vandals started stealing the letters from the town sign. How Lenbrg, like a few Northern Fringe Towns, had avoided the inevitable gang control and lawlessness of the Fringes to become a haven for people trying to make a decent life outside of the Chosens.

We continue along a footbridge stretching over a dying stream—nothing but a pathetic trickle left. A group of linen-clad Fringers tends to a garden on the far side of a brown field. I can't imagine what they could possibly be growing. I'm surprised they're trying at all.

"Straight up through here." Bobby leads us under a balcony and into an enormous, two-story complex. I relish the temperature-controlled air as we step inside. A slew of people bustle around the expansive, partially-lit cafeteria just below the entryway. The sign at the edge of town said that there were more than 700 residents in Lenbrg. I think they're all in this room.

We head down a ramp and file into line with hundreds of hungry Fringers. I shove my hands in my pockets again, keeping my head low. The smell of grilled vegetables and chicken streams out from the kitchen about twenty people away from us. This line can't move quickly enough.

"Do all you Shippers wear fancy clothes like that?" Bobby touches the wilting, ragged collar of my shirt. The thing's half-unbuttoned and spattered with dirt. Hardly fancy.

"It was a special day at our school," Avery answers. "We're not normally in suits."

Bobby drums his restless fingers on his hip. "You go to school?"

She nods. "Of a sort."

I glance around at the people in line in front of us. They stare back, not even trying to conceal their nosiness. All of a sudden, my heart races at the thought that maybe these people aren't flaunt with us being here after all. Maybe it's all a plot to fry us up for dinner or something. I don't wanna be a burger.

Bobby catches me looking and shoves my shoulder. "Don't worry, man. Just gawkers. I've brought people in before." He turns and waves at the onlookers, who respond by questioning and criticizing him with unblinking stares. Thankfully, that's all they do.

The queue shuffles forward. I try to change the subject. "So where do you guys get all this food?"

Bobby grabs a plastic tray from the nearest countertop.

"Got a small farm up at north campus where the football field used to be, but loads of it's scavenged from deserted towns. You should see our collection. Boxes and cans up to the ceiling." He passes trays to Avery and me. "Every once in a while we get Skyship food. Pearl trades, Tribunal food banks ... stuff like that."

I crane my neck to see into the dining area. Rows of lengthy cafeteria-style tables stretch down the wide, carpeted room. The place is half full already, and mass loud. A whole bucket-load of eyes laser onto my face. I dart back behind a stack of dishes. I guess if a newbie showed up at the Academy we'd all be staring too, but that doesn't make it any less uncomfortable.

We pass under an old ratty American flag hanging from a banister that runs along the ceiling. No Skyship flag. No Unified Party emblems, either.

"Hope you don't mind using your fingers," Bobby says as we near the serving counters. "We don't bring the silverware out too much."

I look down at the line of plates filled with vegetables and hunks of chicken. Right now I'd lick the plate like a dog if it came to that.

"Not much to choose from," Bobby whispers as a lady spoons food onto his plate. "Hope you like potatoes."

Once we're served, we make our way down a second ramp and into the dining area. I keep my attention fixed on the food on my plate, trying to ignore the rows of people staring up at us. Bobby drags us all the way to the end of the room, heading for two older men who sit alone in the corner. They're deep in conversation, but Bobby squeezes in close anyway.

"George," he taps the shoulder of the nearest guy, motioning for us to sit next to him. "Yo George, what's up?"

The man stops mid-sentence and glares at him. "Can't you see I'm busy?"

"Yeah, sure." Bobby grabs a piece of chicken and tears into it. "I got cargo for you."

Avery and I exchange looks. Cargo?

George removes his glasses, rubs his eyes, and glances at us. "Ain't never seen you kids around here before."

I meet his wizened eyes. The guy's got to be pushing fifty, with a receding hairline to prove it. There's a curiosity in his expression that's a little off-putting, like he wants to stuff us and prop us up in his room for display.

"Skyshippers." Bobby's voice quiets to a whisper. "Pops didn't like me bringing them in, but what are you gonna do, right?"

George pushes his empty plate to the man sitting across the table from him. "Go see if they've got more of them potatoes, Jim."

Jim nods, standing up and leaving the table. George leans forward. "*Again*, Henderson? Thought you'd have learned your lesson from last time."

Avery grabs a carrot from her plate. "Last time?"

Bobby sighs. "I met these kids from the Chosens. You know, runaways. Big deal."

George scoffs. "Big deal? They were wanted by the government. You nearly brought the Unified Party right to our doorstep, boy."

Bobby shakes his head. "It was the right thing to do. It's not like they hurt anyone. Stupid government laws. Went outside of their work orders. They just wanted a place to hide."

"What happened to them?" I ask.

"Government threatened to take out the town," George mutters. "We turned 'em in. Had to."

Bobby swallows a large chunk of chicken. "Still feel guilty about that, don't ya Barkley?"

"We do what we have to so they'll leave us in peace," he grunts, "something you don't seem to understand, Bobby. Draggin' in strays like this."

"They ain't Unified Party," he counters. "They're just trying to get to Seattle. Told 'em you could help. Maybe."

He frowns. "Is that right? Now what would two sky kids want to go to Seattle for? I thought the idea was to leave the Surface for good."

"It's not Skyship business," Avery replies, "or government. We're on a personal mission."

He chuckles. "Personal mission? Personal suicide mission, maybe. The Colony don't like strangers crossing the mountains, especially strangers from above. Shoulda snuck in down south, or out west over the peninsula. Don't you have shuttles?"

"Not anymore," I mutter.

"That's why we need *you*," Avery says. "The Colony lets you across, don't they?"

"Because we're of the same mind. We're both Fringe. We look after each other. It'd never work with Shippers."

"But we help you guys," I reply. "We send down rations."

"To get your hands on Pearls," he says. "I don't think y'all would be so considerate without that little carrot dangling over your head. Sure, it's not like you're government, but still … we're very different people." He pauses. "Why go to Seattle anyway?"

"I was found there," I whisper, "when I was a kid."

His eyes narrow. "You're still a kid. Place's been deserted for going on two decades now. I don't see any lesions on your skin. No chemical stain."

I tug at the chicken on my plate, tearing off a hunk and shoving it in my mouth. "I don't know. My school found me when I was just a toddler, walking in the middle of the rubble. I don't know my parents. I don't know why I was there, but if I can just see the ruins … maybe it'll jog a memory. Or maybe I'll find something."

Bobby stares at me, mouth agape. "They found you living in Seattle? Like, chemical *wasteland* Seattle?"

I take a long drink of water. "Someone could have brought me there. Maybe they dumped me. I don't know. I keep having these dreams. They're connected."

George grunts. "That's ridiculous."

Avery scowls. "Why would we be here if it wasn't true? You said it yourself... Shippers stay away from the Surface."

"Nobody survived the bombings," George says. "I should know. I had family out west. I've seen the aftereffects firsthand. Even fifty miles outside the city there were people dying from chemical burns. There's no way a child could survive conditions like that."

I shrug. "I guess I wasn't an ordinary child."

He runs a finger along his bottom lip. "You're serious, aren't you? You really believe this."

I nod. "If you'd seen what we've seen..."

He laughs. "Thought I'd heard it all. You kids are something else." He drums his fingers on the table.

Avery glances at me, then back to Mr. Barkley. "So..."

"So," he begins, "if I were to believe you... let's say I even drove you over... there'd be no coming back. I need the space in the van for supplies."

"That's all right," she replies. "We'll find a way back on our own."

"And if the government showed up—not saying they would—but if they did, I'd have to turn you over. I don't want no trouble."

I look over to Avery, smiling. "We'll take our chances."

He sighs. "Awfully strange seeing Skyship kids here in Lenbrg. If this is some kind of trick, I guarantee you'll be paying for it."

"It's no trick," I say.

He frowns. "Eat up. I'll show you the van when we're finished talking."

Avery beams. "Thank you!"

"Didn't say I was takin' you yet," he grumbles. "Now hurry. I should be leaving soon."

37

After lunch we exit the comfort of the dining hall for the oppressive heat of Lenbrg's northern sector. We pass the town farm before coming upon what's left of a torn-down apartment complex.

Avery scoots closer to Bobby as we cross a lonely cul-de-sac. "So, we've met your dad. Where's your mother?"

"Bovine flu hit real bad a couple of years ago," he responds.

"Oh," she whispers. "I'm sorry."

"Hey," he shrugs, "no biggie."

We turn a corner and George's house comes into view—a ramshackle country barn, augmented with its own personal wind farm in the neighboring field.

George pauses in front of the building, resting his hands on his hips. "Don't like livin' inside Uni. Rather be my own man, know what I mean?"

Nobody answers, but he doesn't seem to expect a response. He leads us up the front lawn in silence. Moments later the door swings open and a scrawny, mean-looking boy steps onto the porch.

George smiles. "Hey Danny. Didn't see you at lunch."

"I grabbed some stuff and left," the boy responds quietly, never taking his eyes off of us. "Who are they?"

George heads up the steps and rustles the boy's hair. "Change of plans, son. We've got passengers comin' with us this afternoon."

The boy glares at me like he's possessed by a demon. I half expect his head to start spinning in circles.

"Relax Danny boy," Bobby leans against a wide post supporting the canopy. "They're just Shippers."

The kid's eyes widen at the word. He steps away until he's back inside the house.

"Just a little skittish." George motions toward the front door. "Can't say I blame him."

We follow him into the house. Ceiling fans push the warm air around in funnels. It's not as bad as outside, but nowhere near as cool as the cafeteria.

Danny's already disappeared. He couldn't have had a hard time finding a hiding place. There's stuff everywhere. And not normal house stuff like furniture. Stacks of packing boxes and endless piles of metal parts form a veritable maze inside the living room. Four spare tires lie in one corner while a mountain of cans rests in another. It's an indoor junkyard museum covered in a layer of dust so thick you could knit a blanket from it. I sneeze as soon as we enter.

George takes us through two murky rooms of this

before heading out a back door and down into a sea of junk. Turns out the inside of the house was just the appetizer.

"Got most of this from Seattle," he declares proudly. "City Center's pretty much gone, same with the coast where the water rose. But farther out the impact wasn't as destructive. Chemicals killed the people. Didn't kill their stuff."

"That crossbow was lame, by the way." Bobby runs his hand along a pile of hollow window frames. "Ooh," he pulls a roughed-up, stringless guitar from the next pile. "Can I have this?"

"Don't touch," George says without looking back. Bobby reluctantly lets go of the instrument.

Just beyond the piles of junk sits a large moving van. It was white once, but all the dirt and dust now make it an ugly tan color. It's gotta be one of the oldest looking vehicles I've ever seen. Worse still, there's only room for two in the cabin. Assuming George's son is coming along, Avery and I get to be the cargo.

As we continue winding through the heaps of trash, I marvel at the different scents around me. None of them are pleasant. "This is quite a collection." I stumble past a metal pipe sticking into the middle of the pathway.

"Not everything's useful, of course," George replies, oblivious to the sarcasm, "but Danny and me like to tinker around with it anyways. You never know what'll come in handy."

"Best place for hide-and-seek," Bobby grins. "You get used to the smells after a while."

I wipe the sweat from my face, wondering how any outdoor game could be fun in this kind of heat. The van won't be temperature controlled either. This is gonna be a ride I won't be forgetting for a long time.

When we finally clear the never-ending field of trash, George moves to the back of the van and unlocks the door, pushing it up to the ceiling. Avery and I peer inside the trailer.

There are boxes everywhere, stacked neatly along the back wall but becoming more of a mess the closer they get to us. At least the place isn't crammed with junk. Boxes I can handle.

"It's no luxury liner," George starts, "but this is what you kids wanted."

"Whoo, boy." Bobby shakes his head. "Have fun, guys."

"When are we leaving?" I ask, eager to get the whole thing over with.

George scratches the side of his head. "Soon as we can." He cups his hands around his mouth. "Danny!"

The kid appears noiselessly from behind the nearest junk mountain, running to his dad.

"You got your gloves, boy?"

Danny nods and heads to the front of the van.

Bobby crosses his arms. "Good luck. I can't say I envy you, being stuck in that trailer all afternoon. I hope you find what you're looking for."

Avery grabs his shoulder. "Thanks for all your help."

"Yeah." I smile.

"No prob. Be safe."

George rests his hands on his hips, eyes slit. "Don't go stealing anything while I'm away, Henderson."

Bobby sticks his hands in the air. "Wouldn't dream of it." He leans close to us, whispering. "Not like he'd notice."

Then, out of nowhere, a loud rumble tears through the air above us. Thunder.

My eyes dart up to the sky. There aren't any clouds. It can't be thunder. Lenbrg's the quietest place I've ever been.

Then I see it—a familiar green dot shooting down at us through the blue. Not again.

And just like last time, it's headed straight for me.

My heart does somersaults in my chest, but the pain's gone. I'm in control.

There's only one problem. Pearls don't make noise, not like the rumbling I just heard.

A shadow falls over the empty field beyond us as a government cruiser lowers to the ground a couple hundred feet away. Dust and dirt kicks up as the machine's thrusters batter the earth. I cover my face as it settles down, peering through my fingers at the steadily approaching Pearl.

"Are you gonna catch it?" Avery steps away.

I nod. "I can use it."

The cruiser's engines shut off and the rumbling silences. The sunlight glints off the ship's shiny black exterior. The windows blend seamlessly with the body—an ominous, impenetrable machine. It sits like a shark's fin poking out from the ground, ready to attack. Whether it's after me or the Pearl is the only question. Maybe it's after both.

George jumps behind the wheel of the van. Bobby staggers back into the junkyard, taking refuge among the piles of rubble. The Pearl continues its path toward my hands.

A ramp lowers from the bottom of the cruiser and seven soldiers run into the field. With their dark bulletproof uniforms, they look more like robots than people.

I gaze up at the Pearl, coaxing it forward. The soldiers sprint through the dying grass. Avery grabs my arm. "There's no time! Get in the van!"

"No." I stare up at the Pearl. "I can do this."

She backs away as the energy draws nearer. My fingers buzz. The soldiers' heavy boots clomp through the dirt. Thirty more seconds and they're on us.

Then the Pearl lands in my arms and all hell breaks loose.

38

A line of bullets rains down from the sky behind us, puncturing the dry grass in front of the oncoming soldiers. Even though the guys are protected by bulletproof everything, they stop in their tracks and gaze up over our heads.

I spin around and cock my head to the sky. The underbelly of a second ship rushes over the barn, kicking up a fierce wind that nearly sweeps me to the ground. It's tinier than the government cruiser, but majorly ticked off.

Spinning to the side, it plunges to the ground—landing mere feet from the cruiser.

"It's an Academy transport!" Avery flattens against the side of the moving van. "Jesse, we can't stay here."

"Government *and* Skyshippers?" Bobby marvels from the edge of the junkyard, peering out from the center of a busted window frame. Then he turns to me and notices the Pearl in my hands. "Man, how did you do that?"

I watch as the side doorway's pulled open from the Academy ship's silver exterior. Unlike the dumpy shuttle

Avery and I piloted into a building yesterday, this one's a sleek, needle-shaped agent's transport—more than a match for the cruiser.

The soldiers stop in their tracks, dumbfounded as they stare at me. With all the distractions, I hoped they wouldn't notice my Pearl-catching trick, but it's too late.

The energy from the Pearl intensifies in my hands, getting warmer by the second. Coupled with the triple-digit weather out here, it's all I can do not to drop it to the ground.

Captain Alkine bounds out from inside the agent's ship, landing hard on the grass. He wears a dark bulletproof jumpsuit underneath his long gray jacket—crazy-hot gear for the Fringes. I do a double take as I watch him step forward.

He notices me immediately, probably because I'm staring at him, mouth agape, holding a freaking Pearl. It's not hard to miss. Our eyes meet for a second and I instantly pull away, pretending I didn't see him.

"In the van, Jesse," Avery coaxes beside me.

The soldiers split into two groups, one headed for Alkine and the other breaking off toward us. Alkine leaps into the fray, taking on three of the nearest soldiers with nothing but his fists. A roundhouse kick catches them off guard, followed by a series of lightning-fast blows that send all three slumping to the ground. Despite myself, I stand in awe, watching.

Half a dozen agents jump out into the field behind him. Right in the center are two slightly smaller ones. I squint in the harsh sunlight to see them. Skandar and Eva, each wearing dark bodysuits just like Alkine.

They run through the chaos, separating from the others and heading for the van. Ahead of them rush four government soldiers, closing in on us.

Avery jumps into the back of the trailer, stretching her hand out to grab mine. Instead of grabbing hold, I turn and toss the Pearl to her. I could've exploded it and been done with everything, but I can't risk hurting my friends. Even Eva.

"What am I supposed to do with this?" Avery rolls it from hand to hand, cautious of the growing heat.

A second Academy shuttle bursts into the sky above us, firing down at the oncoming soldiers. Half of them stagger backward and fall to the ground, hit by raptor bullets too powerful for their government battle suits. The two remaining soldiers duck out of the way and renew their frantic pace. Eva and Skandar take a longer route, circling around the battlefield to avoid the flurry of bullets.

"Bobby!" I turn to face the kid, still huddled in the safety of the junkyard. "Toss me something, now!"

He nods, prying a long metal beam from the pile behind him and throwing it to me. I catch it at the middle and wobble to the side, knocked off balance. It's hotter than the Pearl, and much heavier.

I reach down with my other hand, stabilizing the beam and wielding it like a baseball bat. The soldiers don't seem to notice or care. It's just like August Bergmann back at Lookout Park. Let them underestimate me.

They converge on the back of the van, going for the Pearl rather than me. Muscles straining, I pivot sideways and swing the beam at them, letting gravity pull it forward until it connects with the backs of their knees. I hear the loud crack of bones. They tumble over backward, long enough for Avery to jump down and yank the gun away from the nearest guy. The other one loses grip of his rifle. It flies out into the dust. Avery cocks her weapon and points it straight at the two of them, Pearl tucked under her arm. "Back up. Now."

Eva and Skandar sprint up beside me. Eva holds her arms out like she's gonna give me a hug, but I dart out of the way before she gets close enough.

"Jesse," she pants, "we've gotta get out of here."

"Duh," I reply. "That's what I'm doing. You? I'm not so sure."

She frowns, face shiny with sweat. "What are you talking about?"

I cross my arms. "No traitors onboard."

An explosion sends a puff of dust rising into the air several yards away. Skandar grabs my arm and pulls me up to the trailer. "Get over it, mate. We're here to help."

Avery shoots me a questioning look, keeping the rifle pointed at the injured soldiers. There's no time to argue. We dive inside. I spin around to take one last look at Alkine. There's a whole squadron of Skyship agents around him now. Shadows fall over the field as more government cruisers converge in the air. Reinforcements.

Eva begins pulling down the back door. Before she can shut it completely I grab the rifle from Avery, lean outside, and toss it to Bobby. He catches it awkwardly, a scared, wild look in his eyes. I mouth the words "I'm sorry." They wouldn't be enough even if he could hear them above the rising din of battle.

Without waiting for a response, I yank down the rest of the door and secure it. Avery rushes to the front of the trailer and bangs on the wall. The engine rumbles to life and the van backs up and turns dramatically.

All four of us crash into the side wall, flung around like unsecured cargo. I land backward on my arm, twisting it. The Pearl rolls around, hitting wall after wall, leaving small dents in the metal. The inside of the trailer glows a soft green, humming with Pearl energy.

George guns it. Without a chance to grab onto anything, we're thrown against the back door, settling in a misshapen heap. Gunshots and explosions echo all around us—some near, some far. Several shots rebound off the corner of the van as we speed away. We jostle up and down through bumpy, uneven grass. I dig my fingers into the metal floor, but there's nothing to grab onto.

After a minute of stomach-churning mayhem, we roll onto steadier ground. Pavement, hopefully. The explosions fade behind us, replaced by the continuous grumbling of the old van.

Eva scoots forward and hugs me. I can't get away this time. "Fisher, you're alive."

I struggle free and push her away.

She lands in the corner, rubbing the back of her head. "Jesse?"

I grab the Pearl from beside me, clutching it in my arms. "Why is Alkine here?"

She purses her lips. "He just—"

"And don't lie," I interrupt her. "I know everything. How did he find me?"

She moves forward slowly, crawling along the width of the trailer. I let her approach, cautious.

"Don't move," she whispers, then reaches up to the top button on my shirt and yanks it off, holding it in front of her face. "Microchip tracer. It went offline for a couple of hours last night, but it's working now."

I stare at the insignificant button. Tracked, all this time. "Disable it."

She nods, twisting the button until it comes apart in two pieces. Inside is a thin round chip. She removes it and snaps it in half. "I was only doing what they asked."

"Yeah." I glance over at Avery. "Seems like a lot of that going around."

Eva sighs. "I'm sorry, Jesse. Skandar and I begged Alkine to let us come down with the battalion. I want to help. I told him that we'd have the best chance of convincing you to head back to the Academy—"

"Wait," I interrupt. "If you—"

"—but I'm not here to convince you of anything," she continues. "We're here to have your back. I promise."

Skandar stares at the Pearl in my arms, laying his finger on top of the swirling energy. "Man, where'd *you* manage to get one of these?"

"I caught it," I reply, keeping my attention on Eva. "So what's Alkine's plan now?"

"He was hoping to pick you up," she responds. "I guess the Unified Party had the same idea." She pauses. "Wait a second, did you just say you *caught* it?"

I nod.

Her eyes widen. "Alkine was right. There is something different about you. Back at Lookout Park … that was you, wasn't it?"

Before I can answer, Avery swears, cradling her forehead.

Skandar glances at me. "What's wrong with her?"

I lay my hand on her shoulder. "Headache again?"

Avery nods, speaking through clenched teeth. "They're getting worse."

Eva frowns. "Why is *she* down here, anyway?"

I rub Avery's back. "She knows what's going on," I mutter, "from Madame's side."

"From *Madame's* side?" Realization dawns on Eva's face. "Wait, she's a spy, isn't she? I always thought there was something going on there. Flunked out of the program, yet you know how to hack into our com-pads."

"She's not a spy," I lie. "She's my friend, Eva. Drop it."

Avery runs her hand through her hair, managing the pain. "I work for Jesse," she whispers. "No one else."

Eva nods. "Then I guess we have something in common."

Skandar elbows my side, grinning like this is all some fun little game and I've just won them both as prizes.

Eva sighs. "How did you find out about Alkine, Fisher?"

"Air vent," I say. "Your little closed-door meeting wasn't as secret as you thought."

"Then you saw how much it was killing me to do it, to follow you around like I was your mother. I swear I didn't know anything. Alkine asked me to protect you. I thought it was some sort of mentor thing."

"Yeah," I reply. "Well, I don't need your protection."

She nods. "We're going to Seattle, I assume."

Avery takes a deep breath. "What's left of it."

"Alkine will follow us," Eva starts, "with or without the tracer. Watching your path so far, he realizes what's happened. He knows that you know. He'll try to stop you from doing something stupid."

Avery scoots closer to me. "With those cruisers dropping out of the sky one after another, he might not have a chance."

"He'll get there," I say. "It's just a matter of who gets there first. We'll need to—"

A voice interrupts me, words I've never heard before, swirling around my head. Whispers. I close my eyes and try to focus on the sound. There's no one else in the trailer. A string of nonsense echoes around me.

"We'll need to what?" Eva asks. "Jesse, are you all right?"

I set the Pearl on the ground between my knees. The whispers stop. Everything's quiet. I open my eyes. Everyone's staring at me.

I glance around the trailer, then place my hand on top of the Pearl once more. Whispers again. Nothing but cryptic babble. I lift my fingers from the surface. Silence. Somehow, the voice came from inside the Pearl. These things just get weirder and weirder.

"I'm fine," I mutter.

"Oh!" Skandar digs through his pocket, "I almost forgot." He pulls a chain necklace from inside and drops it into my hand. Attached is a silver key. I run my finger over the curved metal head. It's the same as the one from my dreams.

Eva clears her throat. "I swiped it from Alkine after the meeting. It's important, I think. He always talks about it when he's mentioning Seattle."

I hold the chain between my fingers, allowing the key to hang above the Pearl, glinting with the reflection of the wavy green light. "Thanks."

She shrugs. "I told you I was on your side."

I pull the key up into my fist, clutching it tightly as our van speeds out of the city and toward the mountains. "We were so close to finding answers without the Academy."

Eva sighs. "The Academy's not your enemy, Jesse."

"Yeah," Skandar says. "Alkine's worried sick."

I scoff. "Alkine doesn't get worried."

Eva nods, her eyes pleading with me to understand. "I know. And *that's* the scary thing."

I bow my head, getting lost in the Pearl energy, and try to convince myself that everything's fine. But I can't ignore the cruisers back in Lenbrg, or Cassius's grim determination to find me. This isn't just some fancy scavenger hunt amidst the ruins. There are weapons involved. Armies.

I *should* be worried. I should be mass worried.

39

Cassius laid on the accelerator, propelling the sports car up the side of the mountain pass. He'd found a gun under the passenger seat and used it to snatch a canister of water and a quick meal from a pair of Fringers on the outskirts of the nearest town. He'd dumped the guy's body from the trunk as well. Less weight in the car.

Now he sped along a narrow road between miles of dry forest, much of it blackened by continual fires. The Northern Cascades—once a lush, snow-clogged drive to Seattle, now a thinning forest fire waiting to happen.

He felt strange sitting behind the wheel of a car. The warm breeze pushed against his face through the half-open window. Families used to take trips in automobiles before the Chosen Cities—radio blasting, hands sticking up out of the sunroof. Now everyone crowded onto the Chute system, except those lucky enough to afford a shuttle of their own. Driving felt all right. Freeing.

He drank from the water canister before dropping it onto the seat beside him. The motor puttered up the steep incline. He prayed it wouldn't give out entirely. Still, if he had to get out and push the fraggin' thing, he'd do it. The sooner he got to Seattle, the sooner this nightmare would be over.

Suddenly, he saw movement in the forest ahead of him. He slowed down slightly, peering out the dust-caked window.

Then, a heavy whoosh. The trees crashed to the left of his car, bending forward to let something through. He watched as a large, dark shape flew through the forest up into the air, casting a shadow against the hood of his car.

He slowed to a stop as a boulder the size of an oven smashed into the pavement, fracturing the already busted road and nearly pancaking the front end of the car in the process.

The trees settled back into place, swaying gently in the breeze. All was quiet and still.

Breathing hard, he stared at the giant rock blocking the center of the pathway up the mountain. He looked at the sky, half-expecting something else to fall. But the boulder hadn't come from the heavens. *People* had done this. He wasn't sure how, but he wasn't alone on the mountain.

He grabbed the gun from beside him, surveying the woods.

Nothing.

With one hand on the wheel he backed up, swerving to

the left. Shifting gears, he curved around the right side of the boulder, darting his head from window to window.

Halfway around the rock, a gunshot rang out from the forest and nicked the corner of his bumper.

He sped up immediately, rocketing around the boulder and back onto the road. A second shot shattered the passenger window. Glass spilled onto the seat. He ducked, car weaving as he tried to stay on the road with one steering arm and limited vision.

He glanced at the rearview mirror and watched as several gangly figures bounded out from the trees onto the road, running after him. He kept his head low and stomped down on the accelerator, flying up the hill as fast as the car would take him. The figures fired shot after shot, some of which hit the back of his trunk. Others ricocheted off the pavement. He longed for one of the government's concussion grenades, or even a proper shotgun instead of the peashooter he held now.

He kept a constant, breakneck speed, whipping around a cluster of dying trees before straightening out once more. Then he saw it, half a mile ahead, stretched across the road. A wooden barrier. It was at least a foot thick, with two words carved in jagged marks on the bark. *Cascadia Territory*. It'd crush the car no matter how fast he was going.

Two choices: stop the vehicle and defend himself, or off-road it.

He glanced over to the right. The forest ended, replaced by a vast rocky basin—an evaporated lake, no doubt.

Without giving himself time to reconsider, he swerved to the right, flying off the highway and down to the basin. The car was airborne for no more than a second before smacking into the dirt. Hard.

His chest bashed into the wheel as the front tires bounced on the rock, but he managed to keep control and steer the vehicle safely into the basin. Once he was level again, he gunned it, kicking up dirt and rock as he sped onward—a tiny red insect in the middle of a massive, empty hole in the Earth.

Lucky for him, the Cascadians hadn't booby-trapped the basin. The chances of someone being reckless enough to try and steer their way through the uneven landscape were too slight. But Cassius had exploded twice in the past week. Nothing was too reckless anymore.

He took a quick right to avoid an outcropping ahead of him, which led him up a mound of rocks that sent the car flying through the sky once more. He landed with a crash, bumping his head on the ceiling.

Once he was a mile beyond the barrier, he headed back for the highway, climbing up over the gentlest slope he could find and tearing through the backyard of what used to be a ski cottage. He rejoined the roadway at a downward slant. Beyond was the West Coast. Within minutes, he'd be off the mountain.

No more bullets or boulders. He'd made it, though the small victory didn't mean much. The mountain pass would be nothing compared to Seattle. Things were going to change down there, one way or another.

He watched the speedometer soar until he was in triple digits again. The Cascadians were long behind him. He didn't look back.

40

After an hour of driving over relentless potholes, our van slows to a stop. The inside of the trailer reeks. In all the run-for-my-life excitement I didn't realize the smell until we were about twenty minutes out of town. It's like a skunk took a bath in two-month-old milk. Once we get out of here we're gonna smell like this for days.

Even worse is the heat. It's like a dark, smelly sauna. We're breathing each other's air, leaving puddles of sweat on the already dirty trailer. A meager stream of air flows in from the cracks in the doorway. I need someone to let us out. Like, now.

The van slows to a stop. I hear footsteps approach outside, then a soft muttering from up front.

"It's the Cascadians," Avery whispers.

I nod. "Bobby said something about a toll. We better not be part of it."

Eva and Skandar exchange confused looks, but don't press us for information. I steady the Pearl with my ankles, making sure it doesn't bang against the metal and make any unnecessary noise. "If Barkley opens the door and turns us in, then we run. No questions... just bolt into the forest."

Eva smirks. "Look who's giving orders now."

We wait and listen. I hear George's voice, but the words are muffled. There are at least two others outside. One is a woman.

The conversation lasts a few minutes and ends with the slam of a door. The engine rumbles. I breathe a sigh of relief. Getting over these mountains is the first thing that's gone right all day.

Skandar stretches his arms. "Anybody else think this place needs some in-flight entertainment?"

"Here," I hand the Pearl to him. "Hold this."

He cradles it in his arms, staring at the radiant glow coming from within. The van lurches forward. We're heading down.

"I don't know what we're gonna find in Seattle," I start, "but if you really wanna help, the best thing you guys can do is cover for me if Alkine shows up."

Eva shakes her head. "He's not here to stop you, Jesse. The cat's out of the bag."

"Has he told you anything? About a lab?"

She shrugs. "Listen, what you heard at that meeting is all I know. As far as I can tell it's all he knows, too."

"There's a lab," I mutter. "I saw it in my dream." I wind my fingers around the chain necklace. "It's where I was given this key. I think it happened right before Alkine found me. I remember Seattle, covered in mist."

"The chemicals from the bombings," Avery interjects.

I nod. "And I remember the lab. Everything in between is blank."

"So you're going to try to find this place?" Eva stares at the key lying on my chest. "You think it still exists?"

"It's all I've got to go on," I reply. "Maybe the key opens the door. Maybe there are answers inside. Why else would I be remembering it now, after so long?"

Skandar frowns, holding the Pearl in front of his face. "Meanwhile, there's gonna be a whole army of Pearlhounds looking for this thing."

"I'm not worried about them."

Eva laughs. "*Jesse Fisher* not worried about an army of government soldiers? Do I need to remind you about what happened back in Syracuse? And that was just *one* of them. A trainee, no less."

"Yeah," I start, "*that* was back in Syracuse. Besides, you'll hold them off."

"Hold them off?" She grimaces. "What do I look like, a freaking tank?"

Avery scoots closer to me. "You owe him, Rodriguez."

"For what? For saving his butt for nearly three years?" She crosses her arms. Apparently the generous, guilt-ridden Eva has left the trailer.

"For lying to him," Avery responds.

She rolls her eyes. "Coming from you, that's rich."

Skandar darts his head around the side of the Pearl. "I never lied to you, mate."

Eva sighs. "That's because you're incapable of lying, Harris. It would require a level of self-awareness that's completely beyond you."

He glares at her, confused.

"It doesn't matter," I say. "If you're with me, be with me now. We'll talk about everything else later."

"If there *is* a later," Eva mumbles. I pretend not to hear her.

Other than the occasional attempt to get a conversation going, we spend the next hour in silence. My mind attempts to formulate some sort of a plan, but it's impossible. I have no idea what I'm getting myself into. If there's a lab—if there's *anything*—I don't even know where to look.

And all the while Skandar plays with the Pearl like it's some kind of toy. I know what's really inside—a concussive force strong enough to flatten an army. I've seen it happen, triggered by my own hands. I'd never heard of a Pearl exploding before last night. These things have been poked and prodded, dropped off buildings and transferred to reactors, but never once exploded. Until I caught one.

The van comes to a sudden halt.

We freeze, careful not to make a sound. My heart thumps double-time, urging my body to get out of the tight space.

I hear the driver's side door open and shut in one motion. We're here. We must be.

Someone shouts, followed by a flurry of voices. George's isn't among them.

I press my ear against the wall. Just like back on the mountain, the individual words are too muffled to make out.

A loud blast rips through the air. The trailer wall vibrates with the echoing sound. I stumble backward, slamming my elbow on the metal.

Then it's quiet again. I listen for George's footsteps to come around the side. I wait.

Nothing.

Instead, the voices come back, murmuring at the front of the truck. The hairs on my neck stand on end. Avery squeezes my arm, sensing my tension.

Footsteps make their way from the van's cabin to the side. Suddenly, I realize that we're trapped. There's no way to open the back door from inside the trailer. If this is who I think it is, then we've just cornered ourselves. Big mistake.

The footsteps tread around the van until they've reached the back door. I hear breathing, followed by the jangling of keys. The lock turns and clicks open.

We scoot back as the door rises, a crack at first. Even with my heart in my throat, I relish the breeze that streams in from outside. Polluted Surface air has never felt so amazing.

But as the door continues to pull open, my worst suspicions are confirmed.

This isn't George or his son. It's not Alkine.

It's a mini army of soldiers wearing Unified Party combat gear.

They've got guns.

And they're pointing them directly at us.

41

The soldiers' faces are shielded by government gas masks, their bodies hidden behind thick, genderless uniforms. They're completely anonymous.

The ones in front reach in to grab us but the leader motions them to stop, stepping forward and extending a gloved hand.

"The Pearl. Surrender it." The voice sounds robotic and alien from behind the gas mask.

I glance over to Skandar, who clutches the green orb close to his chest.

"Count of three," the soldier warns. The mass of weapons beep and whirr as they lock onto our chests. "One..."

I turn to Skandar, motioning for him to toss the Pearl to me. He shakes his head. "I'm not letting them have it."

"Two..."

I dart over to him, yanking it from his arms. The soldier stops counting and watches me scoot forward.

"Place it in my hand." The soldier takes a step forward.

I look up at the gas mask, searching for a face behind all the hardware. Eyes, a nose ... something.

They don't know who I am.

The thought strikes me out of nowhere. If they knew that Madame wanted me, they'd forget about the Pearl altogether and pull me from the trailer without hesitation. Of course, it doesn't change the fact that as soon as they get the Pearl, they'll drag us all off to a Security Center anyway. If they don't shoot first.

Not gonna happen.

"Get behind me," I motion to the others.

Avery grabs Skandar and Eva by the shoulders and pulls them to the empty boxes at the front of the trailer. Eva tries to fight her way back to me, but Avery pins her down.

As soon as they're safe, I close my eyes and focus, hoping that Portland wasn't a fluke.

My body's not screaming bloody murder like it did back in the alleyway. I know this is a crap shoot, trying to control something I don't even understand, but I continue on, feeling the Pearl's energy meet my own.

"Weapons at the ready," the soldier orders. I do my best to ignore the sounds of the battalion.

I hold the Pearl in front of me, feeling it grow warmer with each passing moment. I press in on it with my hands, squeezing between my fingers, and imagine a straight line from my chest down through my arms and into the Pearl.

And then it happens. I open my eyes and watch the

Pearl drift away from my fingers, floating toward the open trailer door. The closest soldiers take a cautious step back.

I squint, eyes fixed on the hovering Pearl. When it reaches the back end of the van, I ball my fingers into fists.

The Pearl explodes, shooting a wave of green energy out into the city. The soldiers topple over in its wake, pushed to the ground like paper dolls. The sides of the van bubble out in an ear-piercing grind of metal. But behind me, it's still. Like last time, my body deflects the energy.

I claw my way forward, watching as a pair of legs disappears up over the top of the trailer, soaring into the air and out of sight—just like in the Portland alley. I catch sight of the figure just in time. It curves up past the layer of chemical smog and out of sight. Definitely humanoid this time.

My fingertips pulse like they're ready to shoot lightning bolts. I feel like I could single-handedly power an entire Chosen City.

The others stumble out from behind the pile of boxes, mouths agape.

Skandar moves to the edge of the trailer, staring down at the sea of unconscious bodies before looking over at me, dumbfounded. "Jesse, you're the man."

Eva moves to his side. "Have you done this before?"

I ignore her, and turn to Avery. "It didn't hurt this time."

She nods, flashing an encouraging smile.

Eva steps down from the trailer, laying her hand on the unmoving shoulder of the nearest soldier. "Jesse, you just destroyed a Pearl."

I scoot closer to the edge. "Now you can see why I have to find answers. The Unified Party's not gonna like what I can do."

Avery joins me. "Neither is the Tribunal, for that matter."

"You're like a human bomb or something," Skandar whispers.

"I have to have a Pearl," I reply. "But I can sense them ... control them. I brought one straight to me in Portland, without even realizing what I was doing." I step out onto the pavement, trying to ignore the bodies below me. "And I think there's something inside."

"Inside what?" Avery follows me.

I turn to face her. "Pearls. Something or ... someone. I've seen it twice now, with both explosions. Flying up out of the energy, there's a figure. It's like I've hatched something."

Skandar cranes his neck to look at the sky. "I don't see anyone."

"It's gone." I stare at the wispy layer of clouds above. "If it was ever there."

Avery backs away, curving around the trailer until she comes upon a pair of bodies lying on the ground beside the cabin. She crouches, pressing her fingers on George's neck. "They're stunned. Both of them. They won't be waking up for a while. I hope they get some good dreams out of this."

I sigh, relieved that the soldiers hadn't killed George and his son. Without them, we'd have never made it over here. Without a word, I make my way through the pile of soldiers, stepping over limp arms and dodging legs. The air's thick with remnants of chemical smog. Not enough to be lethal—at least for a couple of hours—but enough to keep a deep, sulfurous smell in the air.

The van had stopped on top of a maze of crumpled roadways and overpasses surrounding the city. Colossal slabs of concrete rest in heaps around us, crushing anything beneath them. Colorful bits of vehicles lie smashed between boulders—confetti on an ever-dark background.

We stand on one of the only remaining elevated highways. The ground's caved in from the dividing lines on, joining the pile of jagged boulders below us. The road itself has a nasty slope to it. A narrow strip of concrete travels down into the city to my right. It's the only accessible route.

I move to the edge of the highway cliff, staring down at the remains of Seattle. Several skyscrapers stand like skeletons around the edges of the city, chunks missing from all sides. Most buildings are toothed stumps now, poking up from the carpet of rubble lying in piles around them. Farther away, water seeps in from the coast, creating dark, disease-ridden rivers between islands of junk. A gray smog hangs over the city—an incessant, unmoving drizzle replacing the once-red chemicals from the bombs. I can't see much beyond the water.

Far off to the right, surrounded by a septic sea of green, are the remains of the famous Space Needle, reduced to a pointed spire. There's not a hint of vegetation in sight. No trees, no bushes, no grass. The clouds keep their distance but the dark mist drifts into the city like a runny watercolor.

I try to picture the city that once was. People lived here—and worked and went to school. Then came the Scarlet Bombings. No warning. Not one person knew what had happened. One moment they were going about their normal business, the next they were dissolved into nothing. I can't imagine being dissolved from the outside in. Can't even go there.

The others join me at the edge of the cliff, staring out at the wreckage. Nobody says a word. Words can't really describe it.

After a moment of silence, I turn to face them, speaking softly. "We'll need weapons."

Eva nods. "There are plenty back there with the soldiers."

"Find a pair of com-pads, too. You guys need to stand watch up here."

Skandar groans. "Man, that is not cool. I wanna do something."

"If anyone shows up, I'll need to know," I say. "If all four of us are down there, it'll be too easy for them to take us by surprise."

Avery grabs my hand, clutching it tight. "I'm going with you, Jesse."

I nod. "Avery and I will go down alone."

Eva glances at our hands, muttering. "Yeah, I bet you will."

"Please don't argue," I reply. "For once."

She sighs, reaching over to Skandar and pulling the com-pad from his belt.

"Hey!" He scowls.

She ignores him, tossing the device to me. "You don't want Pearlhounds tracing you. It's safer to use Skyship-issue."

"Fine." I clip it to the side of my frayed pocket.

"I don't like this, Fisher," she grumbles.

"Yeah?" I let go of Avery's hand. "Well, you're gonna have to deal. All this time protecting me, you should be pretty good at it. Protect me now by standing watch."

Skandar frowns. "No offense, buddy, but maybe you need us down there. I mean, that Pearl trick was mass impressive, but you're running on empty. We can help."

"You're more helpful up here," I say. "You can see everything. Once we get down below the smog it's gonna be a mess."

"Jesse's right," Avery starts. "We need eyes above the city."

Eva sighs, crossing her arms. "You're right. For once in your life, you're actually right."

I smile. "Right when it counts, huh?"

She lays her hand on my shoulder, shaking her head. "Just ... be careful down there. Keep in contact. If you need us, don't hesitate."

I nod.

"Come on, Harris." She turns to the pile of soldiers. "Time to get suited up."

Skandar pauses for a moment, then steps forward and smacks my arm. "Good luck, mate. I hope you find what you need."

Then he's off, joining Eva beside the van.

I meet Avery's eyes. She smiles, weaving her fingers between mine. "You ready?"

I reach up and tuck the silver key under my shirt. "Let's go."

We stumble down the road, careful not to wedge our feet in any of the cracks.

Five steps down and the screeching of tires on pavement interrupts us. Something screams from the top of the highway.

I spin around to see a red sports car come speeding down the uneven road like an out-of-control monster. A cloud of dust trails its pathway, kicked up into the already coarse air.

I don't have time to think—to *move*, even. The strangeness of seeing an old-fashioned car in such nightmarish terrain knocks me off guard. For a moment, all I can do is stare.

But as the vehicle draws closer, shock turns to dread. I recognize the driver immediately. No mistaking the gritty expression on his face.

It's Cassius, and he's headed straight for me.

42

If I was thinking clearly, I'd react. But all I can do is watch his face until it's too late.

"Jesse!" Avery dives out of the way.

My feet are glued to the ground. He found us. So close, and he found us.

Cassius slows down, then peels out to a stop right in front of me, the bumper of his car inches away from my legs. He sits there for a second, staring at me, hands gripping the wheel. I shake the fog from my head and prepare to strike a bargain.

He doesn't give me a chance. Before I can move out of the way, he lays on the accelerator.

My legs buckle as the bumper slams into them. I'm thrown up onto the hood, yelping as my ankles seize with pain.

Cassius accelerates again, sending my body flying against the windshield. I grab onto what's left of the wipers to avoid flipping over the vehicle altogether. Face down,

I hunker against the car, staring at Cassius through the glass. Our faces are a foot apart now. He doesn't smile. His expression is blank. Terrifying.

I bang on the window with my fist, shouting for him to stop. Instead he rockets down the pathway into the city. The wind beats against my back, tearing through the legs of my ripped up slacks.

Just as I'm about to balance myself, he makes a sharp left at the bottom of the roadway to avoid a massive pile of boulders. My body lurches sideways, feet hitting the passenger-side mirror as I struggle to hold on to the wiper blades. They bend to the point of snapping off until Cassius straightens out the car and I twist back to the left, colliding with the windshield again. A crack spreads from the middle. One more direct hit and it'll shatter.

Piles of rubble fly by on both sides, dwarfing the speeding car. The mist settles in around us. All I can see is the hood as I desperately cling on. The engine heat roasts the skin under my shirt.

We travel until the overpass is long out of sight. It feels like hours. Slow motion. But it's over in seconds.

Cassius slams on the brakes. The force flings me back instantly. The wiper blades snap and I fly over the trunk. Landing on my feet's not an option. With the moments I have, I cover my head to minimize injury.

I hit the pavement hard. And it isn't like Syracuse. This time it steals my breath. This time the pain rings through my body with such intensity that I'm afraid I'll pass out.

I let my limbs fall to the side and lie on my back, struggling for air. My shoulders throb. *Everything* throbs. It feels like somebody punched me all over with a concrete glove. My head spins. The thick smog threatens to reach down and choke whatever's left of my lungs.

All it took was two moves for Cassius to completely immobilize me.

Cassius shuts off the car and bounds from the driver's side, slamming the door behind him. The sound echoes along the ravaged buildings.

I move my fingers, trying to lift my arm. My legs are brittle and useless, but I pull them in anyway, pushing at the ground with my heels. Anything to get away.

Cassius marches toward me, faster than I have any hope of escaping. In one violent movement he reaches down and grabs the front of my shirt, yanks me from the ground, and pushes me into the pile of rubble behind me.

"What the hell did you do to me?" he shouts, his face red, eyes ablaze.

I grab onto his wrist, trying to pry myself from his grip. My body feels like a rag doll, muscles shut down.

"I told you," I stammer through fractured breaths. "I don't know what happened."

"Why would she lie to me?"

"Madame?" I kick at his shins. "Madame's crazy. She's not who you think she is."

He lifts me up another inch until the shirt starts to cut into my neck. "Don't talk about her like that!"

"I'm ... I'm serious," I choke. "She's using you."

The com-pad at my belt hisses to life. Eva's voice comes out muffled and small. "Jesse, are you okay? Jesse? Avery's coming down after you. There are—"

Cassius rips the device away, chucking it into the rubble. "Back in Portland you said you were sick, like me. Why haven't *you* exploded?"

I cough as the smog creeps into my lungs. "Put me down and we can talk."

His eyes narrow as he considers it. With a sigh, he lets go of my shirt. I crumple to the ground. Not exactly what I meant by "put me down."

I pull my aching body to a crouching position and rub my shoulder. My knees are raw, my scuffed slacks stained with blood. "What do you mean, *exploded*?"

"On the Chute," he mutters. "Fire."

I stare up at him, searching his stony face for an answer. "That was you? *You* blew up the train?"

"Every time I get close to you," he continues. "Ever since the rooftop." His fingers clench into a fist at his side. "Fire. From everywhere. From inside."

I take in a mouthful of air. "You're ... you're not exploding now."

He looks down at his hands, shaking. "She said if I found you I'd be cured. She said you were the reason, that you're dangerous. What the hell's so dangerous about you?"

I frown. "My incredible knack for getting my butt kicked?"

He scowls. "You think this is funny? I crawled through the desert because of you! I... killed an entire train of..." He trails off.

I sit in silence, watching him control his expression.

He crosses his arms. "So what happens to you? What happens when you get sick?"

I look over to the side. I shouldn't tell him. It's stupid to reveal anything that could be used against me, but there's a desperation in his eyes that even he can't control.

"Pearls." I hold my fist in the air, letting my fingers fall open. "They explode. Boom. Then they're gone."

His eyes widen. "You can destroy Pearls?"

I nod.

His expression becomes cold once more. "She's right. You're a danger to the country. You're just what the Shippers need to weaken the Unified Party and gain control." He reaches forward.

"She doesn't love you," I say, hoping that I can get him to pause for a second. I remember what Avery said outside Lenbrg. *Madame's really done a number on Cassius.* I can't take him physically, but maybe there's another way.

His hand freezes.

"You're not her son," I continue. "Not really."

"That's none of your business." He sneers. "Why did you come here? Why Seattle?"

"Skyship found me here when I was a kid."

He shakes his head. "Madame knows. She'll be here. She'll find you."

I grit my teeth, inching back against the rocks, building up what little energy I have left. "I'm a good hider."

He chuckles. In that instant, for the split-second he's unguarded, I kick him right in the stomach. He staggers back a few paces, out of breath. It's long enough for me to push myself up and limp around the nearest boulder.

"Big mistake!" He wheezes behind me.

I keep my attention forward, dipping under a crumbling entryway into a narrow, dirt-stained alley. Strength failing me, I dart behind a piece of wall, clutching my chest. My organs burn, working overtime. The air stings as it hits my skin.

It's quiet for a moment.

Cassius flies around the corner of the wall and punches the side of my face. I lurch farther into the half-building, feeling around the inside of my mouth with my tongue to make sure I've still got all my teeth. I gag on blood. Metallic. It tastes horrible.

Cassius smiles. "Time's run out."

I hunch over, breathing hard. He approaches slowly and watches me struggle.

"Help me find the lab," I choke. "Maybe there'll be a cure."

"Madame has the cure." He pushes me backward. "All she needs is you."

I trip over a beam sticking out from the ground. "She's playing you. It's all for Pearls. I can control them. Once you bring me to her she'll forget about you."

Before I can stand up, Cassius grabs my arm and twists it behind my back. I shout out in pain. He twists harder. "Prove it."

"That girl I was with," I sputter. "Her name's Avery. She's like you. Madame trained her, raised her, and got rid of her. You're just an accessory."

"I've never seen that girl at the Lodge," he whispers. "I don't believe you."

"That day on the rooftop," I continue. "We triggered something in each other. It brought me here. You, too. Help me find the lab. We're connected in some way."

"You're crazy," he replies. "There is no lab. The Unified Party's sifted through these ruins hundreds of times. Everything was destroyed."

I elbow him in the stomach with my free arm. He stumbles back, allowing me time to break free.

He's about to lunge at me again when a soft whimpering cuts through the silence. Both of us pause, listening to the crying.

"Do you hear that?" Cassius whispers.

I nod, coughing. "It's coming from the other side of the alley."

Without responding, he walks to the edge of the building and peers out a large hole in the side of the wall. I limp after him and turn the corner into the alleyway.

The crying grows louder.

I toy with the idea of attacking him again. His back's

turned, but even without the injuries I'd be no match for him. It's safer to run.

And that's just what I'm about to do—until I step into the intersection.

I recognize it immediately from my dream. No, not dream. *Memory*. Everything's where it should be, each concrete skeleton positioned as if I had stepped back in time. The green mist has cleared. It's lighter now, but the same.

Then, crouching on the sidewalk next to a blown-out window, I see her.

A girl a few years younger than me sits with her back to us, dwarfed by a jagged, barely standing wall. She senses us immediately. She quiets and turns around to stare.

She wears loose-fitting pants and a shirt, unadorned and simple. Once white, they're now smattered with dust and dirt from the ruins.

We approach her carefully. Something about her demeanor demands caution.

There's something off about her. At first I don't see it, but as a faint glimmer of sunshine pokes through the smog and illuminates her skin, I notice the glowing.

Green. Hazy, but undeniably green.

The energy pours from her like a beacon. Pearl energy.

The pieces fit together perfectly in my mind, even though if I sat down and thought about it I'd realize how crazy it sounds.

I know who this girl is.

She flew out of a Pearl on the overpass. I freed her.

43

The girl staggers forward, looking at us like we're a pair of strange animals. She squints as she pushes through the mist, jerking her head side to side. Her bony shoulders are hunched over. She's malnourished, to say the least.

Cassius and I stand in silence. I watch the girl stumble on bits of rubble. She seems disoriented—out of place.

The sadness and uncertainty in her eyes make her look like a child. Her wispy blonde hair floats in the breeze, sticking to tear-dampened cheeks. She wipes it from her face and allows herself a faint smile as her eyes meet mine.

Then she runs, an awkward lope toward me like a baby learning to walk.

Her first words are unrecognizable—strings of sounds like the ones I heard coming from the Pearl in the trailer. But as she falls forward into my chest, there's one distinct word buried in the clutter. "Key," she says.

Before I can react, she wraps her arms around me in a tight embrace. At first I try to pull away, but as her skin touches mine my body buzzes with warm electricity. My knees scab over and smooth. The throbbing in my ankles retreats. Every last drop of pain fades into a memory. She's healed me.

After a few seconds, she lets go. I fight the urge to grab her again and hold her close. It's addicting, the energy.

"The. Key." Her words come out fractured.

"Oh." I fumble with the chain around my neck, pulling the key from under my torn shirt. "You mean this?"

She glances down at the silver key for a second before looking back up at me, brows furrowed. She shakes her head.

I pull the chain over my head and cradle it in my hand. "The key, right?"

Her eyes narrow and she points her finger into my chest. "The. Key."

Cassius steps up behind her, grabbing her shoulder and spinning her around forcefully. "Who the hell are you supposed to be?"

She pushes away from him immediately, pulling her arms up around her shoulders. She glances back at me before scanning Cassius from head to toe. Then me again. Then Cassius.

I place the necklace around my neck again. "Do you know anything about a lab?"

She cocks her head, eyes focused on a point far off in the distance.

"Do you understand me?" I continue. "Do you speak English?"

Her eyes shoot back. "I … learn … English. Learn. Ed.

Learned." Then it all spills out like I've flipped a switch inside of her—a jumble of words thrown together so fast that they become a single sound. "Carbon-bench-green-supervisor-episode-age-sea-setting-plenty-small-escape-crunchy-umbrella-orbital-police-future-run—"

"Okay," I try to interrupt her, "that's enough."

"—radius-church-shiny-given-convict-rhythm-lost-lecturing-abhorrent—"

Cassius glares at me. "Shut her off!"

"Don't you think I'm trying?" I grab her shoulder, hoping to shake the crazy out of her.

"—silverware-dance-shipping-amaze-cry—"

I grip onto her other shoulder and spin her around so we're face to face. Her eyes roll back, gazing up at the sky. All I can do is watch for a moment as her lips move effortlessly to accommodate each new word—faster and faster until I have to shout to be heard over her voice. "Have you seen a lab?" She ignores me, eyes still far away, so I repeat myself. Louder. "Did you come from a lab?"

The girl stops. Just as suddenly as it had begun, the string of words becomes a tense silence. Her eyes drop to meet mine, her voice soft. "Came from energy transport."

"From a Pearl. I know."

"Key *should* know." She reaches up and rubs her chin, clenching her teeth. "Before transport, there was a lab."

I drop her shoulders and clench my fist. "I knew it! Where is it? I think this key might open something inside. If we can just find—"

"Wrong." She grimaces. "Incorrect." I watch as she moves her tongue around in her mouth, opening and closing her jaw. "Untrue. Transport laboratory is many moons away. You should know."

My fingers fall loose at my sides. I run through her words again and again in my mind, trying to convince myself that there's another explanation.

Cassius scoffs. "This is ridiculous. I'm supposed to believe that this girl came from inside a Pearl? That's the stupidest thing I've heard in my life."

She turns to him. A hint of green still lingers around her.

He shakes his head. "Pearls are energy. Electricity. They're not people. They're resources!"

"Transport energy," she replies, eyes dissecting him. "Body and soul broken. Electrons, neutrons, dancing inside... waiting... waiting to reform. Waiting for sanctuary." She reaches her fingers out to his arm. "Your wrist. Bare."

Cassius pulls back his hand. "You don't seriously believe this crazy chick—"

"I saw her fly out of the Pearl," I reply. "And it's not the first time. Back in Portland..."

Without turning around, the girl lays her hand on my shoulder. Again with the pleasant, almost tranquilizing buzz. "More of us. Where are they?"

I shake my head.

"Key," she continues, "Key unlocked them. You know."

Cassius moves forward to grab her arm. Before he can

do anything, her hand darts up and he's forced back by an invisible energy wave.

"The others," she whispers. "Thousands. Where?"

"I don't know," I stammer. "I ... didn't know."

"Key. You know."

I stumble backward in realization of what we've done. I breathe deeply. "All of them. Every single Pearl we've used to power a Chosen City or a Skyship, they've all been people, haven't they? We've been killing *people*."

The girl's eyes bore into mine.

"I ... I was never anything special," I continue to back away. "You've gotta believe me. I was just an ordinary guy until—until I met Cassius."

Her eyes widen with a sickening realization. Her fingers fall limp at her side. "Trigger. Trigger never happened."

Cassius steps closer, careful to keep his distance. "What trigger?"

Her path wobbles and she lunges at him, grabbing his hand and running her fingers along his palm in circles. He struggles, but her grip is too strong.

I watch sparks shoot from his hand as she continues to touch his skin. They pop into the air like mini fireworks. Then, after circling his palm half a dozen times, she conjures a tiny flame. It flickers half an inch above his skin. He doesn't cry out in pain, doesn't even wince. Instead, his brows furrow and he pushes her away with his free hand. "No, no! You don't know what you're doing—"

She stumbles back but quickly regains her balance.

"Only several days old. Power should be strong." She shakes her head. "Not right."

He closes his fist. The flame extinguishes. "You know something about the fire?"

"Displacement of energy," she mumbles. "Conduits. Reaction. Not right."

"Slow down." I move to her side. "You're not making any sense."

"Separated," she continues, paying little attention to me, "separated immediately. No trigger. Everything ruined."

"*What's* separated?" Cassius moves in.

"Thousands of us," she crumbles to her knees. "Gone. So many. Separated."

I grab her arm to prevent her from crashing to the ground. The right side of my body hums with energy. "I think she's going into shock."

She shakes her head, tears streaming down her face. "Failed us. They failed us."

Cassius crouches down beside her, swearing. "*Who* failed you?"

Before she can answer, her eyelids flutter and she loses consciousness. I set her on the ground.

Cassius sighs. "Well, that's just great, isn't it? Babbling like a crazy person ... "

I glance over at him. "I don't think she's crazy. She knew about your power."

He clenches his fist. "It's impossible. She drew it out of me without an explosion. She controlled it."

I pause, hearing footsteps behind us. Cassius notices it too. He darts up from the ground.

I stand, just in time for Avery to bound at me, nearly knocking me off my feet. "Oh Jesse, thank god you're alive!"

"How'd you get down here?" I struggle for breath through her monster hug.

Instead of responding, she releases me, and stares into my eyes. Then she kisses me.

It takes a moment for my mind to register what's happening. After so much stress, so many missed opportunities, I can't bring myself to believe that *this* is how it's happening. Now.

Still, I don't pull back. Her lips tug mine. She draws me forward and it's like breaking the Pearls all over again. Mass powerful. Buzzing.

I hug her shoulder, wishing that I'd never have to let go. Wishing we weren't in the middle of a war zone.

In that moment, any remaining doubts about Avery shatter inside me. Then she pulls away, eyes wide. "They're coming. Unified Party ships pulled into the city just as I started running down."

Before I can respond, the sky rumbles. The outline of a cruiser cuts through the mist overhead, bathing us in shadow. Then another, from the opposite direction. We're surrounded.

"How charming," a woman's voice echoes from the alleyway behind Avery. "It's comforting to see that teenage hormones are alive and well in these trying times."

Avery spins around to watch the woman enter the intersection. Her tailored jacket is spotless, like she's managed to dodge all the dust in the air that's clogged up the rest of us. Her hair blows softly in the breeze, framing an intense expression of down-turned lips and narrow, mesmerizing eyes. She wears long gloves over porcelain skin and an expensive suit beneath the jacket—completely at odds with her surroundings. I recognize her immediately from pictures at the Academy.

It's Madame.

44

Madame marches through the intersection, kicking a scrap of metal out of her way as she approaches us. Shadows of cruisers dot the vacant street, growing larger as they find breaks in the rubble to settle down.

She glares at Avery, hand at her side. "What a terrible disappointment you've turned out to be."

Avery grips my shoulder. I grab onto her arm, never wanting to let go.

Madame stops and smiles. She grips a small rectangular control pad. A tiny red dot flashes below a thin antennae. I watch her finger caress the buttons on the front end, then flip a switch at the bottom.

Suddenly Avery jerks away, cradling her forehead. Her eyes close in pain as she crouches to the ground and bottles up a scream.

I drop to her side, keeping my eyes on Madame. "What are you doing to her?!?"

Madame holds up the control pad, smiling. The flashing dot is now a constant light. "Correcting behavior."

"You're killing her!"

"Again with the adolescent dramatics." She outstretches her hand and cradles the controller in front of her. "Here. Come and take it from me if you're so concerned. Be the hero."

"No, Jesse." Avery grips onto my wrist. "It's a trap."

"Preposterous." Madame moves her thumb along the side of the pad and presses a silver button. Avery's body falls limp. "Too late. Better be on the ball next time, young man."

"No!" I crouch by her side, running my fingers over her cheek. Her eyes are shut—arms lifeless at her side.

"Relax," Madame says, "she's not dead. Yet."

I gently set Avery down on the ground, take one last look at her unconscious face, and stand to confront Madame. "If you hurt her ... "

She laughs. "You'll do what? Tackle me? Mr. Fisher, I've been tracking you since the minute you left the Academy. I could have had you dead a thousand times over by now. There's a chip in her head capable of disrupting brain patterns. With the press of a button I could reduce her to a vegetable. You will do nothing unless I tell you to." Her eyes shift to Cassius. He stands behind me, fingers drumming nervously on his thighs. Her voice softens. "Cassius. What a job you've done. A test, and you passed it brilliantly."

"Why did you send me on this mission?" His voice

comes out quiet and meek. "If you knew where Fisher was—"

"Ah." She raises a hand to silence him. "Your brother survived the fall from the building in Syracuse because the two of you triggered your abilities. He was bathed in Pearl energy. It protected him. But it's a process, Cassius. Your bodies needed to adjust in order to accommodate your new abilities. You were both dangerous, but not to each other. Not directly, at least. You were the perfect person for the job."

"Wait," I start, "did you say *brother*?"

Her eyebrows raise. "Didn't you know? Two children without family, drawn together by Pearl energy. Etcetera, etcetera. I thought it was becoming quite obvious."

Cassius glances at me, then frowns at the realization. "You . . . you sent me to kill my own brother?"

"Not *kill*," Madame replies. "*Recruit*. I sent you to find your brother and bring him back where he belongs. I couldn't have done it without you, Cassius."

"She's lying," I say. "You're expendable. Just like Avery."

She chuckles, voice calm and steady. "Now what would give you that idea? On the contrary, you're very valuable to me. One half of a very exclusive set."

I glance at Cassius. He doesn't smile, but he doesn't try to stop her either.

She steps forward, gripping the controller pad. "The two of you are going to help me save the planet, ensuring the continued strength of the Unified Party."

I scoff. "Like I'd ever help the Unified—"

"Twelve years ago I found you, Cassius." She ignores me. "Our radar picked up an anomaly over Seattle. I came to investigate. I didn't know there was another until I took you back to the Lodge. By then it was too late. Fisher had already been rescued." She sighs, continuing to step forward. "By Jeremiah Alkine, no less.

"You were wearing a curious bracelet, Cassius. The rest of your attire was so simple, but the bracelet ... I'd never seen anything like it before. Deep and dark and endless. I nearly got lost staring at the seamless material. It was cold to the touch. Didn't want to part from your arm, either, but I had my methods."

I stare at Cassius, watching him squirm as Madame approaches. Like usual, he tries to control his expression. But it's not working very well. He's crumbling.

"It wasn't from Earth," she continues. "Neither were you, for that matter. But I didn't discover *that* until two nights later, when the bracelet began to glow by my bedside. I watched as text scrolled across the band—illuminated characters unlike any known language. Seconds later, the writing translated itself into English, as if it knew that *I* was reading." Her eyes fall on me. "And that night I learned about *you*, Jesse Fisher."

I look to the side, trying to avoid her eyes.

"For many years I was convinced that you'd been knocked off course, sidestepping Earth altogether. I was relieved. As long as Cassius didn't develop his powers, our planet would be safe." She sighs. "And then I got word from

Avery. Just fragments of information—strange little orphan child that all the teachers were whispering about—but enough for me to connect the dots. The mystery boy was alive." She frowns. "He was a Skyshipper."

She shrugs. "As it turned out, we'd still dodged a bullet. The Hernandez Treaty kept the two of you separated for a handful of years, but it was bound to happen eventually. I only wish I'd acted sooner." She pauses. "The rooftop changed everything. Pearls are treacherous now. They are capable of being unlocked. By *you*. We're in danger of being overcome by your people."

"Our people?" My voice comes out as a whisper.

"That's right," she replies. "Alien. Extraterrestrial. *Invader*."

My stomach turns. I fight back nausea as the words repeat in my head. I feel like I'm not really here now, that I'm watching someone else's life.

Alien. The word doesn't sound right. It doesn't sound real—just something made up by people with too much imagination. Groups like Heaven's Rain. But as my heart starts to slow, I realize that I know it's true. I've known it since I saw the girl.

The girl. I look down at her, lying unconscious in the rubble. She looks so … human.

Cassius scoffs. "Aliens don't exist."

Madame shakes her head. "There are things we don't talk about, remember? Your past is one of them. You are one of *them*."

"No," I sputter. "No. I've been here my whole life. I would've remembered—"

"You were very young," she interrupts. "The first. The first Pearls and the means to unlock every one that fell after."

I look down at my hands, the hands that destroyed two Pearls already.

"And that makes you dangerous," she continues. "An enemy to both the Surface and the Skyships. To the entire planet."

I clench my fists. "You're crazy."

"Am I? Or am I the one unlucky soul who must carry this secret?"

"No," I respond, "you're crazy."

Her eyes narrow. "Tell that to the millions of people who died the day our country exploded, the day your chemicals nearly drove this planet to extinction."

Cassius steps up beside me. "The Scarlet Bombings. But terrorists did that. You said ... "

"There is terror beyond this planet." She frowns. "The invaders were sneaky, disabling our radar systems to mask their location."

I shake my head, unwilling to believe that anybody related to me could be responsible for killing millions of people.

Cassius frowns. "But the government's retaliation efforts—"

"I told you I must carry this secret, Cassius. Our people demanded revenge. *Someone* had to pay. That someone happened to be a group of people that had been troubling our country for far too long."

"Skyship was right," I say, gritting my teeth. "There were no terrorists. Your retaliation … it was … murder."

Madame pauses. For a moment I think that she's gonna defend herself, but she just shakes her head, eyes shut. "No one knows what Pearls really are, what they carry inside. And nobody knows the terrible sins we've committed better than me. It's our duty to correct our mistakes … to use the energy from the invaders to make this world livable."

"And kill people in the process," I say.

"They are not people," she counters. "It's Homeland Security. They've prepared this world for colonization … triggered environmental change and pitted us against one another. They thrive in heat, Jesse, and they'd prefer we lie down and die before they arrive. I cannot let them win."

I look up at the charred, skeletal buildings around us, trying to imagine chemical-filled missiles shooting down from space. The only missiles I can imagine are the ones deployed by America after the bombings. It's true what the Tribunal always said. The Unified Party is more than dangerous. They destroyed an entire chunk of the world. They'd do it again if they had to.

I cross my arms, glaring at her. "So what are you gonna do? Kill me?"

"No," she replies. "Not unless you force me to." She places her hand on her hip. "I've been watching you, Jesse Fisher. As soon as I saw what you were capable of in Portland, I had my team move into action. We caught the invader you freed and disposed of it. I nearly pounced on you then, but decided it was better to wait. You were heading to Seattle, after all. What better place to have this conversation? Vacant buildings all around us. No one need know."

"Captain Alkine's on his way," I start. "My friends—"

"Oh?" She holds the device up to her lips and whispers into it, smiling. "These friends?"

Footsteps surround us. I notice movement among the rubble and watch as Unified Party soldiers approach from every angle, forming a wall around the entire intersection. Their uniforms blend into one another until we're surrounded on all sides by a dark, unmoving circle. Two particularly large soldiers approach farther, positioning themselves on either side of Madame. One grips Skandar. The other pins Eva close to his chest. Handcuffs, leg restraints, gags. The whole deal.

Madame's eyes dart from side to side, then settle back on me. "Your so-called Academy really needs to raise its standards." She cranes her neck, snapping her fingers to get the attention of the soldiers behind us. Before I can turn around, they creep up and drag the Pearl girl away into the ruins. Avery lies peacefully beside me. Skandar and Eva stare at me with wild eyes, struggling with their restraints.

"I can destroy everything you love," Madame says, "so I suggest you listen closely to what I'm about to say."

I glance around at the ever-increasing wall of soldiers, so many that the ones in the back fade into the smog.

Several hundred, at least, and only one of me. One

snap of Madame's finger and they'll rush in. I don't really have a choice.

"Join me," she continues. "We need you. You can control them . . . bring Pearls to us and away from the Skyships. We'll restore America to what it once was. A beacon of hope, of progress."

I grit my teeth. "Why would I want to help the Unified Party?"

Her eyes slit. "Because it is the winning party. Because we alone have the capabilities to harness your power and use it where it is most needed."

"No," I say. "Not you. I won't help you."

She scoffs. "Perhaps you're not understanding. You're not in a position to be disagreeing with me. If you don't turn yourself in, I *will* kill you. Sure, it'll make things harder on my end, but I can't allow you to exist if you're not working for me. It's a matter of survival." She advances. "Without a Pearl you're just a scared little boy." She glances up at the sky. "And I don't see any Pearls falling, do you?"

Cassius shifts beside me, clearing his throat of the smog. "You lied to me."

Madame stops in her tracks and turns to him as if she had forgotten that he was standing there. "Excuse me?"

"You said you'd find a cure," he mutters. "You said you didn't know where I came from. You lied to me."

She shakes her head. "I was looking out for you, Cassius. I was protecting you."

"No," he continues, "you didn't protect me on the Chute. You didn't protect me afterward, in the desert."

"There are very important things that you don't—"

"There is no cure, is there?"

She sighs, dropping her hands to her sides. "This is what you are, Cassius. The reaction. Your brother unlocks the Pearls, you channel whatever energy he's unable to control. It manifests itself as fire, an element native to this planet. I didn't want this for you, but there's no going back."

He stares at the ground, dodging her eyes. "That's what I am to you, then. A reaction. An afterthought?"

"That's not it, Cassius. You're very powerful."

His head darts up and he shoots out his hand. A fireball erupts from his palm. Madame staggers back, shielding her face. The fire dissipates almost as quickly as it had appeared. "That's right," Cassius says. "I'm powerful."

Madame adjusts her jacket, then motions for another soldier to approach her. This one carries a black cube half a foot long on each side. When he's close enough, he tosses it to Madame. Cassius watches her catch it with great interest.

"The cube I brought to you in the infirmary," she says. "It's not a lie. When your bracelet had finished decoding its warning it ... transformed—melted and dripped from my fingers right down onto the floor." She cradles it in her hand. "Into this. *This* is your bracelet, Cassius. There's one keyhole at the top, that's all. Nothing will open it."

I feel the silver key press against my chest beneath my torn shirt.

"Join me, boys," she continues, "and we'll unlock it together. We'll see this country flourish. We'll take care of our people down here, every one of them, and we will be a family. You've always wanted a family, haven't you Jesse?"

I watch Skandar and Eva kick at the soldiers holding them captive, then glance down at Avery, still unconscious on the ground. Some family.

I shake my head. "People in Fringe Towns, you've forgotten them. You're trying to start a war with Skyshippers. That's not family."

Her expression hardens. "Cassius?"

He glances off to the side. "I don't know . . . "

She sighs, pivoting to face the two closest soldiers. "Very well. We'll start with your friends, Jesse." She nods to her men. The soldiers' hands move to Eva and Skandars' necks, closing in and gripping tightly. Their expressions strain as the soldiers choke them. Their arms are secured tightly behind their backs. There's no way they can break free.

I rush forward. "No, wait!"

Madame raises a hand. The soldiers' grip weakens. "Second thoughts, Mr. Fisher?"

"Don't hurt them," I say. "Please."

She smiles. "Then you'd better do as I ask."

"Let them go."

"Not until you are escorted safely onto my shuttle."

I mentally curse myself, wishing I had a Pearl in my hand. Or something . . . something to distract her.

I take one last look at Avery and step forward. Madame

motions for the nearest soldier to grab me. I hold out my fists. The soldier removes a pair of shackles from a compartment on the side of his belt. Madame smiles.

Then a voice cuts through the silent city, calling my name in the distance. The soldier turns, distracted. A figure breaks through the line of soldiers, stumbling into the intersection.

The smog lifts from his grizzled features and I see Captain Alkine's concerned face locked onto mine. He walks with a noticeable limp, a dark sack slung over his shoulder.

Despite my anger with him, the sound of his voice instantly raises my spirits. It's the voice of safety. Reinforcements.

I wait to hear an agent shuttle overhead, or see a battalion of troops come bounding through the line of soldiers to help me. But with each fragile step Alkine takes, my optimism wanes. And then it hits me. This is not the rescue I was hoping for.

It's Captain Alkine, all right, but he's completely alone. And worse yet, unarmed.

45

"Jeremiah." Madame shakes her head and chuckles like she's staring at some pathetic little kid. "It's been too long."

"Not nearly long enough," he mutters as he staggers over my way.

She watches him approach, smiling. "Got a little limp there, I see. Not as spry as you used to be. Training children for so long must have tempered your fighting spirit."

He ignores her, his eyes latched on to mine. "Jesse, I'm sorry. I should have told you everything. I never meant to put you in danger."

Madame rolls her eyes. "It's too late. You may have underestimated the boy, but I haven't. Look around you, Jeremiah—250 fully equipped Unified Party soldiers, with more on the way if necessary. I will not let this go."

He continues to approach me, ignoring her. "You see why we were protecting you now. They want a war, Jesse, but only if you're on their side. Only if you'll bring them Pearls."

"Nonsense," Madame scoffs. "The Skyship Community is just another terrorist organization masquerading as a gang of peace-loving idealists. They're every bit as dangerous as the invaders."

Alkine shakes his head. "You know that's not true, Jesse. We're your family. Come with me."

Madame laughs. "You're in a funny place to be making demands, Alkine."

He glances at her, sneering. "You kill me and it'll be the beginning of the end."

"I'll take my chances."

He limps closer, unafraid of her. "Let the kids go, Jessica. Do what you want with me, but let them go."

Eva and Skandar squirm in their captors' grip. Madame's eyes slit. She raises the control pad and whispers something into a tiny speaker. Before I realize it, three soldiers creep up behind Cassius and me.

Expecting them to attack, I jump away, fists ready to fight.

But they're not after me. One removes a rifle from his side and points it at my heart. The others lift Avery by the arms and drag her off into the rubble.

"Let her go!" I rush toward them, but the guy with the gun fires a round into the concrete inches in front of me. Another hefts Avery over his shoulder and steps farther back. "Please," I turn to Madame. "Let her go!"

"She'll be waiting for you at the Lodge," Madame replies, turning to the soldiers beside her. "Kill the children."

I watch in horror as fingers tighten around Eva and Skandar's necks once more. Both struggle for breath, faces white and panicked.

"Wait!" Alkine shouts. "You're forgetting something, Madame."

Madame motions for the soldiers to loosen their grip. I crane my neck to see Avery, but they've already taken her away into the mist. The soldier with the rifle holds his position. If I move, he'll shoot.

Madame strides forward, sizing Alkine up. "And what is that supposed to mean?"

"Reinforcements," he mutters.

She chuckles. "Oh by all means, please bring your reinforcements."

Alkine's eyes dart up to the sky, to the layer of mist above the city. I follow his gaze, but there's nothing to see. No shuttles or transports. Just the foggy ceiling.

Madame shakes her head, motioning for her men to raise their weapons. "Take him out."

I hear the click of artillery. Hundreds of guns lock onto our small group. It's a shooting gallery, and there's no way of escaping.

Then the mist begins to swirl above us. A deafening roar, like a thousand freight trains, forces my hands over my ears. The sky darkens. Unnaturally fast. It's at least an hour until sundown. This is more like an eclipse.

Madame looks above her for the first time, taking two steps back and mumbling to herself.

A jagged point pokes through the layer of churning mist like a knife reaching down to stab the earth. It's needle-thin at first, but widens as it lowers. Soon it's as thick as a tree trunk—then a rocket.

Waves of smog spread away from the vast object, revealing a canopy of dark weathered metal that blots out the sky above us—a constantly lowering ceiling to what's become an intersection enclosed on all four sides. Rocks tumble down the sides of buildings as the behemoth settles down. The engines rumble above us like never-ending thunder.

Alkine smiles. He says something, too, but the thrusters above our heads are too loud to make out words. But I don't have to hear him to know what's happening. I've approached the hull of this ship enough times to recognize the scuffed underbelly.

Skyship Academy.

I back up, dwarfed by the shadow of the approaching Skyship. The southern spire drills into the ground, kicking up chunks of rock and dirt. I can't believe it. The Academy...on the Surface. The engineers must have been working overtime to keep it cloaked from Madame's cruisers.

Madame pulls in her jacket as the wind from the thrusters pummels the pavement. Her perfectly styled hair blows into a mess, sticking to her teeth. "You have no idea how many laws you're breaking," she shouts.

Alkine shrugs. "Never did like to play it safe."

The thunderous engines die down to a low rumble and the bottom level of the Academy opens up. Shuttles shoot from all sides, bursting from around the perimeter like flower petals. Everyone in the intersection ducks. The soldiers lose their grip on Skandar and Eva. I spin around, looking for Avery. She's long gone. I don't know where they took her.

The Academy ships bolt out into the city, then loop up in the air and reverse their path, barreling down on the intersection. Explosions rattle the pavement.

Madame gives her troops the attack signal. They spread out, quickly filling the intersection like a hive of dark insects. Some run back to cruisers. Most raise their weapons and fire, aiming for the shuttles that dart underneath the Academy's expansive hull.

Trapdoors open from below the shuttle. Agents rocket down into the intersection, aided by upturned ankle boosters that slow their descent until they land on the pavement with the grace of acrobats.

While she's distracted, I lunge at Madame, grabbing the control pad from her hand and chucking it away into the chaos. "Where is she? Where did you take her?"

She slaps my face, pushing away and grabbing a small pistol from her belt. "This is not what I wanted for you."

"No!" Cassius tackles her from the side, knocking her to the ground. She keeps her grip on the pistol, but the black cube tumbles into the intersection. Cassius dives to retrieve it, then grabs my hand and pulls me away. "Come on." He drags me through the dense battle zone. Agent versus soldier, more of them every moment. Shots ring out through the intersection. An explosion pummels the ground to our left, sending up a fountain of debris. Shuttles whiz by overhead, dropping detonators on large swaths of government forces.

A soldier bumps into me, pulling my hand from Cassius's and dragging me back through the crowd. Seconds later, he slumps onto the ground, a bullet through the chest. I turn to see Alkine brandishing a gun in the distance. He tosses his bag to Eva, shouting something. I'm too far away to hear it. Then they're both swallowed by the crowd.

Another explosion pulverizes the pavement behind me. Soldiers fly into the air. Cracks spread from the ground, snaking toward me. The concrete wobbles, then slants into a diagonal. I jump forward, careful not to be swallowed by the sinkhole, and collide with a Skyship Agent.

I turn to see August Bergmann standing before me, armed like the ultimate soldier, his buzzed hair already glistening with sweat. "Oh man." He frowns, and for a second I'm convinced he's gonna punch me in the arm. Instead, his frown curves into an amused smile. "Jameson was right. This *is* a rescue mission. Takes a freaking army, huh Fisher?"

I meet his eyes for a second but don't respond. I'd like to see *him* survive what I've been through. Bet he wouldn't think it was so funny.

"Relax." He slaps my shoulder, nearly knocking me to the ground. "And don't die, okay? Don't be your usual stupid self."

Then he's gone. I look around for Madame. A hand grabs onto my arm. I push away before realizing it's Cassius.

He frowns and motions for me to follow him between two walls of fighting soldiers. I watch as beams of energy shoot from cannons emerging from the hull of the Academy.

Cassius releases my arm. We squeeze between the remaining soldiers and sprint through what's left of an empty alleyway. On the other side I see a line of cruisers, also empty. Every soldier Madame's got has joined the fray back at the intersection. The alleyway's dark, shadowed by the Academy overhead. Cassius cradles the cube under his arm. I grab him by the shoulder, stopping his mad dash to freedom.

He spins around, glaring. "What are you doing?"

"I can't leave without Avery."

"Madame'll kill you," he responds, keeping one eye on the far-off intersection.

"I thought that's what you wanted."

He shakes his head. "We have to get away."

"Alkine will—"

He grabs my arm and yanks me backward, just as Madame bursts into the alleyway.

Her jacket hangs halfway off her shoulders. Her hair is mottled with dirt and sweat. She breathes heavily, aiming the pistol at my heart.

"Come on," Cassius coaxes, pulling my arm.

"Don't move," Madame warns as she steps forward, "or it will be the last thing you do."

Cassius releases me, clutching the cube tightly under his arm.

Madame sighs. "My dear Cassius. I have regrets. I should have kept you out of this. I should have let you stay at the Lodge. You're confused, as you have every right to be. We'll sit down and talk when this is over. I'm sure that—"

She's interrupted by Eva, who stumbles into the alleyway holding Alkine's dark bag. Her arm restraint hangs from her left wrist. A large scratch runs down the side of her face.

Madame rolls her eyes, pivoting slightly and pulling the trigger. Eva lunges toward the wall and presses herself against the brick. The bullet whizzes past her and into the intersection.

"Don't hurt her!" I shout. "It's me you want."

Madame turns back around, reloading the pistol and aiming it at me. "There are cruisers directly behind you. Step into one, and we can continue this conversation elsewhere."

I watch as Eva tiptoes forward, grabbing something from inside the bag. A faint green light illuminates the back of the alley. Madame doesn't see it. Yet.

"Okay," I respond, trying not to stare at the Pearl Eva's holding. "Okay, I give up. Just don't shoot."

Madame's head cocks to the side, a suspicious frown on her face. "Into the cruiser."

I nod and take a small step back. Eva comes closer.

Then Madame sees the glow coming from behind her.

She spins around, but before she can do anything Eva hurls the Pearl into the air. It makes a wide arc above Madame's head and shoots down to me.

I stretch out my right arm, tense my fingers, and stop it in mid-air.

The Pearl hovers between Madame and me, nearly blinding us in the dim alley. I motion for Eva to run back to the intersection. She lingers for a moment, watching me, before backing away.

Madame keeps her aim steady, approaching cautiously. "This isn't funny, Jesse."

I back up, focusing on keeping control of the Pearl. I wave my hand back and forth. The Pearl follows like a pendulum swinging in the air. Left, right. Left, right.

Madame watches, and for the first time I notice fear in her eyes. She knows what's inside the Pearl, but I bet she doesn't know what happens when it's freed. Not firsthand.

I move my hand more dramatically and the Pearl follows course, slamming into the brittle walls on either side of us. Loose brick tumbles in piles onto the ground as the alley starts to cave in before me.

Madame stumbles back. "Stop it."

I don't. The Pearl continues to smack the walls with the force of a wrecking ball, adding to the pile of rubble in front of us. It's nearly up to Madame's waist now, blocking her path.

Then, just as I'm about to bring the entire alley down around her, I hear a gunshot and feel something prick my shoulder. I look down to see a silver dart lodged into my skin. She shot me. She actually shot me!

The Pearl wobbles in the air as my concentration fractures. Whatever's in the dart races through my bloodstream. It's all I can do to stay standing. Madame laughs. All other sounds fade into nothing.

I clench my fists and the world explodes in front of me.

A shower of rubble rains over Madame, burying everything in the alleyway—including her. The walls crumble around us as the Pearl energy tears through the derelict buildings, streaming out into the intersection. A glowing figure shoots into the sky, soaring up around the Academy and out of sight.

I fall backwards, watching as the Skyship's hull absorbs the brunt of the Pearl's force. Sheet lightning dances along the dark underbelly, illuminating the mist around Seattle. Just like that day—the day Cassius and I first landed on Earth.

Then, as the last of the energy dissipates, I lose consciousness.

46

She's got me. She's escaped somehow and she's got me.

It's the only thing running through my mind upon waking. My back's pressed against a leather seat. A belt stretches over my chest.

I'm in a government cruiser. Never been inside one before, but the Unified Party emblems etched into the control panel are a dead giveaway.

Dark sky forms a wall outside the window. I turn to my left, praying to see Alkine. Eva. Skandar. One of the good guys.

Cassius.

I jerk away from him, my mind still on survival mode.

"Relax." He glances over at me, frowning. "She's not here."

I watch him pilot the cruiser for a moment in silence. His hands grip the wheel tightly. His steely gaze focuses on the path ahead of him.

"You've been out for over an hour," he mutters. "Tranquilizer. It's meant to keep you down for longer."

I cough. "Where are we?" My throat's still clogged with dust from Seattle.

"Halfway over Kansas, according to the radar." His eyes shift to my face, then back to the front window. "Wichita's on your right—below us."

I look down at the Surface—an unending abyss punctuated only by pinpricks of light far off in the distance. Directly below us sits a cocoon of white lights, stretching up from the ground like a bee's nest. Wichita. Chosen City #27.

My mind flashes back to Seattle. The alleyway. "Are you—"

"I'm not taking you to the Lodge," he interrupts. "Nobody's taking you to the Lodge from the looks of it back there. They're outnumbered. Despite all of Madame's planning, the Skyship took her by surprise. I didn't think it was possible to surprise her."

I close my eyes and see the pile of rubble crashing down on Madame. The thought of it makes me sick. "Was she...? I mean, did I...?"

"I didn't check," he replies. "I just left."

I rub my eyes and try to wipe the image from memory. "She's unconscious, that's all. People like Madame don't die."

He scoffs. "I wouldn't have thought you'd care."

I look down at my lap for a moment. It's not caring, definitely, but I don't like the thought of killing anybody either. Even Madame. "Look, I didn't want to hurt anyone."

"Don't apologize," Cassius says, and that's the end of that.

I shift in my seat, wondering if I should just shut up and let him do his thing. He's not exactly the most approachable person in the world. But I can't stay quiet. There's too much I need to know. "So if we're not going to the Lodge, where *are* we going?"

He sighs. "Somewhere people can't find us."

I groan inwardly. The last thing I want right now is another chase. My body couldn't handle it. "Running again?"

"You got a problem with that?"

"I—" I catch myself and try to choose my words carefully, unsure what could set him off. "It's just that … my friends. Avery."

"She's gone," he replies. "They could've dragged her to any of the Unified Party's compounds by now. Finding her would be impossible." He pauses. "Your friends will be fine."

I shake my head. "I should have been quicker. I should have stopped them from taking her."

He frowns, his voice devoid of any expression. "You did what you had to do. You saved yourself. Now take a look at this." He reaches down and grabs something from beside his seat. Before I can argue, he tosses Madame's small black cube into my lap.

I catch it, expecting my muscles to strain. They don't.

The cube's unnaturally light, like paper or cardboard. I run my fingers across the smooth, cold exterior. It's solid as stone, and seems like it's been the same shape since the beginning of time. Not so, if what Madame said is true.

"Open it," Cassius coaxes.

I glance at him in confusion. But then I remember the silver key around my neck. I lift the chain over my head and feel around the top of the cube for a keyhole.

Cassius reaches over and turns on the lighting panel above my seat. A dim glow falls on a narrow slit in the center of the cube. I grab the key and lower it into the hole.

That's all I have to do.

Deep lines begin to form on the surface, starting from the center and spreading out on all four sides like a compass rose. It's like watching an invisible knife cut through the material. Impossibly sharp. Within moments, the top of the cube's portioned into four equal squares. The lines reach the edges and continue to cut down the sides of the cube. The key crumbles into dust, dissipating into the air. The roof of the cube blossoms out from the center, revealing an opening the size of my fist.

Cassius keeps one eye on the cube the entire time. When all the fanfare's over, I shift my attention to him. He glances up at me, then back to the crumbled cube in my lap. "Go ahead."

I nod, then cautiously reach through the hole and pull out a reflective disc the size of my palm. At first it looks like a hand mirror, but as soon as I touch it, an image flickers to life on the shiny surface.

It's an electronic photo. A man and woman sit together,

smiling. I hold it closer and notice two bundles of cloth cradled in their arms. Babies. It's a mother and father.

Our mother and father.

I can tell instantly. My eyes. Cassius's chin. Both of us are right there, in our parents' faces. Mom's fair hair has a slight curl to it, like mine. The determined look in Dad's eyes could set the world on fire. Both wear untroubled, cheerful expressions, but beneath their expressions is something else—a slight downward tug in the smiles, a hint of worry in the tensed eyebrows.

Still, the four of us look like any normal, American family. No one's got antennae or green skin. We aren't wearing shiny silver jumpsuits or bulbous space bubbles.

I hand the disc to Cassius without a word. He stares at it for a moment, eyes fixed on the picture. "It's true, then," he mutters, "what Madame said."

I nod, but before I can respond the open cube quivers in my lap. Worried, I lift it from my legs, but as soon as it touches my skin it melts like wax. Dark beads slide down the sides. My hand tingles with an iciness as the cube drips into a thick mess.

I crouch on the seat as the dark liquid falls between my fingers, only to lift up again like a yo-yo. The puddle breaks into two. A glob of blackness shoots across the cabin and clings onto Cassius's wrist. What's left coils around my arm. Another second and the material hardens into two smooth bracelets—one for each of us.

I claw at the thin band, searching for a break in the

material to pry it off. It's seamless, and too narrow to fit around my hand. For a moment my wrist is overcome by intense cold, but soon the temperature adjusts itself to meet the rest of my body.

I sigh, digging underneath the bracelet. "Well, that's just great."

Cassius places the picture-disc on the front console and flexes his arm in front of him, keeping one hand on the steering wheel. "What did you do?"

"Me? I didn't do anything!"

He glares at me, but then something on the radar screen catches his attention. "We're being followed."

I turn in my seat, craning my neck to see behind us out the window. Madame. It's gotta be Madame.

"It's coming up fast," Cassius continues. "It'll be on us in a—"

Before he can finish his thought, a brilliant green glow overtakes the cruiser. The cabin flashes dramatically as something hurtles overhead. We shake with turbulence, though I hardly notice it. I'm too focused on the green figure soaring through the air ahead of us. Losing altitude. Fast.

I point out the window. "It's the person I freed in Seattle! Follow him!"

Cassius shoots me a questioning look but brings the cruiser down, speeding up to match the pace of the glowing traveler in front of us. I watch as the figure plunges to the dark Surface, leaving a trail of energy behind like a shooting star.

"Pearls," Cassius mutters. "I think I liked them better when they weren't shaped like people."

The screens on the control deck flicker on and off as we follow the energy trail. The cabin lights power to full capacity until I have to squint to see through the brightness.

"Power overload," Cassius says. "The cruiser can't take all this energy. If this keeps up we'll have to pull off course."

I look down at the crazy light show in front of me. "Can't you shut some of this stuff off?"

He shakes his head. "I didn't turn it *on*." He glances at the altimeter. "We're getting close. Two thousand feet and dropping."

I keep one eye on the green figure—an oversized firefly shooting through the night. Then in an instant, it disappears. The energy trail fractures into tiny sparks of light around us, evaporating into the air. It's dark once more. Mass dark.

"Frag it." Cassius switches on the emergency beams and pulls up on the wheel. I jostle in my seat as a wide rooftop comes into view just below us, spotlighted by our ship. We almost crash right into it, but Cassius stops us just in time.

After a moment floundering in the air, we make a cautious landing in the center of the roof. The surface beneath us bows with the weight of the cruiser. I wait for it to cave in altogether, but it holds. For now.

Cassius shuts off the power—everything but the emergency beams, which shoot across the rooftop in two horizontal pillars.

We've set down in the middle of a Fringe Town, and we're the only light for miles. I hope we're alone out here.

A man crouches on the rooftop between our beams. Back turned to us, he slumps over the ground, resting on his knees. His outline is utterly still. From what I can see, he looks human.

Cassius raises his armrest and strides back to a small locker protruding from the wall. After plugging a code into a nearby keypad, he pulls it open and rummages around inside.

I unbuckle my belt. "What are you doing?"

He turns to face me, inspecting the barrel of a pistol. "Protection."

"No." I stand, glancing back at the man on the rooftop. "Leave it."

His eyes challenge me, but he says nothing. After an uncomfortable silence, he sighs and returns the weapon to the locker. "Fine. We'll do it your way."

I look down at his clenched fist. Sparks dance along his fingertips. Not enough to start a fire, but enough to tell me exactly how he's feeling.

He shakes his head and walks to the side of the cabin, punching the button to release the doorway. Sweltering night air streams into the cockpit as the door slides open.

I step out first, knees shaking as my feet touch the rooftop. The air is humid, without even a hint of a breeze. Apart from the distant chirping of insects, it's silent, too.

I round the front of the cruiser, eyes fixed on the figure

spotlighted by our beams. Cassius follows close behind. As sneaky as we try to be, our footsteps echo like drumbeats in the tranquil night.

"Uh … excuse me?" My voice breaks, barely above a whisper.

The figure's head darts up and slowly turns around to stare at us. He squints through the beams, his lips down turned.

Cassius and I freeze. The man's eyes drill into us. Then they fall on my wrist—the bracelet. He recognizes it.

Immediately he jumps up and bounds toward us. A string of noise pours from his lips, nonsense words recited with the conviction of a lunatic.

Cassius and I back away until we're pressed up against the front of the cruiser. Cassius holds out his hand, trying to get a flame going.

The man stops, inches away. He gapes at us for a moment, eyes wide and crazy. My breathing quickens. I try not to look at him, but his expression draws me in.

I take a step to the side, trying to get away, but he's too quick. He grabs onto our wrists, fingers wrapped around the bracelets. His head shoots back until he's looking up at the stars. A trail of energy leaks from both bracelets, streaming up into the atmosphere and plunging into the alien's open mouth. Then, out of nowhere, he speaks English. Or rather, the *bracelets* speak, channeling words through his larynx.

"My boys," his tone is robotic and expressionless, like a computer trying to recite a poem. It doesn't fit. "If you are hearing this now, then you have safely made it to Earth. Your father's transport system worked. You are the first, and the means of unlocking each that follows you."

He pauses. I glance at Cassius. *Father.* This is a message for us, a recording of some sort, from our . . .

I don't let myself finish the thought. There's no telling who this is from. I can't get my hopes up.

The bracelet sends shockwaves up through my arm. It doesn't hurt, but it keeps me frozen in place. "We wish we could be there," the voice continues to spill from the guy's mouth. "We *should* be there, but fate has not allowed it. In our stead, I have programmed this device to guide you until you are old enough to take care of yourselves. Any of our people will know how to activate it, though this message is set for playback as soon as the two of you reunite. It will lead you to food and shelter. You will be lonely until others arrive, but you will need that time to build trust in one another and develop your powers. One to create, one to destroy: a shared burden to channel and transform the transport energy. It will grow easier with time."

Cassius grabs onto the guy's wrist and tries to yank his hand from the bracelet. But it's like trying to move a tower. The guy stays utterly still, possessed by the words streaming from our bracelets.

"I didn't want this for you," the voice continues, "but you would have surely perished if we'd have kept you with us any longer. Our world is crumbling. The Authority seeks to colonize and conquer Earth. We cannot let that happen, so we must stay and fight … try to get as many members of the Resistance as possible off-planet before we take down the Authority once and for all.

"Of course, this means nothing to you. You're only children. I'm sorry that it had to be children. An adult body would have rejected the serum necessary for transforming you … for giving you the power to manipulate transport energy."

"Pearls." I look over at Cassius. His arm goes limp, giving up on trying to break free.

"You were still growing," the voice continues. "We needed bodies that were malleable enough to survive the triggering process. I would have done anything to keep you here, but you were our only hope of getting safely off-planet in time."

Energy continues to erupt around us, feeding the man the next words. And with each new phrase I grow more and more certain that this is her. This is our mom speaking.

"The Authority is everywhere," the voice continues, "and now that they've discovered your father's energy transfer, this civil war is getting bloodier by the hour. They've already attacked Earth, leaving us free to jettison you to safety among the ruins. From all we've been able to assess, the planet should provide you with stable living conditions. And when this war is over and we have won, we *will* join you. I wish there was another way. I hope you will be able to understand. And forgive. Your father and I love you very much."

Mom. It's Mom.

The man releases our wrists and staggers backward. The voice stops. So do the coils of energy.

Cassius and I stand in silence for a moment, dumbfounded. As loony as it all sounds, everything fits together like some messed-up jigsaw puzzle. A few days ago I would have laughed it off as some elaborate joke. But I've seen too much.

And then the dread sets in. Every fallen Pearl an extinguished life from our home planet ... wherever that is. Madame knew, and still she kept Cassius from me. Pearls were more important to her than the truth ... than *lives*.

Suddenly the thought of her buried beneath a pile of rubble isn't so horrifying. Screw this so-called "Authority." People like her are the real enemy, trading lives for energy to power Chosen Cities. One of those lives could have been my mom's. Or dad's.

The guy stumbles to the ground, hand over his face. Then for the first time he speaks in English. Two words. That's all it takes.

"All gone." His face crumbles as he crawls into the darkness. "All gone."

Cassius shakes his head. "We can't just leave him here."

I consider my options: grab the guy and take off on the run again, or contact Alkine and head back to the Academy. As angry as I am at Alkine, he was there when it counted back in Seattle. The Surface is too dangerous right now, with or without Madame.

"I'll take him up to the Academy," I respond. "It's the only safe place."

I wait for Cassius to argue, but all he does is nod.

I glance over at the invader, face still buried in his hands, then turn back to Cassius. "You should come with us."

He scoffs. "That's not a good idea."

"Why? Don't you think our parents would have wanted it?"

"I can't go up to a Skyship. I belong down here."

I frown. "With the Unified Party?"

"I didn't say that."

"Look," I step forward, "if I'm gonna start freeing these people, I'm going to need your help."

He glares at me. "I just spent the past few days trying to kill you. Do you realize what you're asking?"

"People change."

He gives a cold laugh. "You're optimistic. What happened to that scared little kid hanging off the rooftop?" He walks back to the side of the cruiser.

I follow him. "Are you saying we're supposed to be enemies?"

"Fisher, you and I *can't* be enemies anymore. That doesn't mean you should trust me."

"But our mother said—"

He bangs his fist on the dark metal. "That was just a recording. A trick."

"That wasn't a trick, Cassius."

He shakes his head, keeping his face obscured by darkness. "You wanna believe it, don't you?"

"You've seen what's happened."

"It's ridiculous." He sighs, staring at the ground. "They abandoned us," he mutters. "Left us with this stupid, impossible mission. They should have known we'd be separated."

"They're still coming," I lean against the side of the cruiser. "They'll be here."

He glances up at me, eyes slit. "You have no idea what you're talking about."

I ignore him, peering inside the cabin. "You got any long-range CPs that could tap into the Academy's frequency?"

He nods, steps into the cruiser, and comes back with two palm receivers. He tosses one to me.

"They're closed circuit," he mutters, "but you can change the frequency. Play with the dial at the bottom."

I look up at him. "Are you gonna keep the other one?"

"Why?"

"If we need to get in touch ... "

"And what? Plan parties while the parents are out of town? Get real, Fisher."

I keep my eyes locked on him. "Promise you'll keep it."

He says nothing, but slips the receiver into his pocket. Then he moves to the door handle, preparing to pull it shut.

"Wait." I hold out my hand. "What are you doing?"

"There's something I wanna take care of," he replies. "You said you knew how to contact the Academy. Is there anything else you need?"

"No..." I start. "I mean, is this it?"

He sighs. "You start breaking Pearls again, you know where to reach me."

I nod. And without a goodbye, he pulls the door shut and moves to the driver's seat.

I back away from the cruiser, over to the alien, and watch as the landing gear retracts and the ship rises into the sky. Another moment and it retreats into the darkness, rippling my battle-torn visitation suit as it speeds away.

I clutch the com-pad in my hand, holding it in front of my face and taking refuge in the meager light provided by the touch screen. He's angry, that's all. In shock. I'll see him again.

But for tonight, it ends on a rooftop between Cassius and me. Just as it began.

47

Cassius Stevenson snuck through the shadowed hallways of the Lodge, looking over his shoulder with every corner he turned. He had changed into a fresh suit upon arriving, eager to leave the dirt and dust of the Fringes behind.

It was three in the morning, much too early for most to be awake. Without Madame, the Lodge was quieter—less of a fortress and more of an old, lonely mansion.

His mind rushed back to childhood memories. Birthdays. School. Training.

It would be the last time he'd walk these hallways.

After changing clothes, he'd broken into the student infirmary and managed to run a full body scan. Ever since he'd seen Madame reduce Fisher's girlfriend to a puddle with the press of a button, he knew he'd need to make sure she couldn't do the same to him.

Sure enough, the scan detected a chip. Not in his head, luckily, but in his wrist, directly below his identification code. He'd stuffed his pockets with supplies. The chip would have to come out. Not now, but soon.

His next stop was the Office of Research and Discovery. Last time he'd entered, it'd been to leech the energy from a Pearl—to destroy the life inside. Now he was heading straight for the central radar system used to track Pearl landings. He wouldn't be able to stop the Unified Party outright, but he'd be able to slow them down.

He paused at the doorway, questioning if he was on the right side. It had certainly been easier following orders, working toward a clear goal. Right and wrong.

But he had been lied to. Now it was impossible to know who to trust. The only action that made sense was to level the playing field.

He locked in the code on the wall beside him. The door clicked open. He grabbed the handle, pulled, and slipped inside. The security crew would have spotted him on the cameras already. They'd be down in minutes to see what a trainee was doing inside the office.

He didn't worry. All he needed was a few minutes anyway.

He passed by the long bank of computers on his way to the radar system at the far side of the room. Rounded bookcases bordered the tight space. Kindling.

The central computer sat on a raised platform in front of the far window. Without it, the six remaining radars around the country would lose their connection to the

Lodge, making Pearl discovery infinitely more frustrating until it was repaired.

Upon arriving at the platform, he gritted his teeth and clenched his fists, summoning up the fire inside him. Ever since the alien girl had drawn out his power in Seattle, he found it much easier to control. But a tiny flame wasn't going to suffice now. He needed a blowout.

So he closed his eyes and let all the revelations of the day flood into him. The angrier he became, the more intense the burning inside of him. He conjured up emotion—betrayal, jealousy, rage—and dared his body to teeter on the brink of destruction.

Madame knew. She knew he had a brother and she would have been content to destroy him. All she wanted was power. She never cared. Not really.

When the fire inside of him reached its breaking point, he lifted his hands and channeled it, concentrating on the tips of his fingers.

Boom.

Streams of fire shot from his fingertips, lighting up the room in torrents. The force of it sent him staggering back. He crashed into the nearest computer, pushing it off the table.

Within seconds the entire room was ablaze. Wood and paper went first, joined by computer systems and file cabinets. Explosions ripped through the office as hardware went up in smoke.

The room became more unrecognizable by the moment,

folding in on itself like a crumpled piece of paper. Cassius felt woozy, drained from the inside out.

He clenched his fists and shut off the fire. Then he reached for the central computer, yanking it from its station and throwing it into the hungry blaze.

The warmth inside of him dissipated, spreading out into his system until his body temperature normalized. The flames triggered the sprinkler system, but they were too late. The inferno was ten times more powerful than the one he had set off in his dormitory. It would take human intervention to contain it. Serious manpower.

Alarms blared in the background, but Cassius was protected by a wall of fire. No one would find him. No one would know who was responsible.

Still, he needed to escape before he was too exhausted to run. He climbed up onto the platform beside the window and crossed his arms in front of his face. He paused a moment, taking one last look at his home. Then he jumped through the window.

Glass shattered as he flew through the air. He landed hard on the dew-stained grass outside, shards raining down around him. Without pausing to check for damage, he picked himself off the grass and ran away from the Lodge as fast as his aching body would allow.

48

Captain Alkine leans back in a large leather chair behind his office desk. A window of blue sky fills the wall behind him. It's twelve hours since they picked me up in Kansas. I've barely slept. I haven't even had time to process. And Alkine thinks it's a good idea to pull me into a meeting.

"I've spoken with our medical team," he starts. "Except for some residual energy floating around his skin, your friend seems completely normal. Human, even."

"Who said he's my friend?" I slouch down in my own far more unimpressive chair.

"Wrong choice of words." Alkine pauses in thought, staring off into the corner of the room. His right arm's bound in a dark cast. "I want to apologize, Fisher."

"No need," I reply. "I get it. You wanted to keep me safe from Madame and the Unified Party and all the other big bad monsters of the world."

"That's true," he says, "but I should have done more. We all should have. We were so concerned about Pearls that we neglected to consider the personal effect this would have on you. When we found you down in Seattle all those years ago, I was convinced that there was some sort of connection with the government, or the terrorists even. I never dreamed that it would stretch any further than that. I should have spent more time investigating. If we had known the truth about Pearls ... "

"Yeah? Well, now you have a chance to make up for mistakes."

"My thoughts exactly." He nods. "Beyond your mother's message, we've been unable to extract much from our visitor. His English is limited and comes out in spurts. As soon as we know more, we'll have a better idea how safe these people are." He sighs. "I hope you believe me, Fisher. We had no idea what was inside of Pearls. Everything would have been different if we—"

I raise my hand to stop him. "It's okay."

He nods. "Now that we know what you're capable of, we can tailor our resources to help you. We're more than able to take on this rescue mission. That is, if you're interested."

"You're asking me?"

He shrugs. "After so many years of keeping things from you, it's only right that I give you the choice."

I drum my fingers on the armrest. "What about the Tribunal?"

Alkine sighs. "As soon as they find out I broke through the Skyline to help you in Seattle they'll be furious. I've decided to go off-grid for the time being. We've already begun to move westward. By the time they realize we're gone, we'll be out of Skyship Territory and over the Pacific."

I wince at the thought of it. Going against the Unified Party is one thing. We're used to it. But running away from the Tribunal is something mass new. I never thought Alkine would make such a bold move for me. Maybe I was wrong about him. Maybe he *is* looking out for my best interests. But if he really wants to help, there's one more thing he needs to do. "Avery," I say. "We have to find Avery."

"Likely back at the Lodge by now," his voice lowers. "I had my men search the city, Jesse." He grimaces. "Look, I know you two were close, but it's not in our best interest to—"

"*You* don't wanna find her," I interrupt. "You're afraid she's still working for Madame."

"That's not it. We're not even sure if Madame's alive. But launching a full-scale assault on the Lodge would be a huge mistake. I'm already pulling operatives from several Chosen Cities. We need to disappear until we get this thing figured out."

I grit my teeth, meeting his eyes. "I don't wanna go without Avery."

He shakes his head. "They would be expecting us, Fisher. We're outnumbered."

"So bring the ship down like you did in Seattle."

His eyebrows raise. "Over a Chosen City? They'd blast us out of the sky without so much as a warning, cloaked or not. We're not Atlas, Jesse. A Skyship this size doesn't stand a chance against a Chosen. We got away with it over a deserted area. It won't happen again. Even so, I'll be paying a price for it. Now it's your turn to give something up. Avery Wicksen's a smart girl ... sneaky, too. She can handle herself. You have more important things to worry about right now."

"My parents," I mumble.

"Excuse me?"

"They're coming to Earth ... if they're still alive. They could be in any of them ... any of the Pearls."

He nods. "Then you better be damn sure the government doesn't get their hands on them first."

I take a deep breath, realizing that he's right. It's a matter of time. And we don't have much time to waste.

I glance out the window at the wisps of clouds streaming by. "So where are we going?"

"Eastern Siberia," he responds. "I have contacts there. Survivors of the fallout from the Chinese-American War. Both the Tribunal and the Unified Party will be looking for us in the air. We can hunker down for a while and get this project up and running. We'll need supplies, and a space for our ... visitors to settle."

I bristle at the word "visitors," and wonder if that's what Alkine thinks of me, too. A visitor. A tourist on my own planet. "You really want to go through with this, then? I mean, it'll change the world."

His eyebrows raise. "Is that really such a bad thing?" He clasps his hands. "I want to do this if you think you're ready. If it's safe."

I nod. "It's safe. The people I've met so far … they don't want to hurt anyone."

"We'll confirm it, and we'll move ahead cautiously. I'll instruct all units to prepare for Project Pearlbreaker. And you will need to get your butt in training. Slacking off is not gonna cut it, Fisher. This is important."

I sink down in my chair. "Project Pearlbreaker?"

"Military code name," he replies. "Gives the people a sense of purpose."

"No uniforms, right?"

He smiles. "Not unless you want one."

I shake my head, pausing for a moment. "Are people gonna know? About me, I mean."

Alkine chuckles. "Fisher, this is Skyship Academy. People are going to know. In fact, I've heard a few rather unpleasant rumors filtering around the ship already. You might want to nip that in the bud."

I tense up, imagining what people like August Bergmann are going to have to say after what happened in Seattle. *Puny Jesse Fisher needs an entire Skyship to save him from a middle-aged woman.*

"I'll keep you informed if we manage to extract anything useful from our friend down in the infirmary. No more closed-door meetings, Jesse. I promise you'll be involved from now on."

I fidget in the chair. Even though he's being all warm and fuzzy, I still feel like I'm at a meeting with the principal. Plus, Alkine and promises don't exactly fit together the way they should.

"Took a lot of guts going down to the Surface," he says. "Initiative. I hadn't seen it in you before. It suits you."

I force a smile, realizing how strange it feels to be complimented by Captain Alkine. He clears his throat and crosses his arms. "Is there anything else we need to discuss?"

I shake my head, eager to leave the conversation on a good note.

Without a goodbye, I pull myself up out of the chair and head for the door. I feel Alkine's eyes bore into the back of my head as I leave. Creepy. As. Ever.

———

Late evening. A blanket of stars stretches around the ship beyond the Level Five windows. I stand in the outer corridor, hands in my pockets, and stare out into the night. I wish I had a telescope so that I could see farther.

I try to imagine hurtling through the stars, on my way from the laboratory of some unknown planet. It's too ridiculous to visualize, but it happened. Pearls—I was inside one of those things.

I lay my fingers on the fiberglass and trace the stars. Connect the dots. There are worlds out there, maybe hundreds of them. Worlds as chaotic and troubled as our own. Worlds where people lose things they love. Worlds with families and children. Sisters.

Brothers.

I hear footsteps down the corridor. A voice interrupts the silence. "I'd kill to know what's going through your mind right now."

I bring my hand down to my side and turn around. "Eva."

"Evening, Fisher. I thought you'd be in your room."

"Nah. I needed some space."

She joins me at the window, peering down. "Nothing but hundreds of miles of water below us. Gotta make you a little nervous."

"Huh?"

She grins. "I know what kind of swimmer you are."

I shrug, turning my attention back to the stars.

"Hey," she lays her hand on my shoulder, "you did well today. What a difference a week makes, right?"

I chuckle. "Yeah, everything's changed now."

"Aw, don't be dramatic," she replies. "Not *everything's* changed. You're still the guy I've gotta look out for."

I scowl at her. "I did all right on the Surface."

"Sure you did." She smiles. "But you've got a lot to learn. Alien or not."

I lay my forehead against the fiberglass. "Please don't use that word."

She laughs. "I thought you'd be used to it by now. It's not like you've ever been normal, right?"

"Is that supposed to be a compliment?"

She shrugs. "Take it for what it is, Fisher. At least now you've got a reason to be different."

I turn to respond but notice Skandar sprinting toward us through the corridor. A heavy cast covers his right arm. He swings it around like it doesn't hurt at all.

As soon as he's within striking distance, he grabs my shoulder and spins me around, using me as a human shield. "Is he coming?"

I yank my shoulder free. "Is *who* coming?"

"Bergmann." He crouches. "He was talking trash about you, Jesse. I nailed him right in the jaw." He shakes his bandaged arm.

Eva rolls her eyes. "You punched him with your cast?"

He smiles. "Duh. It's a lot harder than my fist."

She shakes her head. "That arm doesn't deserve to heal."

Skandar stands up straight, staring over my shoulder. "I think I lost him outside the library."

I wince at the thought of August Bergmann coming after us. "You don't have to defend me."

He grins. "Oh, don't worry. Bergmann won't be coming for you. I told him you could explode his head. You know, like a Pearl."

Eva leans against the window. "That is the stupidest thing I've ever heard."

Skandar shrugs. "Seemed to believe it."

She sighs. "You're a moron."

My front pocket buzzes. Skandar notices it first. "That you, mate?"

Confused, I reach into my pocket and feel smooth plastic. The com-pad. Cassius's com-pad. I'd nearly forgotten about it.

"We'll have to talk later." I step away from the window.

Eva's eyes narrow. "Jesse, what do you have in your pocket?"

I back away across the corridor, heading for the elevators. "Just trust me for once, okay Eva? I'll ... uh ... see you guys tomorrow."

She steps forward, intent on following me, but Skandar juts out his uninjured arm and holds her back. I turn and race through the hallway. When I reach the elevators, I pull the com-pad from my pocket and answer it.

"Hey."

There's a pause, long enough that I figure the connection cut out. Then I hear Cassius's voice, small and quiet coming from the tiny speaker.

"Hi."

Another pause. I struggle to come up with something to say.

"Is there something wrong?"

"No," he replies.

"Okay." The elevator doors open and I arrive on Level Three. I crane my neck up and down the hallway, looking for agents. It's empty for now. Still, I hurry toward my room.

"Listen," he clears his throat. "Can we talk?"

I plug in the code to my room and open the door, slipping inside. "About what?"

He sighs, voice still low. "You know, just ... *talk*. About things."

"Yeah." I slump face down on my unmade bed, turning the speaker's volume up and setting it against the pillow.

Time to meet my brother. For real this time—without Madame or Alkine telling us what to say or do.

Two kids standing on opposite sides of a cold war. And still we managed to find each other. Now, linked across thousands of miles by little more than a shared frequency, we're united. It's just like our mother said. We need the time to build trust. After all, we've got twelve years to make up for.

I close my eyes and focus on his voice ... imagining a future where all of us are together. Cassius. Our parents. Avery.

"I took down the Lodge's central radar system," he mutters in a tone that doesn't sound quite happy *or* sad. "They'll be off your case for the time being."

"Thanks," I reply. "Where are you heading?"

He clears his throat. "I'm gonna try to sneak through the Canadian Border ... maybe head up to the Polar Cities until I can figure out what to do next."

"We're on course for Siberia," I start. "You're welcome to—"

"Not yet," he interrupts. "You go ahead. I need some time to think."

"Is it safe? I mean, what if Madame's still alive?"

"You let me worry about that," he replies. "Just ... if you find them ... if one of those Pearls you break is our mom or dad, let me know. Okay?"

"Of course."

"Even after all I've done," he continues. "You've gotta let me know."

"Yeah," I say. "Sure."

Sirens blare through the com-pad's speaker, interrupting Cassius's voice. Then rustling. Panting.

I grab the receiver and hold it to my mouth. "Cassius, are you okay?"

The response comes seconds later. "Fine. I've gotta go, all right?"

"All right. I'll talk to you—"

The connection fractures. I set the device on my pillow and sit at the edge of the bed.

As Skyship Academy drifts over the Pacific, away from Fringe Towns and Chosen Cities, I try not to think about what lies ahead. Siberia's only the start. Getting away with this . . . breaking Pearls while the Unified Party remains strong—I can't do it alone. Cassius can't either.

They'll want to shut us down, come at us from every angle until we're both under their control. Or worse yet, dead.

I recline on the mattress and stare at the ceiling, exhausted. One thing's for sure: I've really gotta start taking my training more seriously.

About the Author

When he was a young boy, Nick James's collection of battle-scarred action figures became the characters in epic storylines with cliffhangers, double crosses, and an unending supply of imaginary explosions. Not much has changed. The toys are gone (most of them), but the love of fast-paced storytelling remains. Working in schools from Washington State to England, Nick has met thousands of diverse students since graduating from Western Washington University and braving the most dangerous job in the world: substitute teaching. Luckily, being dubbed the "rock star teacher" has granted him some immunity. He currently lives and teaches in Bellingham, Washington.